There was the shadow of the building and the blue circle of the pad at the end of it. The boat was not so small, when seen close up.

Why had he done this? Upon waking this morning, he had no idea to leave Tawlin Estate, let alone Hovart Clan. Let alone T'chishett. Let alone Neunacht. This hop felt like any other: small jolts to the stomach and lots of boredom. He might have been on his way to Southbay for any of a number of reasons, instead of leaving his home world, for no reason at all.

Wanbli felt calm enough. Collected. But he kept chewing on the question of why he had done it. Not why he had left Tawlin: that had been brewing for a year and more. Not even why he had done it today: the price of an aircar changed everything. The flea-bite, unendurable question was why he had chosen this particular method of cutting his life in two parts, heading off into black space without planning. No return ticket.

Other Books by R. A. MacAvoy

**Tea with the Black Dragon
A Trio for Lute**

The Third Eagle

LESSONS ALONG
A MINOR STRING

R. A. MacAvoy

BANTAM BOOKS

NEW YORK · TORONTO · LONDON · SYDNEY · AUCKLAND

*This edition contains the complete text
of the original hardcover edition.*
NOT ONE WORD HAS BEEN OMITTED.

THE THIRD EAGLE
*A Bantam Spectra Book / published by arrangement with
Doubleday*

PRINTING HISTORY
*Doubleday edition published February 1989
Bantam edition / January 1990*

ISBN 0-553-28356-1

Published simultaneously in the United States and Canada

---

*Bantam Books are published by Bantam Books, a division of Bantam
Doubleday Dell Publishing Group, Inc. Its trademark, consisting of the
words "Bantam Books" and the portrayal of a rooster, is Registered in
U.S. Patent and Trademark Office and in other countries. Marca
Registrada. Bantam Books, 666 Fifth Avenue, New York, New York
10103.*

PRINTED IN THE UNITED STATES OF AMERICA

OPM   0 9 8 7 6 5 4 3 2 1

For Dio Santiago, Clara Minor and Machdia Towee
With thanks for all help

and for Anthony Villiers

The Green Sky

ONE

"Out of the black and shining vault,
   The black void, the shining night,
   To the golden mother, painted with light,
   We were born out of the belly of our father
   To the grace of two mothers,
   Bright beads on the Strings.
   We are like none other: the people.
   We are Wacaan."

THE RISING sun licked Wanbli's bare back. He faced not the sun itself but west, where it was opening and revealing the estate to him. Tawlin's flat-topped buildings went from mud color—they were mud—to white, glistening with the mica in the plaster. The stripe of cloud at the horizon, beyond Hovart and the single mountain in the plain, lit up in pink and purple as it prepared to dissolve.

3

Though not a single alio stalk had exploded open for the day, there were already four black motes in the sky, leaving steam trails. One was close enough so that Wanbli could make it out as a private two-seater.

Now, as he opened his mouth to continue, he heard the first alio pop.

> "Other men are the birds of the air.
> Other men are the hogs at the trough.
> We are those who live. We are those who die.
> We are those who remain people.
> We are Wacaan."

He spoke perfectly audibly, but not as one speaks to be heard. He took another breath, which wanted to become a yawn. He had to urinate very badly. Every morning when he recited the invocation and came to the word "void," he was reminded of his full bladder. Nonetheless, Wanbli did not wiggle or grimace, and his hands on the hilt of the stone knife were steady.

> "I invoke the six directions upon this morning.
> I invoke the sun.
> I invoke the moons and their little sister that
>   is coming,
> Who is my little sister.
> I am of the people of the sky. I am Wacaan."

He lifted the knife above his head so that the sun struck it and lifted from its obsidian blade a different glitter than it gave to the buildings. The light it reflected was green and red, like the growth on the golden soil of T'chishett.

Wanbli lowered the knife in a more casual manner and laid it on his little altar cloth, which was spread out in front of his knees on the roof of his house. Flip, flip, left and right, top and bottom, he slapped the corners of the cloth over the blade and tied all ends in a knot that spanned the middle. He was protecting himself in all directions; enclosing himself in the earth as the knife was enclosed in the napkin. He did not feel particularly protected, however:

only badly folded. Tawlin T'chishetti had been at it all hours of the day and night, and of course his Wacaan shared that burden with him. Now the Wacaan came to his feet with a groan and cracked his back with one brick-brown hand at his hip. He walked to the edge of the roof, snapped the toggle of the insect screen and urinated over the side.

One very bad morning, after Tawlin T'chishetti had been especially troublesome, Wanbli had forgotten the toggle and had had to hose down the entire roof. Why he had to finish the invocation before voiding he did not understand. Usually it meant he woke himself up in the middle of the night so it would be easier to wait in the morning. Maybe that was the reason for the custom—to make him a light sleeper.

Now he could yawn without offense to the earth or the sky. Or the sun or the moon or the six directions, separately or together. He yawned six times, once for each direction and then once more for good measure. Down below, one of the alios in the herbal border popped, shooting out the ratchett that had sheltered in its armored petals all night. The little creature landed rolling and then running. The darter that nested in the eaves missed it, but not by much. Wanbli watched without taking sides, and then turned away from the edge. Replacing the insect screen, which was invisible except for a slight shimmer and which also kept out dust, he stepped to the hatch and went down.

The first place he went was to the kitchen, for a cup of tea. He made it strong and added a childish amount of milk and sugar. Sugar was more or less taboo for the Wacaan, and for that reason, he enjoyed it immensely. Long after the dextrose had let him down, the knowledge of his sin would keep Wanbli bright-eyed and smug. (He knew this about himself. He knew how and when to sin. He had learned it in school.)

The next place he went, cup in hand, was to the full-length mirror in the dormitory. There he examined his image critically but with some enjoyment.

His skeletal proportions were very balanced. Of course. He was a Wacaan. His muscular development left little to be desired also, and that was more his own doing. His coloring, which might have been café au lait on another, colder world, was bright russet, and the black hair shone with red highlights, even under the cool artificial light of the room. The eyes with which he regarded himself were dark, and of a garnet shade.

This much was a given. So was his perfectly nice Wacaan face (to outsiders they were peas in a pod). It was not his face or head or even his general physique that held Wanbli's attention, but his tattoos.

Starting at the dimple at the base of the throat and running under the length of each clavicle were tattoos of feathers—long feathers, black with gold edging, which ended only at the top of the arms.

Below, drawn from the solar plexus along the bottom of the rib cage and drooping gracefully down almost to the navel, was another pair, this time of blue just touched by green, like the dusty sky of T'chishett. It was also edged in gold.

Lower, where they would be covered by any shorts or breechclout, were a still more graceful and drooping pair of feather tattoos, and this pair was entirely gold. Wanbli glanced down at this tattoo and had to grin, even though he had won it almost a year since. He had been known to suffer quite a bit of pain to pluck out pubic hairs that threatened to obscure the gold feathers.

The training of a Paint was a very challenging thing. Many young Wacaan found themselves turning to other occupations: crafts, farming, even digging into the crumbly yellow sandstone of Southbay for its sparse minerals, rather than completing the ten years of study, workout, privation and ordeal that led to the Journeyman Eagle. Wanbli, who had earned all three Eagles in that same length of time, thought he was rather special among Paints.

His education had been rewarding. He could wish the working life of a Paint to be half as much fun. Ten years climbing a ladder to find nothing on top. Nothing but day after day.

His reflection was looking sour. He changed its expression.

"You'll do for one more day," he said very severely to his

image, and went to his shelf to decide how to cover his golden pride this day.

For the different weathers of Neunacht he had three sorts of outfits: G-strings, breechclouts and thigh-length shorts. Nights were colder; at night he might wear a blanket affair with a hole in it for his head. It was not comfortable, but it was custom.

As it seemed a temperate sort of day, he chose a woven breechclout. First he spread it down on his bed, along the striped blanket, made a small bunch in the middle of it and raised his fist. He hit the bed a blow that shivered the batting from one end to another, but the little hollow he had created in the fabric of the breechclout remained rigid. Then he poked it gently with a finger and it collapsed, as fabric should.

It was a bother to perform this test every day, but once, as a stripling, Wanbli had found himself neglecting it and had gone out into practice with a broken seat belt. The first solid blow to the crotch had put him out of training for a week and made him the butt of jokes through his whole clan sept. He hated to be made fun of, so now he was careful.

On the waistband of the breechclout he snapped his holster, which contained a stocky little gun with a funnel-shaped barrel: his blunderbuzz. On the other side went his wallet, a small leatherette bag containing his personal logic pad, his case knife, a pack of chewing gum and various items of magical import. Off the estate, he might also carry money. Most of the citizens of T'chishett wore their wallets around their necks, but the painted Wacaan made a taboo of that. One might be strangled by the cord, was the official explanation, but in fact the cord need not be heavy enough to be dangerous; the truth was that a wallet so hung obscured the wearer's Eagles.

Mimi's bed was next to his, partitioned only by a half-wall. It was an unmade nest, as usual. Wanbli could close his eyes and see Mimi as he would be in another ten minutes, toppling into it; no doubt he was thinking of his bed even now. Had the T'chishetti continued acting up all night and into the rising sun? It was drugs again. Drugs and perhaps Ake Tawlin T'chishetti's pride in his own bad reputation.

A more substantial wall separated Mimi's place of mess from Vynur's cubby. Vynur had given notice over a month ago, but Tawlin T'chishetti had made no move to replace her. No doubt it would have to be taken up in Clan Council. Vynur had been out interviewing for two days now, which made it difficult for the other Wacaan. Perhaps she would not come back, and that was a scandal against all the Paints. But Wanbli was her first cousin and school-fellow and Mimi was at least an old lover. They had not said a word of protest (except between themselves). What else could the woman do, after all, when her employer refused to look for a replacement? Once she had found another berth, they could howl in unison, and Tawlin would run the danger of losing his Wacaan entirely.

Sentence of death.

Wanbli gazed lazily through the deep-set window, finishing the last of his tea and watching a pink sky. Had he not been so tired, Wanbli would have wakened before dawn and seen the stars out. As much as the day sky, he liked the sight of the stars.

Out of the wind now, his ears could pick up snatches of orchestral music: not freestanding music, but the uneven sort that accompanies theatricals. The old man wasn't asleep yet. Poor Mimi.

Of course, the old man behaved that way because he was bored. Wanbli could understand that. He himself was bored. He behaved better about it, being Wacaan, but he *was* bored.

He went out.

The new sun was soft on muscles that were growing very stiff. This would make the third day he had had no time for training, and on the third day a painted Wacaan began to feel insecure. On the third day he started to lose ground. Wanbli rubbed his hand over his Journeyman's tattoo—the green one—and he scratched surreptitiously over his gold. His fingers did not move quickly enough to engage the seat belt.

T'chishett is in the equatorial regions of Neunacht, and

except for one short season, there is no rain. The sunlight lifted Wanbli's under-eyelids, making his eyes into garnet-brown crescents and in later years it was sure to give him the fan pattern of wrinkles the Wacaan called "wisdom."

Wanbli called it "headache" instead, but his ancestors had seen to it that he was built for the sun and it did him no real harm.

From the outside the main buildings of Tawlin were very white and simple. They seemed to be floating on a shimmer of the air. If one took the main, sculptured, alio-lined path to the door (as Wanbli never did, on principle), one had the impression that Mount Hov rose out of the roof of the reception hall.

Wanbli thought it a very silly effect.

He came to the pale building through the loose sand, indirectly as a cat. He touched the blank wall and followed it to the door, which knew him and opened. Before entering, Wanbli took his blunderbuzz out of the holster and thrust it before him into the doorway. The air erupted in racket; he drew the gun back again and snapped out the battery, which he shoved under a rock among those in the border design. He could as well have hidden the logic module, since it was the combination of armory logic and power source that triggered the house alarm, but it suffered more from dust than did the battery. Wanbli's only purpose in bringing the gun into the house was to test the alarm. He placed the inactive weapon into a box fitted into the inner wall which opened to the hands of the Tawlin Wacaans only. The shell of Mimi's gun was still lying there.

Inside, the desert lightness and the airy sense of infinity was squashed by Tawlin's collected clutter. Ake Tawlin greeted the visitor with a two-meter-high blue statue of an ugly dog with bulbous eyes, ears, nose and teeth, which was pawing a flattened sort of ball which looked much like a second nose, equally bulbous. This dog, in fact, had bulbous everything except its hind end, which was completely inadequate to its size. It was this hind end which the Wacaan first saw, coming into the hall at change of shift. The creature was a reproduction of a relic of Tawlin's Earth heritage, Wanbli had been told.

Some relics deserved to be lost.

The walls were lined with edged weapons, some of which were from Earth also, but none of which had any identifiable connection with the line of Tawlin. Wanbli disapproved of these displays more than he did of the blue dog. There was no place for random weapons in the household of one of the T'chishetti merchant princes, and especially one as unpopular as Tawlin. They were all in a shocking state of decay, but they could still cut his pouchy throat.

He felt his second stab of disappointment that morning: that life should lead to nothing more than this. If it were not for the fact that Wanbli's mother had worked here, and that he had been as good as raised on these grounds and apprenticed at Tawlin, he would have left with Vynur. For a moment he wished he had.

Wanbli glanced around the room smoothly as the fiber mat sucked the dust from his feet. Panels with rotten scrolls. Perhaps reproduction rotten. Maces, morning stars, a labrys that could never have been used as a weapon (it was so big), a row of ash urns—they would have put his mother in one of those, thinking it a privilege—one lamp in the ceiling out, a tapestry of Mount Hov in raintime over two lost-looking rattan chairs, a recliner in cracked leather, two standing suits of radiation armor around a stone fireplace and a much-larger-than-life-size bronze of a sort of prehistoric darter which was called a dragon. Under all was a very busy multicolored carpet depicting the settlement of Neunacht (to be read from the left right and the top down), which had been imported at expense from the planet Selim FC, where they make such things.

Other visitors took their shoes off at the door, but the Wacaan were by practice barefoot, hence the mat. Having one's bare feet matted was unbearable to some people, but Wanbli was not in the least ticklish; he rather liked it. He stepped off onto the aniline red of the carpet, which felt slippery in contrast, and he padded toe-heel down the long room.

No one ever came in this way except during formal receptions. Formal receptions had stopped entirely as Ake Tawlin aged and lost interest. This was exactly the reason

Wanbli entered via the memorial hall so often. He was me-
thodically unpredictable.

The long passage running along the library had two more
lights out. One of the Wacaan would have to talk to the
housekeeper. "One of them" meant Wanbli, of course. The
poor housekeeper was too frightened of the other Paints to
be reasonable in their presence. Wanbli himself was very
approachable; that was one of his vanities.

At the end of the passage began the personal living space
of Tawlin himself. The moisture screen nipped at Wanbli's
lips and eyes as he passed in and his nose felt a moment of
oddness, as though he'd been crying.

Ake Tawlin T'chishetti had gone in for ferns a few years
ago, and the huge things squatted spiderish against the wall
or stood like open parasols on stands. To Wanbli these
looked predatory. They offered concealment of which a Wacaan could not approve.

They were concealing Mimi right now, though not from
the eyes of Wanbli. The night guard was a very tired rufous
arc squatting against the white wall, under an opulent
Nephrolepis. He looked up at his mate as one might look up
at a savior on whom one had quite given up.

"Long night, Aymimishett?" asked Wanbli. He poked the
man lightly with his knee. "He never made it no easier?"

Bad grammar was a Wacaan tradition.

Mimi pulled his lips back: a gesture that would have to
do in place of a grin. "The last guest left a dec or two after
midnight . . ."

"I know, I heard the cars."

"But he been waltzin' out on his own since." With Mimi,
the erratic grammar was not merely tradition, it was all that
he knew.

He was a sad man, much older than Wanbli. Standard
two Eagle Wacaan. He'd been tagged once, at Mondoc
T'chishetti. There he had been happy for fifteen years and
now he could not go back.

Ake Tawlin did not appreciate him. He could not con-
verse.

"He was out there a couple decs ago, catching moons in
his nightie. Peein' the posies."

Urinating on the alios was a boy's game. It made them pop open, even in the middle of the night. It wasn't good for the flowers, however, and sometimes a boy would get hit in the member by a urine-stained ratchett. Sometimes the ratchetts bit.

Wanbli sighed in sympathy. "What's he been doing? Taking, I mean. Povlen? Pipe?"

An odd sort of dignity settled on Mimi's features. Superimposed on his tiredness, it made him appear drunk or very foolish. "What does a Wacaan know about trash like that?"

Wanbli smirked his smirk. "This Wacaan knows quite a lot. Tawlin household is an education."

"You can have it," said Mimi, rising. His back crackled. "This ignorant clanner is going to bed."

"Great. Go wrap yourself in that izzard's nest of yours. Put a gel blindfold over your weary eyes. Commune with the Nine Protectors and return to us with new vitality."

Mimi gave his fellow a suspicious glance. He never knew when Wanbli was serious and when he was making fun. "You shouldn't joke about the Protectors, Wanbli. It's very bad luck."

"Oh, I wouldn't." Wanbli was trotting across the room. He stuck his head in the bath. The private chamber was closed. "He's finally curled his knees up?"

"Half dec ago," answered Mimi as he turned to go. "He tottered away and left the screen on. It's still that way."

Mimi didn't know how to operate the arena projector. He had never tried. "Okay," said Wanbli. "Have good dreams."

This batch of cheapies involved feet. Sex and feet, of course. Wanbli caught the gist of the entertainment as it flashed on the wall in a hurricane of fast forward. The others had feet in their titles: *Pretty Pink Peds, Between Your Toes* . . . Had he not just woken up, Wanbli might have been tempted to browse through; after all, what else had he to do but prowl the house and watch his employer sleep? But he had just woken up, and though it was not too early for sex, it was far too early for feet. Besides, he did not share Tawlin T'chishetti's fondness for the peculiarities of flat-image projection. The man said it gave him remove and a godlike superiority to the action. Godlike superiority. Wanbli snorted indulgently, feeling a little Godlike superiority himself.

Wanbli himself preferred a good Arena Theatrical, even if it meant clearing a room of furniture. He had spent whole days watching AT behind Tawlin's chair or, more likely, couch. It was all in the call of duty. He was interested in all types of AT, because they gave him new insights into people, and even better, into the places they came from. (Wanbli had never been off Neunacht; only a handful of Wacaan had been out for one hundred and fifty years.) Most of the ATs contained some episodes of fighting, which was Wanbli's clan destiny and his occupation. From what he gathered, the standards of personal combat on New Benares, where most of the entertainments originated, were either much lower or much higher than those on Neunacht: lower because the actors moved so slowly and with so much useless flailing. Higher because the moves were so complex, and because it seemed to take so very much punishment to drop them. Considering the matter reasonably, Wanbli thought that probably the local standards were high, but that the actors were not sufficiently trained to carry out the technique.

He preferred the sex-oriented shimmers anyway. Wanbli prided himself as much upon his bedroom games as he did upon the gold tattoo under his breechclout—and wasn't that often called the seducer's eagle? Not that a Wacaan had to try very hard to seduce anyone; all the world knew they were good.

Romantic ATs were a puzzle to him, and perhaps his favorite for that reason. He liked to try to imagine himself in the grip of an unbreakable passion, living or dying for the touch of some woman's hand, like Paovo in *The Garden of Grief.* It was a very foreign and exotic mental exercise to Wanbli: strange as floating off into the air. Someday, perhaps, he would find within himself the roots of a deep passion for some uncaring female who would be cruel to him, and then his understanding of life would reach new levels. (He would also be sent back to the clan hospital in Hovart

13

for ritual cleansing and reeducation, which would look very bad on his record, but what was life for?)

The humidi-field, the deep windows and the white walls turned the bright morning sunlight into a cooler, more crystalline illumination. Wanbli put the wound cords of the cheapies into their thumb-size plastic sleeves and wondered what there was about feet to attract Tawlin. The T'chishetti's own tended toward bunions.

A darter whirred against the window screen. Perhaps the frustrated individual that had missed the ratchett a few minutes ago. Wanbli yawned again, irritated that he had let Tawlin's party disturb his sleep. He disconnected the machine; it was very simple.

Late alios were still popping and the daygrass cut into the breeze. The ferns whispered together as though they were dry, which (the Nine Protectors knew) they were not. A barefoot scuff, sounding lazy on the stone floor among them. Repeated.

Mimi coming back. He would strap him to the chair and force him to learn the controls of the cheapie projector.

No. Mimi would not come padding on his toes like a dog: not after all night standing and watching other people debauch. No energy for it.

No one but the Wacaan walked barefoot at Tawlin Estate.

A car, gliding nearer out of the west. Two-seater, he remembered.

A barefoot scuff, sounding lazy on the stone floor. Repeated. Wanbli was in the air and flying. He was down again on bent knees, silently, pressed against the doorjamb to the long fern hall.

As he was aware of the intruder, the intruder was aware of Wanbli. They faced each other through the doorway of white mud and shining mica. They were three meters apart and so neither put his guard up. The other Wacaan had his hands in fists at his sides.

"Heydoc. Welcome to Tawlin. You should have let me know. I could have saved you the trip. The T'chishetti is in his sealed bedroom and will probably stay there half the day."

Heydoc grinned, not as smugly as Wanbli but with a lot

of teeth. His eyes did not exactly wander from Wanbli's face but they were very aware of the right side of the room around him. "Not so, cousin. In his room, yes, but not sealed. I've already counted coup on your degenerate employer and now I'm on my way out. You can either let me go or get hurt for nothing." Heydoc shuffled smoothly back into the ferny chamber. He glanced right and behind him.

Wanbli stood unmoving, slack-shouldered. He scratched his hip under the waistband. His smile was not fierce at all. " 'Docs, you'll only get in trouble using your mouth; it's a weapon you haven't studied."

"And you have? You do tongue-training exercises maybe? You can touch your nose maybe?" Heydoc had taken one more step back, and now he slowly raised his guard.

"I know very well you haven't counted coup on my old man. He's such an accident of birth no one would stoop to giving him a warning, and he wouldn't take it anyway. And I know the door is sealed." Wanbli moved toward Heydoc. The round-arched doorway was in front of him now.

"And I know, by the way you refuse to look left," he continued, still scratching an old bite under the waistband, "that you're . . ."

". . . not alone!" The hidden woman beside the doorway snapped a chained stick down at Wanbli's head. He did not bother trying to block it; any way it hit it would hurt badly. He shot out of the way, toward Heydoc and around him.

He was between Heydoc and the sealed bedroom door. Heydoc was between Wanbli and the woman with the sticks. "Punch him out, Hey," she called out. She was angry. She had let the flail snap her on the knuckles.

Heydoc moved in with a left guard forward. This was fine —better than tea with sugar for waking one up. Wanbli wasn't afraid of a little fist and kicking work with Heydoc. The Wacaan of T'chishett knew each other, and Heydoc was fast but not deadly.

He was also left-handed, though, which Wanbli remembered well. Left-handed fighters were boxes of surprises and he had memorized the left-handed Wacaan as part of his Second Eagle. Why would Heydoc come on with his left first? Most fighters kept their strong hand behind. And that

15

rear hand of his was cramped in against his chest: not even a proper fist. Wanbli let the left come, and true to prediction, it was only a feint. Here came that odd right, with Heydoc's hip and foot moving forward with it, in a punch to the chin that would just barely miss.

Wanbli did not have to see that little flash of metal to know that there was an inch of blade trailing behind Heydoc's little finger, but see it he did. The unfocused punch to the chin was actually a very accurate knife stroke across the throat. But halfway along its trajectory that punch developed a rider, as Wanbli put one soft hand over the front of it and guided it out. As this was happening, the throat in question was very busy going elsewhere. Wanbli ducked and went left, still with his hand glued to the hand with the knife. That right arm of Heydoc's would not get in the way of his good hand. There would be a kick coming soon, but for now, here was Wanbli staring in at Heydoc's crotch, and such a gift of the Protectors could not be rejected. He reached in, not too fast—not fast enough to engage the seat belt—and squeezed. Not waiting to see the effect of that strike, Wanbli straightened up and his soft grip persuaded the knife hand backward. His flattened right hand struck into the elbow joint, collapsing the last resistance, and Wanbli had Heydoc's arm locked beside his head.

Of course, there was another opponent, and this second and a half had given her time to get around her partner. She held the chained sticks in her hand but did not use them again. Instead she lifted her knee up so sharply it clapped against her chest and brought the weight of her leg and the weight of her whole body down in a bone-crushing kick at Wanbli's knee.

Sensible move. No dramatics. There was no room to get out of the way of this, either, while holding the knife man. Need brought Wanbli's right leg up in a deflecting strike that sent her thrust kick shooting out into the air beside him. His own foot came down on the inside rear of her supporting knee and the woman went down flat. He kicked the sticks out of her hands.

Not quite three seconds had passed since Heydoc had thrown his first punch.

"I want you to think, before you move again," said Wanbli to the woman, whose name he seemed to remember was Susan, ". . . where the knife is at the moment, and how much this flyer means to you. Maybe nothing, but think about it."

Where the knife was, was under Heydoc's chin, over the carotid artery, where it bounced and glimmered with every pulse. Heydoc, whose own helpless hand was holding it there, was staring blankly at the sealed door to Tawlin's room.

The woman lay on the floor and looked and looked at the tiny knife.

"Now, you can both take Tag and get out of here, or Susie can try me again, and maybe I'll be slowed down enough killing Docs here that she can dust me. I don't think it's likely but it is a possibility. The alternative is that you walk back to Hovart and start looking for another job: both of you."

Heydoc said nothing. "I'll take Tag," said Susan on the floor. Her partner slowly let his breath out. "Tag," he said. "Of course."

"And the keys?" Wanbli held his hand out. "Remember —you walk out?"

Susie opened her mouth as though to make some objection, but at last she pulled from her waist pouch a star of turquoise-colored plastic on a flimsy chain. He snagged it from her.

The attackers left as quietly as they had come, Heydoc still with the little bright knife in his hand.

For a few minutes Wanbli stood where he was, his gaze fixed on the floor, fingering the car key in his hand.

He was twenty-four, and despite a lifetime of training for battle, nobody had ever really tried to kill him before. His own people too. Well, who else but a Wacaan would dare attack a Wacaan?

He felt a bit of shock, and waited for that to fade. It was vanity that cheered him up in the end; the Third Eagle—

not universally well regarded among conservative Paints—
had proven its usefulness. Tongue exercises, indeed.

And how many young Wacaan, not even sire-promoted,
had estate cars of their very own? How many Wacaan ever
got so much wealth together? He slipped the pretty key into
his wallet.

It was very difficult to wake up Tawlin, and not even his
Wacaan could break the seal on a night-sealed, windowless
bedroom. He pounded with his flat hand. He used a great
deal of cursing.

"If you don't want to know, then . . ." he shouted (the
Wacaan were very good shouters), "then gut you. Then to
sizzle with you, Ake Tawlin! You might have been crawling
with hungry, happy bugs by now. You might have been
spindleworm food. Darters in your eyes . . . Maggots.
Mealworms . . ."

The slate-heavy door slid open. "Progenitors, how you
talk to me!" said Ake Tawlin, who was a head shorter than
Wanbli. "Are you on drugs, redman?"

As Wanbli was red, Tawlin was yellow, but nowhere near
as decisively colored. "Who would believe it's I who pay
your salary?" He was blinking fast. He used the door to
lean on.

"There were two Wacaan here just now to kill you,
Tawlin."

Now the little man's attention was locked.

"To kill me too, by the bye, but you were the target. Of
course."

Tawlin's eyes, already dilated by stimulant, widened further. His hand shot to the switch and the door began
to close again. Wanbli jumped through, knocking the
T'chishetti into the wall in the process. Both were sealed
into a small room of which the walls were red-and-blue
paisley, like a rather florid sort of shawl.

Tawlin sat down on the bed. "But . . . but they
couldn't. I was sealed in."

Wanbli admitted the force of that. "Lucky for you. But
how could those poor flyers know, when they planned it,
that you had chosen today to exchange day for night?"

Ake Tawlin leaned against his headboard, which, misin-terpreting the gesture, glowed for reading. He wrapped himself up in his own thin arms. "I must say, 'Bli, you show an unexpected sympathy with my attempted assassins."

Wanbli sank down on his heels, using the door for sup-port. "Sure. One of them is my cousin. I very much doubt that this assault was their idea. And after all, they lost a lot."

Tawlin cleared his sleepy throat. "You . . . uh . . . took care of them?" Wanbli nodded, with a rakish grin, but his employer's response was to push deeper into the padded headboard. He ran his hand through his unnaturally thick black hair. "Oh, why did we ever let you people in?" His sigh was deep and rattling.

"It has to remind me of the evolution of the combative male."

Now it was Wanbli's turn to blink.

"Yes, the combative male," continued Tawlin, and he glared. "Some time or other, some wee little vertebrate—a fish or like that—was born with the male of the species outsized and outstrength to all the others. I'm sure it didn't take long before that fish learned to bully all the rest. Miser-able for the whole lot of them, except the outsized male. But he managed to reproduce his mutated genes, didn't he? Didn't he, hey?"

"I guess." Wanbli was wondering whether the little man was even capable of reason at the moment. Perhaps he should have let him sleep.

"Soon the only way a female fish could reproduce at all was to find a big bully male . . ."

"I don't think fish really think like that," said Wanbli, knowing he was wasting his breath.

". . . And all the ordinary, decent, forward-thinking male fish were dead! Dead!" He sat up for emphasis.

"You're not dead," Wanbli reminded him.

". . . Never much good for the species, except for musk-oxen and the rare thing like that. But it outcompeted *within* the species and that was what evolution was all about, eh?

"Almost destroyed the human race a number of times. You think we'd have learned. We do not have to give way to that particular evolutionary twitch. And poor as we are on Neunacht too."

Wanbli took a lungful of very close air. "Then who was it talking about sending Vy and me out against Rall Estate last spring? A very bad idea too."

Tawlin seemed not to have heard. "This wasn't in the Founder's Plan, my bully. Whatever your synthetic legends say. We were sixty happy years on Neunacht with you primitives to yourselves in Southbay . . ."

"To ourselves, all right." Wanbli broke in, but calmly. "Starving by ourselves. No money."

"Whose fault was that? All societies are mercantile, given the latitude to be so. And believe me, with cartage fees for everything imported increasing by mile all the way from Hovart to the string intersection, we have little enough to spare for people playing unrealistic games."

Now it was Wanbli's attention that began to fade. He had been hearing about cartage fees all his life.

"It is ever to be regretted that Siering Mo opened the door to you. It was mere ambition on his part."

Wanbli listened to him denigrate the First Protector tolerantly, but added, "It's true, you flyers did pretty well butchering each other without us. In fact, the assassinations of the early years cut the number of incorporated houses in half. I think you're safer now."

Tawlin's small, bunioned feet sought concealment under the covers. "Safer, yes, as long as we subscribe to your damn protection racket. Keep a dog to protect myself against the other man's dogs."

Wanbli laughed. "Do you prefer your blue dog with all the curlicues?" Abruptly, his face sobered. "Tawlin, my mother died defending your life."

The feet went still. "I know," said Ake Tawlin. There was a short, complete silence in the room. "And now these two red friends of yours are dead attacking it. I don't like the whole thing."

"They're not dead."

Under the silk sheets, one could see Tawlin's toes curl. "They're not? They're still out there . . . bleeding?"

Wanbli laughed with real humor this time. "No, no. I

said I took care of them. They're Tagged. They won't come back."

"Tagged? Tagged?" As Tawlin leaned forward, the unintelligent bedstead put out its light. He squeaked at the sudden dark and slammed back against the headboard. "Dongs, man! They came to kill me and you just let them go?"

"They came a lot closer to killing me than you, Ake," answered Wanbli. His employer's rising hysteria inspired in him a contrasting mood of self-confidence. "And Tagging is the same as dusting a person, at least where you're concerned. They can never, never, as long as they live, lift a hand to do you harm. Nor can they return to their old employers. They might as well be dead."

"I know the theory!" Tawlin's emotions would not let him remain still any longer. He rose from the bed, waved the ceiling light alive and began to pace. Sealed chambers were by their nature small, and so his pacing involved stepping over Wanbli's knees.

"It's not theory," the Wacaan countered. "It's our way of life."

"Hah! Way of life. Then who killed Felix Mo but a Wacaan who had already been spanked and sent away once?"

Wanbli lifted a stiff set of shoulder blades and let them drop again. He stood up to allow the T'chishetti more room to pace. "That man was mad. Besides, when he broke Tag, he was no longer a Wacaan."

"I am not reassured by that." Tawlin was working himself into a good rage now. His emotions seemed to be dredging up the last of the Povlen, for his eyes were wonderfully black.

"We destroyed him, you remember."

"I am not reassured by that either." Tawlin stopped and faced his tall bodyguard. "I tell you I am not coming out of this room until you follow those two thugs down and get rid of them for real."

"Then you will have a restricted life, Tawlin. You cannot send a Wacaan after Wacaan, you know." He put a reassuring hand down on Tawlin's shoulder. It was brushed off.

". . . what I can do and what I can't do! Who thumbs

21

the check around here? Then go after Rall herself. She's the bitch who sent them."

Wanbli sighed. He gazed up at the aimless, buoyant ceiling globes. Without warning he grabbed Tawlin's delicate hand and slapped it against the wall plate. White daylight filled the room, with moisture and the smell of ferns. Tawlin cursed energetically and pressed the panel again, but Wanbli was standing in the doorway, and the door was inhibited from cutting people in two. "Look, Tawlin. It's empty. Bare. Okay. Safe."

"Rall has used both her Wacaan up against you. She will have to apply to Clan Council to be assigned more and until then she'll be in strict hiding. I won't be able to find her.

"And what about you? Without Vynur you have only the two of us, and Mimi is on the edge of exhaustion. Don't you have any more enemies to watch out for? Enemies that might hear about this little tiff today?"

Tawlin glared as though Wanbli was the enemy in question. His expression changed, softened and became desperate and the T'chishetti stumbled off toward the rear wall of the sealed chamber, which slid open and showed him the toilet.

Wanbli sat outside the lavatory door and listened to his employer's empty retching. He had tried the friendly firm hand at the base of Tawlin's neck and had been rudely rejected. He sat and he fingered his new car key and he thought. When the distressing noises eased, he called out, "Tell me, Ake, old flyer: does this male mutation you were going on about have anything to do with feet?"

Tawlin T'chishetti was in no hurry to show his face. He dabbed with perfumed water before expanding the door into the bedroom. "Feet? I didn't mention . . . oh. Right. I can't trust that cousin of yours to do anything for me."

Aymimishett was a clan brother but not a cousin. Wanbli had said as much to Tawlin times without count. He didn't repeat himself now.

Ake Tawlin felt much better. Much better. The Povlen was kept in the lavatory cabinet. "You, redman, are a different tale altogether. To make that connection—even if it was a silly one. No, 'Bli, the history of vertebrate evolution has a great deal to do with feet, but not with foot fetishism. I got that stack of cheapies on special deal—almost for nothing. I'm good at that. Have to be, poor as I am."

Wanbli nodded in good-natured agreement. "You are, goldman, you are." When the Wacaan called the T'chishetti "goldman," the T'chishetti believed they were referring to skin color. Or they pretended to.

"Most Paints wouldn't bother trying to make sense out of the two things—my waking up and talking about mutation and the strange flicks I was watching last night." He gave his Wacaan a very proprietary glance.

"I really should have had you educated. But the noise that would have made . . ."

Wanbli's garnet eyes revealed one moment of real anger. "*Had* me educated? I *am* educated, Tawlin. There are very few of the Wacaan to have passed the Third Eagle on their first try and almost all of those were women. There are no Third Eagles at all my age."

Tawlin strode out of the sealed room into the light, looking neither left nor right. He stroked a fern tenderly. "I know, 'Bli. I've watched your progress all your life. Only to be expected. But I meant real education. In business. Politics."

Wanbli's anger melted into condescension. "You don't know much about Third Eagle training if you think I've missed that."

Tawlin stretched and cracked his shoulder blades in a very athletic manner (Povlen was like that). "I don't know much? You don't know much, my boy. Not about me. Not about yourself, either."

Tawlin had the attitude of a man about to offer revelations. Wanbli had heard Povlen revelations before. He broke in. "I think it's time to take you to Hovart Clan House, Tawlin. Remember—you're short a guardian. Since you repelled an attack today, you have the right to stay there until your house is full again." The key in his wallet felt delicious against his fingers.

Tawlin yawned, growing more alert by the moment. "The Clan House? Oddly enough, that's where you just sent the two assassins who were going to kill us, didn't you? What if I ran into them in the front hallway, heh?"

That Tawlin should run into the pair was unlikely, since they were walking the distance, but perhaps the goldman hadn't made this particular "connection." Wanbli's right to the property brought in the attack was undeniable, but he didn't want to embark on a discussion of it with a Povlen-laced T'chishetti. "Then you could hire them. Perfect solution to the problem." Wanbli only half thought of it as a joke, but Tawlin was full of himself enough to take it that way.

"No, thanks. I don't want losers in my stable," he said. "Besides—I'm only permitted three guardians by law. Remember?"

"Right said. But I'm leaving," said Wanbli, and it became true as he said it. He repeated, "I'm leaving."

Tawlin's glance became even more tender. He turned to the nearest window, plucked a fern frond and played with the shimmer of the field. "Just like that? What a very un-Wacaan thing to do. But then you're not really a Wacaan, are you?"

"It's not so sudden. You've made it sizzling flames to work for you these past . . . What on the Ninety-eight do you mean by that—not really a Wacaan?"

Ake Tawlin sat down on a white wicker chair under the light of the window. He seemed to have forgotten all danger from outside. His ivory pajamas, however, were slightly soiled with vomit. "I mean that the Wacaan are very predictable. They glory in it."

"Not in fighting, we're not."

"Since you fight with each other, the question is academic. But you, Wanbli, son of Damasc, are very different. Bright, questioning, unconventional. You are like me. As is inevitable."

"You know that I am on the T'chishett National Baby Board. And, of course, that I spent years in close contact with your mother."

Wanbli came up behind Tawlin, making the T'chishetti flinch. He leaned past him to inspect the scene out the window, both the desert and the garden. "Are you telling me you decided who my father was to be? I doubt that. It takes a vote of thirty percent in total, as well as a majority of the clan involved, to get the valves opened."

Tawlin giggled, but he also stepped back. "But I myself, redman, have the key to my own balls. One of the privileges of plutocracy: even such a poor plutocracy as ours."

Wanbli said nothing at all.

"Your mother was granted one child and by her choice of three fathers. That was all very conventional. But I was there first. I was there first."

"She must have felt sorry for you," said Wanbli defensively.

Tawlin grinned reminiscently. "What can you know about that? You were the one who said she died for my life."

"That was duty! She died maintaining her own honor, moneybags, and I doubt if she thought of you in the process at all!"

"I've made the Wacaan angry. How odd. The half-Wacaan, perhaps."

Wanbli slapped his hand against the wall, so that the pain would bring him back to himself.

"When you were a baby, you looked much more like me."

"That's because you look like a baby, goldman. Any baby." He had himself under control again. "Watch yourself, Ake. You're bragging yourself into a super-national crime, here."

"Only among family." Ake Tawlin was very happy with this riposte. He let the tall Wacaan loom over his chair and waited for the response. It came in the form of soft footsteps, receding down the hall.

"Wanbli, what are you doing?" Tawlin called. Povlen and lack of sleep made him hoarse.

"I'm being unpredictable again. Go to Hovart or stay here and watch Mimi sleep. I'm gone."

Tawlin sat down again. He decided that perhaps he would take the drive.

25

* * *

The dry morning was glorious now. The air felt bright in and out of his lungs and the sky had just enough pink and green to be comfortable. All the day plants were open, both the armored and the feathery and the darters made small creaking noises under the eaves. Wanbli slouched to the Wacaan compound with his gun in his hand; exhilaration made him cautious. He stood by the window, filtering sand between his toes for a moment.

Home seemed killing beautiful, now that he would leave it. He rolled into the guardhouse through a window, crackling the field.

"Mimi, old flyer, wake up," he said. Wanbli called out from beside the doorway. Not too close: Mimi was overtired and a tired Wacaan could wake up fighting.

He woke up quickly enough, but with no more violence than a protesting bleat. "Pro-tectors, Wanbli, what is it?"

Wanbli came in and sat on the bed. Aymimishett took one look at his face and repeated more querulously, "What is it?"

Mimi did not believe in good news.

"Many things, all pushed into a little half dec," said Wanbli. His smile was so sly that Mimi found it obnoxious. "We have had an assault." Mimi made another little noise. "No harm done, and it's over," continued Wanbli. His fingers drummed on his bare knee. He was so jazzed, he felt he might as well have taken Povlen himself. "Remember Susie, from Rall's?"

Mimi began to grin and then remembered the situation. "And Heydoc? They were just here to kill Tawlin. Heydoc claimed to be counting coup, but that was so much gas."

Mimi was out of bed now and standing at ready, as though there was need for action. "And you took them on together?"

Wanbli chuckled. He did not rise from the pallet. "Oh, I wanted to wake you, but they were pressed for time. I took care of it, though."

Mimi took a slow, calming breath and began to prowl. As Wanbli didn't move and it was Wanbli's story, he had to prowl in small circles. "You're all right?"

26

"Far as I know. I haven't felt any air holes yet. They're all right too, Mimi, except for some minor bumps. Just out of work."

Mimi hadn't wanted to ask. Now he could allow himself to smile at the thought of Susie again.

"And I've got the key to a great big Rall aircar in my bag," concluded Wanbli. There was so much wonderment in his expression that his complacent words were robbed of all insult, even to the unlucky Mimi.

"A car?"

"A very nice car," answered Wanbli, though he had not yet seen it, except out of the corner of his eye.

"What will you do with it?"

When a Paint came into big money like this (and they came into big money in no other way) it was always a question of what to do with it. He could not possibly keep the car, because it would cost too much to feed, and if a Paint needed transportation, he would see that his employer furnished it.

He could buy food, but he couldn't eat that much. He could buy clothing, but he couldn't wear that much. He would not be permitted to buy a house, and if he had been, when would he stay in it, living on the T'chishetti estates as the Paints did? If he were old or merely despondent he might retire to Southbay.

Money would not influence the Council's decision on genetic suitability, which was the true success of a Wacaan. Usually a rich Wacaan gave the money away on his next birthday, eliminating the worry and earning points as a great good flyer.

"What I'm going to do with it," Wanbli began very hesitantly, gathering speed in his words, "is travel."

"Where?" asked Mimi in slightly envious appreciation. More nervously he added, "When? You can't leave until we get both a replacement for Vynur and a temp for . . ."

Wanbli looked at the pallet, not at Aymimishett. This was not easy. "No problem there. Tawlin will have to stop gassing and go to Hovart Clan House now. Today. There it can all be handled quickly. You go with him and pick out two new partners, and get a good rest for once.

27

"I'm not coming back here."

Mimi stared and made fish mouths. He sank down beside Wanbli with one hand on his friend's shoulder. He looked old.

No, this was not easy.

"Wanbli. You were born here," he said, and there was actually pity in the man's words.

"Not actually. I was born at Hovart House. I spent most of my first twenty years, off and on, in Southbay."

"Of course. We all did. But Tawlin is home for you."

Wanbli gave a little sniff, which sounded odd to himself. "No more. I'm leaving today."

"Because of the attack?" Mimi was floundering for meaning, and Wanbli couldn't help, for he didn't understand himself. Not on a level to be explained.

"No. Because I now have the feathers to fly."

"But today? That's not planning. That's not discipline." Mimi's large, fleshless features worked with his thinking. "That's not Wacaan."

"I don't need to hear that!" Wanbli was surprised at his own irritation. It was that accident of birth's damn Povlenwarped suggestion. "It's perfectly disciplined. When would be better, with Tawlin already having to go to Hovart House? Should I wait for him to replace Vynur and for us all to settle into a routine? It'll take a bomb to move him again after all this. Strike while the enemy is hot!"

There were flaws in Wanbli's logic that even Mimi could see. But Mimi had the Wacaan sensibility to know that logic was not at issue here. "So where will you go?"

Wanbli waited in his answer. "New Benares."

Mimi's face wrinkled and then he relaxed all over. "Man, I thought you were serious. Don't wind that around me again!"

This wasn't easy at all. Not at all. "I am serious, Aymimishett, Clan Brother. I'm leaving as soon as I can get a boat out." Wanbli stood and faced Mimi, leaning over him, trying to express his earnest in every inch of his body. "I'm going to make shimmers."

"They won't let you. The Clan Council won't give you

congé for that. They wouldn't okay your going off-planet even if they did."

Mimi wouldn't look at him. Wanbli straightened.

The air was still very sweet. Outside Mimi's dark cubby the sun was rising toward a brilliant noon. "So who is going to tell them about it, Mimi?"

Mimi groaned. "So now I'm a party to all this? On top of overwork and . . . and abandonment? Both you and Vynur. Now I'm to lie to the Council at Hovart and say I don't know where you've gone?"

Tears stung Wanbli's eyes for an instant. "Not abandonment, Mimi. I don't want to leave you behind at all. You could come with me and avoid the whole mess. Let Tawlin interview a whole new trio of Paints. A new 'stable,' as he calls us. You *can* walk out. Why not? We'll see how far the money from the car will take us, and talk our way the rest of the trip."

Still Mimi didn't look up. "I have no interest in being an actor, Wanbli, Clan Brother. Nor a thief nor a tramp." His voice was very sad. Wanbli turned to go.

He was in the doorway when Mimi added, "You are close to guaranteed sire-promotion, you know. As close as any Wacaan ever was."

Wanbli stopped and sagged against the doorjamb. There was so much feeling behind Mimi's words. He had never fathered a child.

What he had said was enormous praise: unlike Aymimishett. It was also true.

Wanbli had always depended upon sire-promotion. He would be a better father than Flammulus had been to him. He would never take employment at the other end of the country from his own son or daughter. He closed his eyes and tried to erase the events of the morning. He tried to forget the key in his pouch.

He found he was out the door and walking.

TWO

THE FLAPS of the cuyo bushes were fluttering around his knees and Wanbli was in a lyrical mood as he followed the track of the Rall assassins backward, carrying only a light pack, his blunderbuzz, and using his interference stick to walk. He sang the Third Protector's song as he went—under his breath, of course. He had been trained very early not to make noise in the desert—and in his mind he heard the Flamedart instrumental recording, all brass and percussion, as his accompaniment. Flamedart was a Wacaan group, but very popular all over T'chishett. Bright, not subtle.

He was not out of the grounds when he heard a growl in the air behind him and turned to see Tawlin's own estate car rise and shoot west, toward Hovart. He glimpsed (or wanted to glimpse) two heads against the blue-green sky. If that dinglehead had left Mimi behind with the servants . . . But no, if Tawlin showed up without Mimi, Hovart House would send him right back for the Wacaan. Within five seconds, the car was only a yellow dot against the horizon.

To the border of the gardens, Heydoc and Susie had come from the north, where they undoubtedly had used the great Pontiac table for cover. It rose up in front of Wanbli now, with sheer, crumbling red sides and a tri-level top that looked laser-planed. It was not the work of man. There was little money on Neunacht for Terraforming, and any reputable company would have done the work more cleanly than nature had.

There were legends connected with the Pontiac table. It was said that the ghosts of Hebe Tawlin and her children walked there at high noon on midwinter, because it was at high noon on midwinter that they had been brought there to be killed. That had been early in the days of settlement: before the Wacaan had come north. Wacaan did not kill children under eighteen and usually waited until the enemy was twenty-one. (T'chishetti of both sexes had developed a habit of underreporting their ages.) Hebe's oldest daughter (the legend went) had been named Pontiac.

Another story said that the tableland was named after an ancient aircar. It did not look much like an aircar to Wanbli as he touched the variegated sandstone wall, but he was willing to allow for imagination.

Here the couple had not yet begun being careful; the big footprints and the littler footprints marked the edge of the wall like a stenciled border. Susie had quite a turnout. She was almost duck-toed. Wanbli wondered if it was a conformational fault, which would be rare among Wacaan, or just her natural swagger.

The darters that nested in the crevices came out to look at him: big ones with their nappy wings and smaller ones which had wings like gauze and the smallest species where the wings were no more than a flicker, like the insect field around the windows. It was the smallest sort of darter that had taken on the responsibility of Wanbli's totem in his first initiation dreaming. He knew that a creature's apparent size and strength had nothing to do with its magical potency, but still, Wanbli was a bit embarrassed about it all. In the closed rituals of his year group, when each Paint had to name himself and leap the fire, he came between Howard Black Dog and Heyatuan Screamer: Wanbli Elf Darter. No one had ever laughed. Out loud. It was a very pretty flyer anyway, at least in the breeding season.

Halfway around the kilometer-long rock, he came to a strange thing; it seemed that Susie and Heydoc had stopped to dance right there on the path. Their feet made confused prints in all directions. There were skid marks. At one spot, Susie had gone stomp, stomp in place. As Wanbli stood and marveled, there came a light tap on his head, followed by a sensation of spreading pain.

It was a darter—not his own totem but a dull beast the length of a man's foot—and it had chosen to resent the presence of humans so close to its nest. Wanbli smacked it away and was out of there and running. A hundred meters away, with his scalp still throbbing, he began to wonder what his own footprints looked like.

The aircar was indeed something. It was long and an ethereal silvery-sand color which faded perfectly into the soil beside Pontiac table. No mere errand car, it seated its two passengers on glistening leather upholstery. Cars on Neunacht were very expensive, because of the amount of metal necessary, but for that same reason, what cars they did build or import were marvels of labor and care. For once the "poverty" of Neunacht would work in Wambli's favor.

He hopped the door and slid into the cockpit. He put the key against the plate with confidence; had the car been booby-trapped, Heydoc or Susie would have had to tell him so when taking Tag. It lifted with almost no noise.

Oh, it was beautiful. What power. Certainly it was no more than a year old, for the glass over the instruments had almost no sand scour and the upholstery was unsoiled. It was traditional that an employer who sent out Wacaan to risk their lives equipped them with the best they had. To do otherwise was to express doubt. Perhaps this was Rall T'chishett's personal car.

Wanbli wasted some time (but was it wasted? No, never

say so) doing tricks in the air, to accustom himself to the controls of the big vehicle, and then he aimed it toward town.

It occurred to him that he could locate Heydoc and Mimi, who had no reason to be stealthy anymore, and drive them into Hovart. But just because he was in a good mood didn't mean they would be glad to see him. Just the opposite, in fact. They'd probably rather walk. Wanbli went on, fast but at height enough for speed not to be dangerous. He was not a wild driver.

There was Mount Hov, standing alone in the plain just begging to be circled. Wanbli gratified the mountain, which twinkled its quartz top at him. Someone had climbed the slope, which was not so difficult a feat, and was standing on the round prominence. This someone waved to Wanbli. It was not difficult to climb Hove, but it took time and wind, so the climber would naturally want to be noticed. Wanbli gratified the climber too and waved back. Then he pointed the "mouse" in its box left and downward, toward the suburbs of Hovart.

He knew he had been taken, when he left the car yard, but he knew he had not been taken anywhere near as badly as most Wacaan would have been, and that, for Wanbli, felt like a victory. Third Eagle victory. His pencil-stub-sized, government-sealed changer showed a balance of twenty-five hundred securtys, three solids and five plus. (Singular or plural, plus were plus.)

Wacaan were not bargainers; their only weapon in commercial interactions was their formidable skill, and salesmen learned very quickly that it was all a bluff. No Paint exploded into violence outside of his work. Only timid old ladies like the housekeeper and the T'chishetti—of course, the T'chishetti—were ever afraid of the Paints. Pushovers.

Had he not been a Wacaan—in fact, had he not been a Painted Wacaan—he would have had to show ownership and registration in order to sell the car. It was well-known how the Paints came by their aircars, and in the dealers' lots the vehicles were stickered: "used, registered as new." No Paint had ever abused the privilege, though there was the perennial story about the Wacaan nursemaid who had painted her chest with nail polish and gone in to sell her employer's car. There was no way of telling whether that story was true, but it did surface again and again, like bubbles on a pond.

Wanbli liked Hovart township nearly as much as he liked the desert. It was all good for a change. The buildings were like Tawlin Estate: white, glistening, round-cornered. They enforced the building codes very strictly here.

He bought a bean rito and a glass of juice at a stand on his way to the spaceport. The vendor glanced down as he fit his belt changer into the male end of Wanbli's changer (the male end was for expenditures, the female for receipts) and he whistled at the balance. His glance at the ornaments on Wanbli's bright and hairless torso was covert, but Wanbli had to smile.

"Don't worry. It's not blood money. Nobody died for it."

The man grimaced and looked away. "Wouldn't matter here. Money's money. Only electrons. But you should do something with all that. Invest it before it dribbles away."

Whenever the people of T'chishett talked about bonds, stock, debentures, investments of any kind, the Wacaan realized their separateness. Wanbli was no different, but he replied, "I'm on my way to do that right now."

The port was only ten kilometers outside of town. Had it not been strong noon, Wanbli would have walked or trotted the distance. Nothing trotted the desert at this hour, though, and he took a ground shuttle.

It was quite a trip, especially for a man of some height, because the T'chishetti elite did not generally use the public transport, and consequently the road was not kept in the best repair. He hit the underside of the roof with his darter-stung head more than once.

His mood shifted from very high to quite nasty-tasting. It was that fried Pov-head Tawlin and his pipe dreams that did it. Wanbli looked nothing like Ake Tawlin. He looked nothing like Flammulated Owl either, and that man was supposed to be his father. Was his father.

Actually, it took a very sensitive eye to decide that Wanbli looked nothing like old Flammul'. To an outsider they were all remarkably alike. But everyone had always said that Wanbli had looked just like his mother, at least as a child.

For all the interest Flammul' had shown in him, he might as well not have been his father. Why should a man accept sire-promotion at all when he had no interest in a son?

Unless he knew something Wanbli didn't.

Oh shut up.

Many men said that having the valves opened, even for only a month or so, gave added zest to sex. Maybe so, but if a man didn't care for kids, wouldn't that eliminate the thrill?

Ouch. Wanbli put his hand above his head and pressed against the unpadded ceiling, keeping himself in the seat. No, it wouldn't eliminate the thrill, he decided. It would merely make it naughty.

The shuttle gave off a great cloud of dust. Darters stitched into the reddish opacity, to see if there was anything good in it. Pijjin darters. Without stings. Wanbli wished he had saved crumbs from his rito to toss to them.

Was that something a Wacaan would want to do? He mulled this question until the port came in sight out the front window and decided: yes, many Wacaan did like to throw crumbs to the darters. Many Wacaan and most human children of all castes and both sexes. It was a fine desire and he decided to be proud of it. If the chance came, he would purchase another rito and throw all of it to the darters.

There was a plump woman with white hair and tired-looking eyes sitting across the aisle from him. As the shuttle came to an uneven stop beside the low, rectangular Port Receiving Building, she turned to Wanbli. "You people always look so dignified," she said. She had a warm, appealing voice.

His mind came down from among the darters. It hit hard. "I . . . It's an illusion, Mother. Partly because we are often worn out."

He had called her "Mother": a clan title, not for use outside the Wacaan. Well, what the hey.

At the jerk of the opening doors the woman rose and

nodded. He followed her down the aisle. "And the rest of it is," he added, leaping over the stairs to the curb, "simple lack of intellect."

He was in the filtered air of the Receiving Building in three long strides.

Hovart's port was not a sophisticated establishment, not even to Wanbli's eyes. The job bulletin board at the Hovart Clan House was a more expensive device. Here was just a four-sided holo kiosk, listing arrivals and departures in white-on-gray, as might have been seen in a station on Earth almost a millennium ago.

It was because they didn't have a string station, of course. That was the universal excuse for anything wrong in T'chishett. On all of Neunacht, probably.

Wanbli had come in a mood to be impressed, string station or no, and since there was nothing else to be impressed about, he let himself be impressed by the station's simplicity. He had been here before a number of times, true, but only to commute to Southbay and back, and once to South Interior for a survival ritual. To catch these short-hop flights one stood out on the pavement, under a sign.

It took him a few minutes to understand the symbology of the flight board, but once he realized that the asterisk didn't mean for him to look for further explanation at the bottom of the page, but instead that the flight in question was repeated every tenday, he made progress. The station affairs were handled by the Truckers' Guild, which didn't care whether they were comprehensible to the denizens of a backwater such as the planet of Neunacht. The station was also climate-controlled to the truckers' standard, and Wanbli was getting gooseflesh already.

It was all very simple, once he understood. There were no scheduled passenger flights out of Hovart. None. Of the three daily flights going anywhere, only one was marked with a delta, which meant that under the proper circumstances the captain would accept supercargo. (Wanbli owed his comprehension of the word "supercargo" to a shimmer, in which the great Paovo had signed on to a ship as supercargo and had subsequently saved the lives of the entire

36

crew and married the captain. Most Wacaan wouldn't have known that much about it.) Six other ships shuttled in and out of Hovart once every two tendays or so, and most of these were delta-marked. One was today. That made two chances in all.

The regular ship went from Hovart to Rondo Bay to South Extension Settlement and then out to Icor, which Wanbli remembered from school as being a nearby rock-exporting colony. He did not know whether Icor was on the route to New Benares; he did not know exactly where New Benares was.

The irregular ship was more of a mystery. The destination column was blank, but the flight designation itself sported a delta, two arrows (facing in opposite directions) and a sign that looked very much like a ring with a jewel in it. Wanbli looked from the kiosk to the single occupied counter.

It was black and shiny and out of the top of it protruded a shiny cockpit, where the agent sat. It was as though they didn't trust the people of Hovart, Wanbli thought. He didn't know why not; the Wacaan never went after Truckers' Guild employees.

The man in the cage was leaning forward, explaining something to a woman in a decent but not flashy gauze sarong. His lips moved so that Wanbli could see his teeth even from where he stood fifty feet away. His motions were exaggerated. A language problem maybe. For many truckers, 'Indi was not the native language. There were two people in line behind the woman, trying, as all T'chishett citizens did, to pretend they were not waiting in a line at all.

To Wanbli, the line was not long enough. He would have felt better in a more crowded atmosphere, where functionaries would not be so likely to ask questions. But it was midday, and the station was not going to get busier. Wanbli walked from the kiosk to the truckers' counter, with the heavy steps of a man on important business. Had he had shoes on, he would have made more noise.

The man at the end of the line wore the cocoa-colored skin and the red shorts of an Intek Clanner. His poor posture made each of his middle vertebrae into a white circle stretched against the skin of his back. His sad, unfocused eyes indicated that he spent much of his time in this manner. Wanbli lay a warm, companionable hand on the man's shoulder. "Citizen," he said. "Hold my place." Then he was off again.

The Intek turned his head in time to get a glimpse of Wanbli's color, bright as the Elf Darter and just that quickly gone.

A Paint. They were an uncommon tribe: the painted Wacaan. Perhaps only five thousand in total on all of the planet, though they received enough attention through media and word of mouth to make up for their small numbers. The Intek Clanner, who was an educated man and really ought not to have been spending his days waiting to have deliveries of parts signed off by bureaucrats who didn't know a heating element from a three-cycle flange, knew that the Paint was not about to destroy or even punish him if he failed to do as requested (requested?) and hold his place in line. For all their tradition and their importance to balance of power in the Mercantile Families, the Paints would not be permitted by the UCs to go about smashing people who disappointed them. Still, the Intek thought he would hold the Paint's place in line.

It was all very well to tap a man on the shoulder and then be off again, but in a situation such as this there were really very few places to be "off" to. There was the tea shop, but Wanbli wasn't sure he would be able to get back into line in time, and delay worried him as much as being held up for notice. And there was the lavatory.

Wanbli stood in the empty lavatory, staring at his bright reflection in the three-quarter-length mirror. His top Eagle shone jet and golden. His turquoise Eagle gleamed like a desert sky. His Third Eagle was a glimmer and a mystery just above the band of his breechclout. He gazed deep into the mirror and his own body was the only non-exotic thing he saw.

Look at this sink, now, which was sort of a bubble and sort of a bowl, and which would probably be just the sort of thing for hand washing in free fall. Didn't know how one would get his face in there, though. Or armpits or crotch or feet, if it was to be a really thorough job. Most T'chishett citizens did not undress completely in public places like lavatories, so perhaps the thing was not expected to handle the whole job. He stopped to appreciate the dryer too, which licked at the wet parts of one with little tongues of fiber. It didn't work very well, but Wanbli enjoyed it just the same.

The woman who had been at the head of the line bumped her way through the door and past Wanbli, not glancing at him. By the tightness of her forehead and the wrinkles under her eyes, she appeared to have a headache. She went into one of the evacuatory booths and slammed the door behind her.

Wanbli emptied his small suitcase neatly onto the counter. At the bottom of it lay a full-sleeved shirt affair which he had earned in the survival ritual. It was covered with tiny beads made of seashell and of ratchett bone, done in the pattern of graphic coordinates of Brawliens 2-98, the star of Neunacht. He thought it might help him pass unnoticed, or if not, that it would certainly warm him up. It was either that or the night blanket, and that commodious vestment would stand out kilometers.

The shirt was warm, but it produced quite an itch over the shoulder blades. It was almost as noticeable as a blanket would have been, but Wanbli could not spend all day dallying before the mirror in indecision.

Exactly as the man who had been holding his place turned (a sour expression on his features) to go to his assigned unloading dock, Wanbli appeared again. The woman who had taken position behind the man retreated from this apparition in a sparkling shirt, which tinkled lightly, like a distant wind chime.

"Good," said Wanbli, as though it were the end of a conversation, and not the beginning. "One for Icor, no return." He said these words quickly but clearly, with no intonation, trying to give them a sort of mechanical inevitability. By pretending to himself that the errand of buying tickets was already accomplished, he hoped he would assure that it was accomplished quickly and without questions. But after one close look at the attendant's face, he realized that he was playing out of his own league.

The attendant was pale—far more pale than most citizens of T'chishett. More pale than most Neunachtians of any nation. His eyes were blue like the center of the sky, where the dust can't reach. He was a foreigner—a trucker—and that put Wanbli at a disadvantage. More, the man was nasty-hearted. He wore nasty in the set of his mouth and the pull of his eyebrows. He carried a nasty cold boredom over him like a ceremonial cloak.

Wanbli remembered how the woman in the lavatory, who had been conversing with this flyer as he watched, had come away and slammed the door behind her. Wanbli smiled. He never slammed doors.

The attendant was smiling too. It was the sort of smile that made Wanbli glance down to see where the man's hands were. They were folded on his counter. "I haven't seen one of your kind here before," the man said.

"Funny. I haven't seen you here before, either," answered Wanbli, and before the fellow could answer, repeated, "Onc to Icor, no return."

That was how he had always bought his tickets to school: "One to Southbay, no return."

The blue eyes stared at him, flat. Very slowly the man asked, "Onc what to Icor?"

Wanbli was sure the man had understood. He heard the woman behind him shift from foot to foot and he felt the itch over his shoulder blades. "One ticket to Icor. On the ship that leaves later today." Very simple, he wanted to add, but he held his tongue. Give the flyer nothing to bite down on.

The attendant rubbed his two pale hands together, insect style. He glanced up at the wall clock. "What exactly are you sending to Icor?" He glanced beyond Wanbli to the two people in line behind, as though to invite them to guess what a man of Wanbli's peculiar appearance and attire would be sending to Icor. Both the waiters shuffled and avoided the sky-blue eyes. Wanbli had the feeling they were regulars in this line and had learned not to trust.

"I am sending myself to Icor. A passenger ticket. Very

simple," he heard himself saying, knowing all the while it was a mistake.

Because the man picked up the phrase before it had fairly hit the counter. "Not so very simple," he said in his slow, drawling 'Indi. He overpronounced his *h*'s, at least to T'chishettian ears. "To begin with, that is not a passenger ship, but a freighter."

This statement, phrased as it was, promised to lead to another and more explanatory statement. The attendant, however, let his mouth close after it and seemed content to wait. More shuffles sounded in Wanbli's ears, and a man at the end, new to the line, let out a sigh.

"It's a delta freighter," said Wanbli, who was sweating fearfully despite the chilly air. Behind him he almost heard the bare feet of the Clan Officers, coming to ask him quietly (it would be ever so quietly) what he was about. "It takes on passengers as well as freight."

The man's eyes flickered, but it was a flicker Wanbli couldn't read. The color put him off. "Those arrangements are usually made a long time in advance."

Now there were five people behind him, and one asked another how long the wait was likely to be. Wanbli heard him perfectly.

He'd got what he'd wanted: a crowded counter. But the strategy had backfired on him, for this sky-blue devil behind the counter (and his veins made even his skin a sort of blue) didn't feel the pressure at all, whereas Wanbli was not used to inconveniencing large numbers of ordinary people. It was not part of the Paint training. "Let's make the arrangements right now and get it over with."

"Can't do that." The flat drawl of the answer sounded like a direct insult, but that might have been only the man's dialect.

The attendant said nothing else. He gazed out beyond Wanbli as at a landscape barren of people. He yawned. This was very insulting, in any dialect. He shifted his hand, which happened to be holding a mouse stylus, and let it click against the field of the cockpit.

Wanbli was very familiar with that gesture. People often checked that their fields were in order when in the presence of a Paint. Ofttimes they were not conscious of having done so. This flyer, for instance, would not likely admit to himself he was nervous about riding Wanbli so hard. He might not even know what a painted Wacaan was, so few of them entered his little truckers' realm. But any human body could recognize a good deal about another simply by the way it moved, and so the man checked his shield.

Not many air-transparent shields would stand against an educated Wacaan.

"So why can't you sell me the ticket?" asked Wanbli, and he was grinning again. Now that he knew things were going to be this difficult, he might as well grin.

"Because this is a freight counter." He said it as though it were the punch line of a joke, which, in a sense, it was. "Next."

Wanbli did not move, and the attempt of the line to move forward ended in a series of hopeless shuffles. Instead, he leaned forward and rested his beaded shoulder against the field. It sparkled prettily. Both his hands moved—not fast, not slow, very peacefully—through the invisibility and settled around the very surprised attendant's arm. He stroked it lightly, against the growth of the hair.

"Get . . . get out of my field!" The attendant's face was ice blue. His eyes did not change.

"What field?" asked Wanbli. His grip tightened slightly. "Tell me exactly how I go about buying a ticket to Icor."

"I'll tell you, dearie." The voice was slightly familiar. It came from behind him. Wanbli released the blue man and turned. The field of the cockpit closed with a grateful pop.

It was the little lady from the shuttle bus. She had been in the line behind him all this time, her paper-wrapped package in her arms. "You go outside and look for a little boat in the middle of a big blue circle—on the pavement, I mean, the circle is. You turn right out of the door and keep at the edge of the long shadow: it's easy to find. When you get there tell the first man you see that you want to talk to the purser. Only the purser. Do you have that?"

"Yes, Mother," said Wanbli, leaning with his hands on his knees.

"Tell him you want a ticket as far as Icor, and that you

42

want it commuter rate. If you don't specify they'll give you
first class, which doesn't mean anything on a flight that
short except a drink with dinner, and you can do without
that easier than pay half again the fare."

"Yes, Mother."

The woman nodded forcefully. "There shouldn't be any
trouble you getting on. They're never full on a Thirdday.
The Sixday flight is different, but today it's probably empty.
Do you want me to write this all down?"

"No, Mother."

"And if anybody else teases you, give them my name:
Matitia Blanding. Now hurry—it would be a shame if you
missed it now."

"Yes, Mother," said Wanbli again. He scooped up his
suitcase and headed smartly for the door. Behind him he
could hear her talking to the attendant. She was saying,
"They're very dignified, you know, and if you keep teasing
them . . ."

The sun made him stop to pull off his fancy shirt. It had
already left the beginnings of a rash on his shoulders.

There was the shadow of the building and the blue circle of
the pad at the end of it. The boat was not so small when
seen close up. Wanbli asked the first man he saw for the
purser.

Why had he done this? Upon waking up this morning, he
had had no idea to leave Tawlin Estate, let alone Hovart
Clan. Let alone T'chishett. Let alone Neunacht. This hop
felt like any other: small jolts to the stomach and lots of
boredom. He might have been on his way to Southbay for
any of a number of reasons, instead of leaving his home
world for no reason at all.

The trip to Rondo Bay took only a half dec, and Wanbli
could not help thinking how he could step out there and
take a commuter flight home. No one got off. No one got
on. Wanbli kept to his seat in the crew's lounge, between the
wash tank and the drinks machine. People came and went,
not ignoring him quite, but not speaking. They were truck-

ers; truckers came in all colors and though they moved their faces a lot he found them difficult to read.

There was nothing else to read. Wanbli was more of a reader than most Wacaan, which was not to say he was obsessive about it. Still, there was nothing at all to read except a sign on the wall, which was very dirty and not written in 'Indi. They lifted from Rondo Bay again.

Wanbli felt calm enough. Collected. But he kept chewing on the question of why he had done it. Not why he had left Tawlin: that had been brewing for a year and more. Not even why he had done it today: the price of an aircar changed everything. The fleabite, unendurable question was why he had chosen this particular method of cutting his life in two parts, heading off into black space without planning. No return ticket. It was really very un-Wacaan, whatever he had said to Mimi.

The thought of Aymimishett hit him hard under the ribs. He wished he had convinced the old flyer to come with him (impossible, even in wishes). He wished Vynur had never left.

He found himself nostalgic for the presence of Mother Blanding.

It was so damn cold in the ship. Surely the savings in energy could not be so much. Since crew's temperature control was usually funneled off the light striking the hull, it should not matter how much heat they allowed into the crew quarters. Maybe they all preferred to trot about the ship with clothing flapping over their bodies and their noses and tootsies blue, but it wasn't Wanbli's idea of fun.

He slipped his blanket out and put it over his head, letting only his face poke through the head hole. If he curled his legs on the chair, it covered all of him nicely.

Now he felt much better. Now he could appreciate that his leaving was an inevitable decision. It had been in the cards long before this morning, and Ake Tawlin's crazy Povlen talk about being his father had nothing to do with it. Wanbli wanted to act in the shimmers, therefore he must go to where shimmers were made. Simple and perfect reasoning. There was no need for excitement. There *was* no excitement.

It surprised him very much that he had to run for the lavatory four times between Rondo Bay and South Extension. It was also very unpleasant. His bowels were not listening to simple and perfect reasoning.

"Who's the dizzy under the blanket? A scrabbler?"

Wanbli had enough trouble with the pronunciation without worrying about what a dizzy was, or a scrabbler. Neither could be a compliment. He raised the face flap of his cocoon.

It was a woman, dressed neck to ankle in drab. A trucker, of course. He had often wanted to meet truckers: people who had chosen or been born to a life in ships with no home planet and few contacts with planet-dwelling people. He had thought they might be different from the rest of mankind, though he hadn't had any ideas how. Now, having met the trucker at the port, he had some ideas. This one fit right in with them.

Her face was a gray-blue-brown and she did not look at all sympathetic toward him. She was answered by another, equally colorless. A man, and off to one side. Not a word of this reply was intelligible to Wanbli. The blanket was suddenly too warm and Wanbli thrust it off him. He unfocused his eyes, to keep both man and woman in view.

She gave a sudden gasp, which might have been flattering to Wanbli, had it not ended in a sort of giggle. "If a scrabbler is a ground dweller, that's me," he said to her. Pointedly to her. "But I haven't been dizzy on a ship since childhood."

She stared at his chest and he let her do so, with the air of a king conferring a favor.

As Wanbli had spoken to the woman, excluding the man, who was standing a nervous-making distance to the left and to the side, so her answer came only for her fellow trucker: "Bright bird, isn't it?"

Once, when Wanbli was nine years old (a Neunacht year was only slightly less than human standard, which in turn is only slightly longer than that of Earth), he had let himself get separated from his class by a strange First Eagle tutorial. It had been his own fault; he'd been showing off and had wandered too far looking for spikepods to throw at the others. Trainee Paints didn't kill each other in their little spats, or not often, but they were no kinder than human standard. That day he had learned very impressively that one cannot beg, smile or fight one's way out of the amusements of the pack: not when the pack was on its home territory. He knew of only one way.

Wanbli was very much in truckers' home territory. If he started kicking ass here, they would eventually come put him down. He sighed, yawned as the counterman had yawned at him and folded his blanket. His interrupter went thud against the floor.

"Have you ever really seen a bird?" he asked. Wanbli had not. They had tried to introduce birds of one sort or another to Neunacht, but the darters always got them. Even through the bars of cages. Dogs did better.

"What's that stick for?" The trucker man took a step closer to Wanbli and folded his arms. His legs were wide and braced, locked at the knee.

Like police, thought Wanbli. Or a very badly trained bodyguard. Did the flyer know how unprotected his knees were, let alone his groin?

"Why didn't they make you check it?"

The purser hadn't made Wanbli check his stick because he had voluntarily given up his blunderbuzz. Admitting the one as a weapon drew attention from the other's offensive possibilities, and the interrupter was a much more useful weapon on a boat. The orange slider skin wrapped around the handle and the twinkling bundle of Elf Darter wings also gave the thing a friendly appearance.

"Why should I check it? It doesn't get in your way, does it?"

Another trucker came around the corner into the tiny lounge: another woman. If they were going to be belligerent, Wanbli was glad it was a woman. Even when the women were Third Eagle he'd rather be facing two women and a man than the other way around. Women almost always waited for the attack and Wanbli could end the game by not attacking.

And if it did not come to fighting at all, he'd rather be faced by two women. Lots.

"I'll decide what gets in my way and what doesn't." The man had many stamps and badges on his costume, which would have been very useful for Wanbli to understand, he was sure.

"You know the rock, if it's you who stumbled over it," answered Wanbli, though he wasn't sure that the man would recognize the proverb.

The new woman—she was yellowish pale, a color that went miserably with the drab uniform—said to the man, "I can't understand his language at all. What's he speaking?"

"It's Hindi with all the *h*'s taken off, and most of the middle syllables slid over."

Wanbli understood this, and was very proud of himself for it. "I never could see the importance of an *h*," he said, being careful to pronounce the middle syllables of every word. He glanced at the clock, the three truckers and one particular door out of the lounge. Soon he would be due for visit number five to the evacuatory. Bad timing.

Two people spoke at one time. The man said, "I want that stick out of here," and the yellowish woman said, directly to Wanbli, "Why do you wear all those tattoos?" By the way the man bit down on his words to let her finish, Wanbli learned something about the boat's hierarchy. He felt justified in ignoring him to answer the woman.

"They are marks of rank, like the badges on your suit." He did not preen for her; for all he knew, she might be the captain, like in *The Garden of Grief*, and although Paovo had begun by offending Captain Satvananda deeply and ended by marrying her, Wanbli was not certain that the bad start was a necessary part of it.

She stepped closer. She was not bad-looking, though spindly. Thin women often had great sexual endurance. Wanbli looked back attentively. Respectfully.

"But how do you change them if you're promoted?" She had to repeat the word "promoted" for him before he understood.

He explained that the Eagles were additive, but he did not explain what they represented. He decided to like this lady; the trucker man was wearing a thwarted sort of scowl. Another trucker came in and opened conversation with the first woman—she of the blue-brown skin—and he was left standing there by himself.

"You seem to have filled yourself up," continued Wanbli's interrogator. She glanced down at his breechclout, where the top of the Third Eagle winked and disappeared with his breathing, and then she glanced away. "I mean, you have no more room for tattoos."

"Yes," he answered her, adding, "Alas." He knew that to be an ancient word, and he threw it out to see whether she was educated.

She giggled: doubtful response. "What happens if you are demoted, once the tattoos are there?"

"Usually that does not become a problem. Usually we are demoted by the fire." It was Wanbli's turn to laugh then, but the laugh did not come out, for into his mind came, with horrid vividness, the memory of his mother's open funeral pyre.

She had been only forty.

"I really do want that stick checked, Captain," trucker man number one spoke into the silence. "Who knows what's in this guy's head. Obviously not civilized. It could be dangerous."

She *was* the captain. Only of a minor-run boat, true, but still that made her the highest-ranking trucker aboard. Wanbli was very bucked with himself for having attracted her.

"Checked? If that is the custom, of course," Wanbli answered in his most civilized tones. He lifted what appeared to be an ordinary walking stick, leather-handled and with bright flashing dangles. Before the fellow could step forward he added, "But be very careful handling it. It has strong magic in it."

"Magic?" The trucker's jaw dropped in scornful triumph. "You believe . . . the thing is magic?"

"It's a ceremonial piece," said Wanbli for the Captain's ears, leaving her to doubt whether he really believed or was only constrained by his own cultural mores. "It could do quite a bit of damage if you handle it with untutored hands," he said louder, to the man.

Speaking the strict truth.

Now the flyer stood in front of him in policeman stance again. "Let's see some magic," he said.

Wanbli sighed, but in satisfaction. It had taken so long to elicit those words. "All right. Coming right up," he said, and his hand dove into his waist pouch. When that hand came out it had three polished gold coins in it.

Chargers were the usual medium of exchange on Neunacht, as on most worlds on the minor strings, but coins were still made and still tendered, though most usually used as gifts for children. Each of these three coins had been given to him on Solstice by his father. Flammul' never thought of anything more original than gold coins.

"Behold, madam. Simple coins of ordinary gold. No trickery possible. I dispose them so . . ."

They went between the first and second, the second and third, and the third and fourth fingers of his right hand. "And with such a gesture of the left hand—which is of course magical in its very nature—I put these coins into the care of the Sixth Protector, who was my own great-grandfather."

The coins were there, and then they were not there. You have seen it a hundred times.

The Captain made a gratifying sort of bubbling noise and clapped her hands together. "He *does* know magic. What a joke on you, Travis. Real stage magic. So much for your unpredictable barbarian!"

"Well, there was certainly nothing up his sleeve," added the new man.

"I want to see those coins again," said the blue-brown woman, leaning very close over Wanbli. She was really better-looking than the Captain, or at least that mud color suited her better.

Travis, his arms still folded, had to grin and bear it, for his pack had broken into lone wolves around him and he really wasn't up for tackling this strange fellow alone. He still suspected he was not entirely civilized.

49

Wanbli extended the coins. "Of course, madam. But I need them back again. They're keepsakes."

These three gold coins he had kept, polished and ready, in his pouch since he was nine years old, when the same coins and the same trick and the same, very same line of patter had won him free past eleven hostile, albeit inexperienced, enemies.

Five minutes and two tricks later, he was able to rise and saunter unharassed into the evacuatory, swinging his stick at his side.

So they were not much different from the people of T'chishett, at least not in their group behavior. Wanbli felt he could handle truckers. As long as he kept his tricks intact. But in his concern with his status on the boat, Wanbli completely missed the moment when they caught and held the string that ran nearest to Brawliens 2-98 and left his home planet far behind. He was in the evacuatory when they engaged what FTL—fiddlehead—engines the boat possessed, and although he didn't miss noticing the lurch when they caught the string, he mistook it for something else he had recently been suffering.

He returned to the lounge to find the entire crew—nine of them—assembled with matching boredom stamped on every face. It was the boat's logic and only that which could hold the minor string and scoot them beyond the speed of light. The crew was useless in this and they knew it.

Wanbli did his best to charm. He ran out of magic tricks very early and told stories instead. He told them about Hebe Tawlin and Pontiac Rock. He explained why the Fifth Protector was also called "Joker in the Pack." He described the lives of his people and the lives of the T'chishetti themselves. He found himself repeating the gist of what Ake Tawlin had said to him: not about the combative males but about how the T'chishetti had no choice but to keep the Wacaan and how they didn't like it. After this he gave the standard Wacaan view, which was that they had no choice but to be kept by the T'chishetti and how they didn't like it. His audience found it all very profound and a good joke. Someone asked whether this was perhaps why Neunacht was so damn poor that it had never gotten a station.

This irritated. Tawlin had cried poor every dec of the day, for as long as Wanbli could remember, and he was one of the richest brokers in the Hovart area. Wanbli himself, owning only what he had worn or carried on his person, had never felt in the slightest poverty-stricken.

It was coming, he answered. The station was coming. He recited for them the invocation. He assured them that they had been paying on the account for seventy-five years. Things would be looking up on Neunacht very soon now. (It was an old joke: looking up, as at the station. He scarcely remembered it was supposed to be funny.)

His audience looked tolerant but unconvinced. Perhaps they preferred the idea of a poor, uncivilized Neunacht. Certainly the string station would mean one less stop for a fiddlehead shuttle, cartage prices being what they were. Perhaps they simply did not believe that things changed. There were people like that. Wanbli dropped the subject.

Instead he described the darter that lived under his eaves and how it waited for the alios to open, so it could catch ratchetts in midair, and the other darter that had stung him in the scalp while he followed footprints.

By this time, the truckers again thought Wanbli was a barbarian, but they had all mellowed enormously toward barbarians.

Dinnertime came and though he had paid commuter, they gave him the glass of wine anyway. Wanbli was very unused to the stuff, but honor seemed to compel, so he drank it, holding his breath to reduce the taste. He lost track of the conversation after that, busy with his own thoughts. Perhaps he could do some positive good for old Neunacht if he could become a popular actor. Actors were very used to promoting things; maybe he could promote his planet. He could well imagine people wanting to visit Southbay, or even the desert around Hovart. Once the station was in, it would be very convenient. It wasn't really picturesque, but with its mornings and evenings of rose and green, it was very homey. Home away from home.

He was going away from home. Right now. It was very wearing, and Wanbli fell asleep at the table, the empty wineglass locked in his fingers. The steward cleared around him, and if he was the butt of jokes, he didn't know it.

When he woke up he was on the floor, curled around the chair legs, and two blankets had been laid catty-corner over him. He had had a dream in which there had been a small child with Ake Tawlin's face, and the child had been very angry at him, with reason. What the reason was, he didn't remember, but he woke apologizing. His interrupter was in the palm of his right hand, where the slider skin's scales had left a strong pattern.

When he returned from the evacuatory (things were getting better) there was only one trucker in the lounge: one he didn't even remember from the evening before. The clock on the wall registered one hour to Icor. Wanbli computed hours to decs in his mind and regretted the glass of wine. He had hoped to get together with the Captain. He decided to look for her.

The boat was small and his steps echoed on the walkways. This was not a fancy vessel. Touching the bare metal froze his feet: no wonder the truckers wore shoes.

He found the Captain in a small, square room which contained a lot of switches, a rather nice holo-mouse control resting on a transparent base and two chairs, the other of which was occupied by the man called Travis. She was turning the pages of a magazine with one hand, while the other hand rested in the mouse hole itself, making oily interference patterns.

Wanbli came in and leaned against the wall. Not even Travis objected. That was odd in itself. Wanbli had been prepared for a protest of some sort from the trucker; he was obviously of the complaining variety.

Perhaps Wanbli had been bragging about his fighting skills a bit the night before. He certainly didn't remember it now.

"You keep things very cold here," he said, and removed his bare shoulder from the wall.

The Captain raised her head from the print. "Ship normal. That's . . . What do you use at home? Centigrade?"

"We use the sun." He sat down on what bare floor there

was. There was at least a felt mat in here. "If you kept it a bit warmer, you wouldn't need all those clothes, Captain."

She laughed. Spindly, yes, but she had a nice laugh. "These outfits were designed by a team of ethnologists, biologists and, for all I know, phrenologists to offend as few local taboos as possible. We'd have to wear them even if it was thirty in here, so why not be comfortable?"

Wanbli gazed at the gooseflesh on his arm and answered nothing for a while. She turned another page. Travis stared at the Captain's hand, inside the mouse run.

"We don't have any local taboos," Wanbli offered casually.

Travis turned in wide-eyed disbelief. "Neunacht? You're full of them. Provincial as . . . as all get-out."

"We," explained Wanbli, chafing his arms, ". . . is not Neunacht. We are the Wacaan. We cover nothing. Except, of course, the privates."

The Captain laughed again, this time less pleasantly, or so it seemed to Wanbli. "That's what they all say. All of them. It's just that no two cultures agree as to what's private."

"Why, the genitals; that's all," answered Wanbli. "What's between the legs."

Travis snorted at this inelegant terminology and added, "And of course, the . . . uh, bosom . . . uh, area."

Wanbli glanced again at Travis. "The what? The chest? Why that?"

Travis's pale eyes said "shame, shame," as clear as Hindi, and again the Captain laughed, this time for a reason neither Travis nor Wanbli could see.

The transparent base lit up blue and the mouse squeaked. Both truckers became very busy and Wanbli sat quiet, afraid of the consequences of disturbing them.

What if nothing were private at all? If every passing stranger could see his pride and dangle and have a pretty good guess at the state of his feelings? He would get used to that—maybe. If everyone else did it too. Men's organs were pretty much alike, and women's, though interesting, mostly obscured by hair.

But if he were prancing about stark, everyone could see

his Third Eagle. That was a different matter; it was *made* to be private. The unveiling of the Third Eagle, though performed nonchalantly, was an act of moment, and only done for special people.

If everyone saw it, then there would be no doubt that Wanbli was heavy medicine, even at first meeting. But everyone could see it already, or guess from the glint of golden down tattooed below his navel. No, there would be no advantage in keeping the real, unmistakable privates exposed.

Concealing the chest, though—women's pretty nipples and baby-handles, men's hard-won flat pectorals, the very tattoos themselves—this was an act of idiocy. It was sad. Wanbli looked at the back of Travis's head and wondered if it was things like this in his upbringing that made the man so difficult. Perhaps the trucker in the freight office came from the same place.

The light in the mouse run went out and the truckers subsided into their chairs again. Bored. It struck Wanbli like a bolt from the black that perhaps the thing that drove people to be truckers was not adventure or an inhuman indifference to place, but only the desire to be bored.

There was so little to do here he considered perhaps they had landed already and he hadn't noticed any more than he had noticed their grabbing the string. Surely, though, someone would tell him if they were already on Icor. They wouldn't want him hanging around.

"Icor," he said aloud. "Is it going to be difficult to get passage from there out to New Benares?"

The Captain swiveled her chair. Her small features registered a confusion which evolved into astonishment. "You're going to Icor on the way to New Benny? Why? Do you have business on Icor first? Oh, you must," she answered herself. "Otherwise you wouldn't go in the opposite direction to New Benny."

"Of course." Wanbli's shoulders sagged so the pop in his right scapula (remains of an old training wound) was audible across the room. He made his face blank, as he had been taught since childhood to do at difficult moments. "Poker" was the ceremonial word for that discipline. "But if I had known I was going in the opposite direction, I might have arranged to . . . take care of that business another time."

The Captain looked as though she might not believe him. "Why are you going to New Benares, my bright bird? Going to become a celebrity?"

Wanbli shook his head and tittered scornfully at what was the simple truth. Having used up the first universal excuse for traveling—business—he now touched on the other. "I have family there."

That might seem unlikely to the Captain, Wanbli being what he was and all, but who is going to tell a man to his face that he does not have family where he says he does? "I see," is what she said. "Then why didn't you ask for the direct route, down at Hovart?"

Wanbli chanced the truth. "That flyer in the booth there. He's a real pain in the . . . I couldn't get a straight answer out of him."

Travis spun in his chair. They were from the same planet, thought Wanbli. Perhaps brothers. Now he had gotten himself into real trouble.

Travis was scowling. "Isn't he, though? Isn't he a real yokel? People like that—always trying to turn every situation into a damn contest—they . . . they just goad me! No wonder they anchored his chain down there in the middle of nowhere!"

"Travis has had many encounters with your freight dispatcher at Hovart," said the Captain, smiling wryly.

"Our . . ." Wanbli snickered. "He ain't ours, Captain. Believe me. Nothing like that lives anywhere in T'chishett. Or on all of Neunacht. When I left the line, Mother Blanding was telling him off, point by point, for the way he . . ."

"Who?" said the Captain, and the Mate. "Who? Matitia Blanding? You know her?"

"She sent me here." Both truckers continued to stare at him, so he went on: "She told me to give her name if anyone gave me . . . I mean, if anyone started to pinch me hard again."

The Captain settled back in her chair, her head resting against one fist. "I wish I'd known that," she said.

"Why? Is she really important? I thought she was just a very nice lady who lived in Hovart. I didn't figure which clan."

"She *is* a very nice lady," said Travis.

"She's my mother," said Captain Blanding. "I wish I'd known last night that you were a friend of hers."

"So do I," said Wanbli, with feeling.

The Gray Sky

THREE

SO LITTLE had Wanbli known about Icor that he had grown up believing the name of the place was pronounced "Eecor," whereas everyone who lived there said "Ayecor." He was now down on Icor and very unhappy about it.

Icor was valuable in parts—those parts which had a certain igneous history and composition—and those parts were being slowly and carefully taken away. There was nothing terribly wrong with the rest of the planet, but it had never evolved life of greater complexity than large worms and small tufted trees; it was boring. As boring as a truckers' shuttle boat. Men who lived and worked on Icor also tended to act like bored men.

The fact that the climate of Boom Port was classified as desert gave Wanbli a feeling of grievance: the only feeling he really possessed this morning, as his fingers and toes had gone numb.

At Tawlin Estate they had occasionally known cold

nights, and the rains of winter promoted the wearing of blanket into all hours of the morning, but the sky of Icor was gray as well as cold and windy, and this at midday. The settlement had no soil, as such, but a surface of red rubble rock which crumbled in the hands and yet sliced through bare feet nastily. The few constructed buildings were made of pieces out of other things: plates from ships roofed by great sending disks, corrugated tubes for shipping machinery, even slabs of plywood. Most of the residents of Boom lived within the rocky skin of Icor itself; Boom was a honeycomb.

Wanbli stood outside the small customs building, which was one of the few that had been built of blocks: a planned thing, and he looked up at a cliff dotted with windows. It must have been ten stories high. He approached it and found himself leaping out of the path of a long, balloon-tired yellow vehicle, which rang an irritated bell at him. Someone he could not see laughed at him.

It was humiliating. It was unfair too, for how could one tell the street from the surroundings when it was all the same red porous rock? He fingered the hilt of his interrupter and examined the front door of the skyscraper.

There was an ordinary steel door: windowless, prehung. Its smooth metal jamb fit very loosely into the hole which had been cut into the stone, and the gaps were filled with ferrofoam. One could clearly see the hack marks. It was sloppy, sloppy. It would never have made it in Hovart.

Someone was following him across the street. Wanbli didn't know whether he knew by smell, radar or simple footsteps. He turned and stepped sideways, so he was not backed into the building by the red-cheeked man, who was puffing crystals into the cold air.

Wanbli had no idea what the fellow said, or in what language he was speaking. He seemed a trifle excited, or even accusatory, but he was a heavy man, and had been running, so that didn't necessarily signify. Since gestures were as culture-bound as language and could get a flyer in trouble, Wanbli merely lifted an inquiring eyebrow and waited.

"I said, you got away from us." The man's 'Indi was even

more drawling than that of Captain Blanding, but at least he didn't sound like a leaky boiler.

"Us?"

"Customs."

Wanbli noted the fleecy blue hip coat (he wore it with the fur side inside), the glistening, bichrome shirt and the quilted, over-the-instep bronze trousers. Impossible that could be a uniform, but who was to say that every official needed a uniform? Perhaps the mufti meant the man was important.

"You didn't even come inside."

"I didn't know I had to." Wanbli could look very innocent. He leaned against the lava-rock wall, and it grabbed the beads on his shirt. "I took one look at this street, and I had to go see if it was real. It's a very interesting place you have here."

The official was not lulled by this vacuous amiability. He was frowning at Wanbli's midsection. "There we go," he said. "That's exactly what I was worried about. Weapons, dammit. Well, come along with me, bouncer boy." And he turned back across the street, his bright bald head lowered against the wind.

Wanbli, who had just gotten his blunderbuzz back, picked up his bag and followed in no great good mood.

What was a bouncer boy anyway? Was it like a dizzy? Or was it no more opprobrious a term than "flyer"? It didn't matter, really. Words.

From the Procrustes bed of their forms, Wanbli emerged as Wanbli E. Wacaan, transient, artist—m. (Luckily they hadn't asked what the "m" stood for, nor the "E" in his name. Let the files of Icor remember him as a painter, if they liked. It would cause less ruffles than martial artist and was spelled close enough to Paint.) His travel papers looked very official, but were meaningless to almost everyone along the Arm, for the Wacaan Clan had been pushed into issuing papers unwillingly, and had done so in the Wacaan ceremonial language, which even Wanbli could only read with a dictionary in hand.

"Neunacht? Where zat? What do they export?"

61

Where was Neunacht? How could he answer that question? He could scarcely point to the proper quadrant of the gray sky. "You've never heard of it? It's very close, along this same string."

"Close along a string has nothing to do with real close," answered the man. His eyes were small in a padded face. Perhaps cold-adapted.

Unlike Wanbli. "And we don't export much off-world. Too expensive cartage fees. We don't have a string station, you see. Yet."

"So. A very small Political Union, ey?" asked the official, whose feet were up on his desk.

"Never seemed that small to me," answered Wanbli blandly. "Not smaller than Icor itself, anyway."

Akavit sniffed. "Icor is not a Political Union at all, Wacaan. It's a corporation." He obviously felt he was saying something very meaningful.

"Oh," said Wanbli.

The customs building was deceptively large, for the little square block was only the tip of a larger building that dug down into the rock. There were two light shafts punched into the wall, in which were dangling houseplants in pots. An entire wall was decorated with knives, swords, and axes, like the Long Hall at Tawlin. This display was much less decorative, however, since the blades of each weapon were fitted into holes drilled into the rock and only the hilts were visible. The entire wall was riddled with such wounds.

Two windows. Houseplants. Weapons display. So Comptroller Akavit was at least that important. Wanbli finished the form, wiped graphite dust from his hands and handed it back to Akavit. He was sitting straight in the hard chair and his feet were flat on the floor, because forms in paper and real stylus always made him feel very ritual. He always expected the clerk to sprinkle ceremonial sand over his writing, or press it with a blotter, or sing a chant.

Akavit did none of these things. He scanned the paper quickly, with a great deal of mouth and eyebrow movement. "So why are you here in Boom, my boy?"

"On my way," answered Wanbli, and reluctantly added, "New Benares."

Akavit's facial play stopped. "We're not on the way to New Benares. We're not on the way anywhere."

Wanbli tried to keep his shoulders from drooping. "I know that now. I . . . got on the wrong boat."

He had to sit there and let the man's doubt roll all over him. He had no tools to convince him.

"Then why didn't you stay on that boat you came on? It swings back to Neunacht every week or so."

Wanbli sighed and settled back. At least it was warmer in the customs house. Not warm, but warmer. "I thought about it. But I don't get to travel often, and I don't want to retrace my steps, you know?"

Or give Clan Council another chance to haul him in.

Akavit's face twitched and jiggled as he considered this. Wanbli was beginning to think all foreigners expressed themselves like that. Too bad it didn't make them easier to read.

"Why New Benares?"

"I have family there," answered Wanbli, carefully casual.

Akavit was looking again at Wanbli's arsenal. "Ah. I thought perhaps you were looking to put your pretty face in the shimmers." When Wanbli let this slide by, Akavit extended one hand. "Let's see the gun," he said. His other hand was not to be seen. Wanbli suspected it was not empty. He looked down, to find that the front of the desk was paperboard.

He unsnapped the holster from his waistband and handed over the blunderbuzz. Akavit looked at it curiously and pressed his thumb here and there without effect. "No laser here?"

"No. Just projectile."

Akavit looked at the gun with a kinder eye. Perhaps he was interested in antiquities. "A real granddaddy, ey? Where's the ammunition?"

Deadpan, Wanbli said he hadn't brought any. The strict truth.

"Then why the gun at all?"

Wanbli risked an apologetic smile. "It's what my people wear."

The blunderbuzz was not a popular sort of weapon. It

was an example of bright engineering combined with the very old idea of projectile weapons. It was cost-effective, but most people would just as soon use coherent light, which sliced and diced as well as perforated. The Wacaan thought lasers were terribly unsubtle.

Akavit returned it to him. "And the cane?" the man continued. "Has it got a blade in it?"

"Oh no. Nothing like that." Wanbli's eyes were round. He was made to deliver it over the desk, where Akavit examined it with more intelligence than he had the gun.

"Ah. An interrupter."

Wanbli's heart sank. He didn't like the thought of being without the stick in a strange place, especially one as forbidding as Icor. But of course the Comptroller would have experience with crowd control, and even decorated with wings and painted leather, a nerve stick was a nerve stick. He was very surprised when Akavit slid the stick back to him, over the granite top of the desk. "You'll let me keep it?"

Akavit scratched his smooth round head and also his smooth round nose tip. "It's no business of the corporation how a man chooses to protect himself. A mining camp can be a mean place."

Wanbli had to grin. Those were the exact words used by the voice-over narrator to begin the shimmer *Hounds of Juna,* starring Al Kyle. "A mining camp can be a mean place." Kyle had proven meaner, of course.

"Then why check them at all?"

Akavit looked slightly smug, as though he'd led Wanbli to that question. Perhaps he had. He opened a drawer, closed it again and then rose to his feet. He stood by the wall of weapons. "Your relationship with other folks is your own business, sure. But what you do to the planet is the business of the Icor Corporation. Look." He drew an ordinary, inexpensive machete from its lodging. It seemed to be sticking; it squeaked shrilly on its way out. Akavit raised his arm and brought the blade down again in a loose, practiced strike. Wanbli winced at the thought of what would happen as the cheap steel struck rock.

It went in—not as straight or as neatly as most of the

blades in their sockets, but it went in. "I wouldn't do this to someone's good blade, you understand. It would ruin the edge.

"But out here a man with a big knife and one too many firefloats in his tum could hack up the side of a house. Rock doesn't heal. It can't easily be repaired: not like wood, or synthetics."

"I see," answered Wanbli.

"And there's another thing. A man with a blade goes out into these hills and in two days he's dug himself a house and we have a hell of a time getting him out."

Akavit seemed to think this was self-explanatory. Wanbli was forced to ask why one would want to get a man out.

Akavit's face stopped its usual twitching. "If Icor Corporation wants you to have a house," he said. "It will tell you it does. And it will sell you one."

His stare was more than challenging; it was threatening. Wanbli refused to let his shoulders rise. Nor did he lower his own garnet gaze. He leaned forward.

"What I really want to know, Comptroller, is where I can get a coat just like yours."

Wanbli crunched his way along the street of pumice, stepping lightly, stepping high. He was amid wind-worn spires and plateaus of lava rock. He was in a city of towers and castles. It was astonishing, and the workmanship was generally bad. There was garbage rolling down the street: metal cans, not perfectly round anymore and making insect rhythms over the stone, scraps of bread, too cold to rot. Somewhere down here was a store, with a sign in Hindi to proclaim it so. Once Wanbli could get in, he would begin to believe in life again.

But was he still on the street? From where he stood he saw cliffsides—or walls—riddled with windows. Most of them were glass, since a field that would hold out that amount of cold and wind was a more expensive proposition than glass, but little of it was transparent. It was white and milky, like old eyes, and even now Wanbli could hear the dry scrape of sand against the panes. Lava sand.

But there were no doors, and doors usually opened on the

street side of a building. If he could go around one of the spires until he found the door, he'd be on the road again, or at least near it. Hands folded into his armpits, Wanbli shuffle-danced forward, keeping his left shoulder to the wall of a spindle tower of rock.

Someone was coming around the other way, startling Wanbli, who had not seen another pedestrian since leaving the customs house. He whipped upright from his cold crouch. His arms flew out. He staggered.

He was one meter away from a creature much taller than he, much broader too, with hide, talons and fangs. On its breast it wore a badge of gold in the shape of a flower. It spread its own immense arms out and hooted at him.

Wanbli sprang back by reflex and landed in guard almost two meters away. He reached for his blunderbuzz, which he had stopped to load with a pebble immediately upon reaching the street, but his hands were not behaving like hands at all. One touch of the cold plastic side of the weapon convinced him he could not use it.

The interrupter was another story. He had it out of its stick pad and armed before his brain had really registered that the gun would not do. It was pointed at the behemoth, but he did not yet squeeze the firing ring.

The check came from his brain, which had been doing other things while his body put him into motion. His brain had been telling him that Icor did not possess wild beasts of this size. It had brought to his attention the golden badge, which seemed to be pinned directly through the hide of the thing and indicated that the creature was either domestic or sentient. It had made mention of the fact that the thing was apparently female, and that female creatures lacking young were less likely to attack. Also more often protected under law. Finally it had noted that when the creature spread its talons wide it had smacked the right one into the rock wall, doing that wall some cosmetic damage and leaving a red streak on the back of the silver-gray paw, and that it was now holding that hand in its other and looking as betrayed as any carpenter with a smashed thumb. Wanbli listened to his brain, backed further away and lowered the tip of the stick.

It was humanoid, though well over two meters tall. It had smallish eyes, with nictitating membranes that worked constantly, from the outside in, sort of like windshield wipers. It had a round, button nose, where noses are set on Earth creatures, and a mouth that was only slightly muzzled and more delicate than seemed fitting, given the rest. Its ears were set low on its head, and the auricles leathery and long.

It rubbed the rock dust from its paw—hand, rather—with a sandpaper noise and it emitted a whistle which was identical to the whistle that would be emitted by a human who had closely escaped danger. The talons of its hand, clean-polished and four centimeters long, disappeared into the first joint of the fingers, which Wanbli had not noticed were webbed. At the same time, rather as though the two responses were conjoined physiologically, a complex organ poked out of the now relaxed slit between its long legs.

It gave a great sigh and said in careful Hindi, "I'm sorry if I frightened you." It had a light, child's voice. "I was frightened too."

Wanbli found he was giggling, and the response embarrassed him. "No, you just warmed me up a little," he said, returning the stick to its position as a walking aid. He did not press the top to disarm it, however. He stepped back over the ground he had lost in his retreat, and he looked the creature up and down and up and down. It was his first real foreigner.

The tall creature looked too, wiping and wiping its eyes. "What are you?" it asked first, barely before Wanbli could ask the same question. "Are you homo sapiens?"

Wanbli giggled again. "Why shouldn't I be homo sapiens?" He leaned on his stick and tried to look as human as possible.

The foreigner hesitated. He played with his fingers. When not in use, he kept his hands pursed, so that the gray, abrasive hide concealed the soft white palm surface. Now they looked like flower buds opening and closing.

"None of the humans I have seen are as . . . beautifully colored as you are."

Wanbli felt himself warming considerably to his first rea foreigner.

"Or . . . or is it only for breeding season?"

Wanbli guffawed and struck a more arrogant stance "Among humans, my friend, all seasons are breeding sea son. This color is the mark of a Painted Wacaan, and that i what I am. We are definitely human. My name is Wanbli."

This time the great soft ears rippled as the hands folded and unfolded. "Thank you for trusting me with your name Wobbly. I am"—the sound was a whistle with two hoot scattered within—"of the Dayflower people."

That was a name Wanbli recognized, though just barely one of the pages in the illustrated book he had used fo elementary cosmography. He had been very fond of tha book, but he remembered the picture as being much les imposing than this reality. It had shown a grayish sort o person of no particular size, with ears held out like ceremo nial fans. Whistle-two-hoots here had yet to stick out hi ears.

"I am very happy to meet you," said Wanbli, and he gave him a Wacaan bow, which did not involve losing eye con tact. "I am a stranger here. I just got in on a shuttle boat."

"I just got in on a shuttle boat," said Whistle-two-hoots "This seems to be a very unfriendly place."

Wanbli, who had been dancing from foot to foot and slap ping himself, agreed. "Don't you find it unpleasantly cold?"

Now Whistle-two-hoots did erect his ears. "And windy too."

Hearts one and loyalty united. The Dayflower dropped his own not very pressing business, and led Wanbli down the lava street and to the Corporation Store.

He awoke from a nightmare in which he was carrying an unbelievably heavy child up the side of Pontiac Rock. It was his child, and he was determined to take care of it, though it seemed they were both going to tumble to their deaths. Then he was at the top of the table, not knowing how he had done it, and he put the baby down, to find that it wore Ake Tawlin's old, debauched face. It was not his child after all, and he backed away from it, though it cried and put out ugly little arms. He was over the edge and falling, but no, really he was only being stung by an Elf Darter. The ugly baby would be stung too, and he couldn't let that happen, no matter whose child it was, but now the windy red rock was bare, though he still heard it cry.

Wanbli sat up and rubbed his head, which really did hurt. He was on the floor of the foreigner's room on the cheap sudsy-foam flooring and covered by a really magnificent fur parka which was his very own. The foreigner was curled on the bed, hanging over a bit in all directions, and he was snoring. The room smelled strongly of leather, though Wanbli didn't know whether that was from his new outfit or from his new companion.

Why should the top of his head be smarting so? He hadn't struck himself on anything. The last insult his scalp had suffered had been—and here he mused and mumbled and remembered his dream—that very darter attack at Pontiac Rock, a long time ago. He tried to count days and realized that he had totally lost track of days. That knowledge raised a sweat under the fur, and a feeling of dizziness. He counted meals instead and decided that two days only had passed since he had tracked the aircar of Rall's Paints to its concealment: that day had ended with his falling asleep at dinner on Captain Blanding's boat, and the next day, or at least spell of wakefulness, had ended on Digger's floor here.

He had decided to call the Dayflower individual Digger, after a large dog that had belonged to his First Eagle School Group. It was easier than Whistle-two-hoots. And as he was reluctant to be called Wobbly for who knew how long, he had asked the Dayflower to call him Red.

The toxins of a good, well-placed darter sting ached for five to seven days. No wonder. Events had just driven that small distraction out of his mind.

It wasn't that bad a pain but still Wanbli sweated. He thought he might have a recurrence of his abdominal problems too. That would be unfortunate in these close quarters, where the evacuatory was sitting right in the middle of the room. Not his own room, either. He breathed deeply and attempted to calm himself. It was difficult; he seemed all out of control.

The attempt at self-mastery at least let him remember exactly what he had been doing wrong in these past few days. He had not been working out. Five days now, with none of the exercises that kept a Paint being a Paint. Worse, he had not done either the morning or the evening rituals. No wonder he was out of kilter.

Wanbli was not superstitious—for a Wacaan. He knew the world would not come to an end if he stopped his observances. Brawliens 2-98 would still rise and set in relation to Neunacht in colors of rose, lime and turquoise if Wanbli became a Pov-head or mentally disturbed and never invoked the six directions again. But Wanbli himself would have some trouble rising and setting in the proper colors.

For a bad moment he thought he had forgotten to pack his altar kit, but then he remembered that he had stowed it first of all, as was his early training at school, and so it was at the very bottom of the suitcase. He divested himself of the parka and of the lovely, soft-tickly fur-lined trousers that went with it, and spread his gear. A compass showed him local north, and from then on it was easy.

When he was finished, he felt much better, and the intimations of diarrhea had disappeared. That was just as well, for he was being watched by Digger's little, deep-set eyes, and the foreigner's ears were sail-spread to catch the whispered words.

"The knife made me nervous at first," he said. Wanbli had forgotten Digger's voice was so peeping a treble. "But then I saw that it was all a magic ritual. A very nice one too."

Wanbli rose with a crackling of knees and took a whiz into the rather primitive urinal. Either Digger had profound elimination taboos or he had been taught that humans did, for he turned his body to the wall and pulled the covers over his head.

"You have your own rituals, I suppose," said Wanbli, just to have something to say.

Digger sat up and the iron bed frame creaked much

louder than Wanbli's knees had. "Not really. Just the religious observances, of course."

Wanbli had been putting the trousers back on over his breechclout, not because he really needed them in the room, but because they felt so good, and he stopped with one leg in the air. "That *was* a religious observance."

"Ah," said the Dayflower individual, in tones that suggested that he could say more but was not going to. He didn't piss at all, but glanced covertly at the facilities so often that Wanbli put on his parka and said he was going out for another glance at Boom.

Much to his confusion, it was just getting dark. Had he slept through a local day and night, or was this planet a very slow spinner? He should have asked Digger.

He was comfy in his fur bundling. He felt bold and frontierish, with only a lingering queasiness by which to remember his nightmare. The street was quiet and the windows in the rock walls and spires glowed white or amber. His breath crackled and crystallized in the cold, moisture-hungry air and the fur (he should have asked what kind) crackled against his ears. His booties with their stainless-steel-weave soles drew sparks out of the lava rock: very cheery.

Ahead was a lamp on a post just beside a doorway. Something hung in the air around it, making dancing shadows. It was not as big as the smallest darter, and this cold would be hard on insect-sized creatures. Perhaps it was not alive at all, but some atmospheric phenomenon. It drew Wanbli closer.

It was a piece of glass in the shape of a pentacle, which was affixed to a stiff wire that protruded from the lamppost. It bounced in the never-ending wind of Icor.

The sign above the door read "Shooting Star" in Hindi and in another script Wanbli did not recognize. On either side of the green steel door was a little window, deep-set into the rock. The foam sealer around these and the door was very messy and the sign was not the best handwork Wanbli had seen, but the light through the windows was a very appealing hearth color. There was a faint ring of music and conversation in the frozen air.

There was something very attractive in the idea of waking up to an evening's entertainment, especially in such an exotic place as Boom on Icor. It was like something out of a shimmer. Al Kyle, in fact, was always waking up just in time to go out on the town again. Wanbli had never done it at all; it was not Wacaan, and thus it was a completely perfect, open experience.

He put his hand to the steel door and the feeling of it startled him. He pulled away with difficulty. Had he pressed harder, he'd have been frozen to the door. He pulled his arm up his sleeve and tried again, this time using the skin as a protection, but found himself suddenly shy. Somebody laughed inside and this made him shyer. What if no one spoke 'Indi at all in there? His fur parka began to feel big and clumsy around him and he found he was scuttling back down the street toward Digger's place.

"It will be fun," he said, or rather grunted, for he was doing push-ups as he spoke. Perhaps it was only for clarity that Digger repeated the word "fun" in that dubious manner. The Dayflower individual had pushed himself back on the bed against the corner of the walls, and his legs were folded under him in a manner that a human would have found very difficult. Very difficult. Wanbli could not have done it, though he could sit flat with his legs pointing north and south.

The room smelled even more strongly of leather.

Having finished his fifty push-ups and one hundred abdominal flutters (he took pride in those; they made his Eagles quiver), Wanbli rose and commenced his basic forms. Many had found these pretty, and one enterprising choreographer in the South Extension had used them as the basis for a ballet. Digger, however, drew more deeply into his corner. The opposite leg of the bed below him unweighted and lifted slightly off the ground. "I keep thinking you're ready to strike. Like a shweet."

Wanbli didn't know what a shweet was, but he could imagine. "Strike? You? I'd sooner throw myself into a sand blaster." Arcing both arms to the left, he sank one knee almost to the shabby floor foam and stabbed downward:

Darter Spears Fish Underwater. "I think we oughta do it. Two young flyers in a strange port, only for a day, and so on."

"And so on what? What would be fun about going to a bar when I can't digest your alcohol and the people aren't friendly?" Childishly, sullenly, Digger squirmed against the wall, acquiring white paint patches on either large, sloping shoulder. The wall suffered worse. The outside leg of the bed was rising higher now.

"Doesn't matter if they're friendly or not," replied Wanbli, with a swagger he hadn't felt standing at the green door in the cold. "They aren't going to make a move against either of us. Believe me. And as for drinking—well, I don't do that much of it, either. The thing is to watch everyone: how they act with one another. And so you can say you done it."

Digger had difficulties with Hindi colloquialisms, let alone 'Indi bad grammar. He sat and puzzled that one for a few moments, his ears waving in the nonexistent breeze. "To whom would I say I did—uh, done it?"

Wanbli felt a touch of irritation at his crony's unshakable naïveté, but in Wacaan fashion this passed into amusement. "To the flyers at home, of course. You know—the other fellows."

The tiny eyes grew even smaller. "I'm a mathematician. None of my flyers have ever been in a bar at all."

Wanbli finished Warding Off Three Sticks, which was the last of the basic forms. He had been very stiff, of course, but still felt he'd done creditably. Too bad this huge block of sandpaper didn't know how to appreciate it. "Well there, you see. You'll be the first one."

Digger sighed and this slight motion was enough to rock the bed out from under him. The cheap metal frame gave one buck that jarred its occupant back against the wall and began to slide, tearing the floor foam under its spindly leg. Then Wanbli was up in the air in a forward flip and crashing down on the unweighted end of the bed with both feet under him. It was spectacular, but then, he was already warmed up. Digger's back and the top of his head were liberally dusted with paint and cellulose foam and he was

much shaken up. He had nearly hit the floor and, heavy as
he was and a mathematician besides, he would surely have
hurt himself. His gratitude made it impossible for him to
resist Wanbli's importunities any longer.

Whoever built the Shooting Star had started out with good
intentions; the front wall was thin, even, smooth and lightly
polished. The rear wall—the wall one saw upon entering—
was a hack job. The two side walls seemed to have been
carved by different hands, one more enthusiastic than the
other, and the ceiling had been finished by large passes with
a backhoe. There was a doorway at one side that no rectangular, round or oval door could have fit, but then it had no
door, and the casual patron could stare through to what
appeared to be someone's private domicile and even to the
kitchen-bath behind the parlor. The bar itself was a section
of girder, one and a half meters high.

Of patrons, casual or otherwise, there were seven. Two
tables of two and one of three. Some wore fur, though none
as nice as Wanbli's. They were all human. The bartender
wore an apron and leaned back with his head resting on the
flange of the bar girder. The place smelled burnt and fer-
mented at the same time.

Wanbli padded in, with Digger scraping behind him. All
looked up, and not at Wanbli. It was unsettling, though
very like a good shimmer, and Wanbli took a chair at one of
the nearer tables and tried to look dignified.

"Here," said Digger. He was sitting at another table, one
near the wall which had a bench at one side of it. Digger
had placed himself directly over the center support of the
bench, and still he sat stiffly, as if he were not putting his
whole weight down. Wanbli made a quick change. "You are
one big kind of flyer," he said admiringly.

Digger pulled in his ears and shoulders, making himself
considerably smaller. He tweeted something apologetic.

"Naw, that's something you should be proud of. Be solid.
Who's gonna stir on you, big as you are?"

This brought the ears up. "Nobody has ever . . . what
is it? . . . stirred on me. I'm a mathematician. And a chess

74

player," he added with a hint of complacency. He was asking Wanbli if he played chess when the bartender appeared standing at the joint which was most like an elbow to the Dayflower.

"What you gents?" he asked, looking at neither of them. His accent was so bad that it took Wanbli a moment to realize that the man was asking for an order rather than an explanation.

He was a person of midrange brown, somewhat overweight and underhaired, but average withal. Wanbli found him easier to read than he had the bureaucrats. The man's emotion was primarily consternation, which could dip to either fear or anger or, equally likely, go nowhere and fade away. Digger was the focus, not Wanbli.

The Dayflower too was opening and closing his little white lotus hands. Claw tips, excellently manicured, peeped out and went in. His ears were back like those of an unhappy dog.

It was Wanbli's own fault. He'd pushed the foreigner, who had lent him his floor, his evacuatory and his lavabo. Now he'd better be able to keep things smooth.

"What you got?" he asked, which irritated the bartender further. Wanbli was recited a list of drinks, smokes and candies, ending with the cheese sandwiches that the bartender did not recommend, as they came sealed from offworld and had nothing like the real flavor.

"I'd like rock candy, please," piped Digger.

The bartender squinted at him, but then, the light in there was very bad. "You mean Pov-lace candy?"

"Ah no, sir. The straight stuff!" Digger's ears went out in unfeigned enthusiasm.

Wanbli had intended to order some sort of fruit juice or a mild smoke, but a glance at the bartender's face convinced him that he had the honor of the table to defend. "A Tearjerker," he said. Paovo had almost killed himself on Tearjerkers after his alien mistress was asphyxiated in *The Garden of Grief.* That was how he wound up insulting the captain of the ship.

The bartender gave him the same look he had given Digger. Maybe it was just his way of looking. "You want full size or pony?"

"Full, of course."

"I like sucrose," confided Digger. His sharkskin face got all puckery, which Wanbli hoped signified pleasant anticipation. "But I'm not supposed to eat it."

Wanbli admitted he wasn't supposed to eat sugar, either. But then he wasn't supposed to drink alcohol, and here he was, about to drink. It was all part of a night out.

"That is fine for you, Red. You are human. It would kill me, though. We possess much more delicate constitutions than you do."

Wanbli's glance flickered, but he did not contradict the monster.

It was warmer in here, though not really warm, and he slipped his parka onto the back of the chair. From where he sat he was in plain sight of the table of three and he knew they saw. He knew it and he put back his shoulders.

"How old are you, Digger? Bet I'm older."

Digger puckered again. "I'm nine years. That's fifteen of Earth."

Earth years—what was that in regular Neunacht? Wanbli took his changer out of his pouch and worked the conversion. When it wasn't plugged in at either end, it worked for things like that. Fifteen made sixteen point oh nine and some. "Protectors! You are young."

Digger squirmed and his ears floated uncertainly. "Not really. Old enough for postgraduate work anyway." When Wanbli didn't pick up on that, he added, "I'd better be old enough by now. I'm only going to make it to Earth—oh—thirty-five or so."

"Make it?" Wanbli echoed. "To thirty-five? What you . . ."

"Or forty, if I'm lucky." He struck the medal that pierced his gray hide with one claw nail. It made a bell sound. "I'm a Dayflower, remember?"

Wanbli did not remember—not for many seconds. Then the information churned up from cosmography class; the

Dayflower were called that because they had the shortest normal lifespan of the seven sentients. Shorter by far.

It had never seemed important in astrography.

"I am the first of my people to make it into IP," said Digger with his mouth full. He sucked noisily. He couldn't help it.

Wanbli's drink stood, tall and foamy, within the circle of his thumbs and forefingers. It was faintly green. The first sip had frightened him, but after that it was under control. He noticed that his friend's ears were taut and glowing cheerily. That seemed to be a good sign.

"Can't pass the tests, or is it a money problem?" he asked the Dayflower. "Money's a real turd."

Digger smiled, just like a human. Perhaps it was rehearsed. "Oh no. My district is sending me. They're all very gratified by my acceptance." He squirmed in his seat, still smiling. An odor of sanded resins wafted off the table and chair. "The standards are very high. But I'm the youngest to have finished my theorocrate at . . . at home." He had stopped interjecting words—or whistles—in his native language into the conversation. It always made Wanbli start.

Wanbli sipped again and decided he didn't trust this drink. It seemed to be separating the meninges of his skull. At least he wasn't cold anymore; he was sweating. But that was okay. "I too am the youngest of my clan to pass all the tests. All of them."

There was a sound of fingers snapping, but Wanbli was staring at the drink he did not trust and so he didn't see Digger slap his ears against his face. "Marvelous, Red! We were meant to meet each other. To what challenge are you turning now?"

There was no reason he could not tell this naive young mathematician–chess player–foreigner that he was going to be an actor, but he remembered the dry voice of Comptroller Akavit—he of the corporation and the pincushion wall. Comptroller Akavit, who had asked him if he was going to put his pretty face in the shimmers and had laughed.

"To the Unknown," he replied, and his laugh was as dry as the Comptroller's.

Digger sat silent for a moment. He stretched his ears to translucency and then he giggled. "We all do that," he said.

"But most of us have some plans how it's going to go." Wanbli found himself getting morose, like Al Kyle. Morose and interesting. He nursed the effect.

Digger sat waving, willing himself to understand. Behind them a man laughed uproariously and the bartender replied in kind. Wanbli was suddenly, grievously lonely. Lonelier than Al Kyle.

"Is it an age ritual?"

Wanbli lifted his face toward Digger's. The Dayflower looked less human than ever, with his ears and the whites of his eyes flushed and his big cheeks suck-sucking on the candy. "A . . . what? An age ritual? No, I'm through with all those. Except fatherhood, and that certainly doesn't require diving off the edge of the planet . . ."

Wanbli's brain caught up with his mouth.

"What's wrong? Did I ask something I shouldn't have? Please remember I have not been much with humans before, though I have studied Hindi for years, so I could easily . . ."

It was the bartender again, and his mood had decided itself. "Look what you did to my table, fellow. Dresh! Dresh! The finish is completely gone!"

Wanbli leaned over and looked at the pale brown streaks where Digger's arms had lain. "Well," he said placatingly, "it was never much of a finish anyway, what with the glass rings and the knife slices and 'Ezrad loves Patty-Pov' colored in with red ink."

"Who the hell made you a critic? If I had myself daubed up that way I'd watch before I made statements about what looks good and what don't."

"You don't like the way I look?" asked Wanbli in sheer disbelief.

Digger, meanwhile, had squeezed in his shoulders (which was unsettling to human eyes) and tried to furl his ears, which were too full of sugar to be hidden. "I'm sorry," he said to the bartender. "I know better than to do that. I just forgot."

"Trouble, Hillary?" The voice and the man behind it

might have stepped straight out of the best sort of shimmer. He walked with a list and a roll. He was large and heavy-handed and he looked uncouth. Undoubtedly he had learned the stance, the walk and the word from a shimmer, and Wanbli, whose taste in entertainment was unusual in T'chishett, felt as if he had finally come home.

"He scraped the top right off my table, and God alone knows what his butt has done to the chair." Hillary, the bartender, reached out and grabbed at Digger.

Very drunkenly, Wanbli got out of his chair. It took very little to get Wanbli drunk. It took more than the two sips he had swallowed, however. "Drunk style" fighting was a cherished branch of Wacaan study. People who think they are fighting a drunk do not fight as carefully or get as angry when hit. Officers of the law tend to be more tolerant with the blinking idiot who seems to have flattened his opponent by accident.

Good technique among strangers.

Most drunks who scramble out of the left side of a chair do so with their left leg first. Obvious. Wanbli, though seeming ever so unsettled, moved his right leg, crossing over, and when his left leg swung out it came down against the back of Hillary's knee. It was a light tap.

"Whoa, flyer. I'm the one that's drunk here. Why'd you fall down?"

The bartender had been meaning to ask that same question. Digger scooted his gritty gray foot under the table, so as not to scratch the fallen man's cheek.

"Get out of here," the bartender said, not moving from the floor.

The heavy-handed stranger was right behind Wanbli now and moving. This seemed to distress the poor Wacaan so much that he lost his balance and landed, elbow first, against the man's middle. He apologized, but now there were two men crumpled on the floor and Digger sat in an almost fetal crouch, making himself small. His back was red with rock dust.

Three of the remaining patrons stood. One held a cigarette in his hand and smoke drifted absently from his nostrils. His eyes too looked absent. Another came toward them throwing chairs out of his way one-handed. He came to the other side of the table and made a grab for Digger's wrist. He caught it. "All right, pachyderm . . ." he began, but the young Dayflower pulled convulsively away and the man's words were lost in screams.

"I've hurt him," peeped Digger.

"Understatement," replied Wanbli, for the palms of the fellow's hands were red and ugly, seeping blood.

Then everyone was up: drinker, hopper, Pov-head alike, and they came at Wanbli. Not Digger, but Wanbli. The men might have been drunk, but they were not suicidal.

He didn't try any more stunts and he didn't let them grapple him. Childish fighters though they were, they were too many for that.

Here came a man with a chair over his head. It hit the ceiling, jammed, and broke a leg on the way down. Wanbli was not there, of course. He tapped the man on the armpit as he shuffled by him, disabling that arm. As an after-thought he knocked his legs out from under him.

The next one came in with a fist. Good-sized fist. Wanbli slipped it on the outside, watched it go by and gave him a moderate smack on the hinge of the jaw. This one didn't go down, but he lost a great deal of his interest in the matter.

The round table to the left of Wanbli was kicked aside with violence. Here came the man with the bloody hands, still game. Wanbli watched him come, red up to the elbows now. The fellow said nothing, but kicked Wanbli as hard as he could. The blow landed on the upper leg; Wanbli had not moved.

"Lift your knee when you kick or you'll wind up with artificial joints before you're fifty," Wanbli said, and he walked back to his table.

"Trouble" was getting up, but his direction was away from both Wanbli and Digger. The bartender was still on the floor, malevolent but passive. The two men who had been hit and the one man who had been scraped kept their places. The smoker had never moved, not since standing up. There was another fellow leaning against the far wall, an old man, declaring his separation from the issue at hand in his every fiber. That made six, plus the bartender. There had been seven, but Wanbli had not been watching the door.

Digger had risen from his bench, but he had not run out, as Wanbli had thought he might. He wouldn't have held it against the Dayflower; he knew a mathematician when he saw one. But he was heartened to see him. He'd finally managed to draw his ears down.

"Amazing that this table didn't get nudged," he said conversationally to all who would listen. He picked up his drink, out of which only two small sips had been taken. He bent long enough to retrieve his stick from under the table.

"Freeze," said number seven, who had been hiding behind the bar. In his hand he had a gun not quite like Wanbli's blunderbuzz, but still an old-timey projectile thrower.

Wanbli moved only slightly: eyes and hands. "Easy to do, in this climate," he replied, eyes searching.

"I could put a hole through you anywhere."

He resisted the impulse to clear his throat. "But why would you want to do that? Even down here it must be against the law to perforate tourists."

The gunslinger was thin and dark, with a long, flat-bottomed jaw that rested against the bar top. The gun too was braced against the bar. Wanbli wondered if it was possible to hit what one was aiming at from that position. His doubtful glance communicated itself and the man rose from his crouch.

"Not when the tourists come busting up the bar," he said.

Digger made a misunderstood sort of sound. Wanbli grinned. "We busted the bar? You sure you were paying attention, flyer?"

"Careful attention." The muzzle of the gun tracked small circles in the air.

Now the bartender started to move, and so did the man who had had his arm stung. Even the hopper with the cigarette took a step sideways. Grinning more broadly, Wanbli squeezed the handle of his stick.

The interrupter made no noise at all, but as the man behind the bar started to sway sideways, Wanbli ducked in place, holding the drink carefully. "Down, Digger!" he shouted.

The gun hadn't gone off. There had been only a slight chance it would. Neural Interruption was like having one's foot asleep all over the body. It was so quick as to be felt only in retrospect.

Everyone who had moved went back to his place.

Wanbli still held the tall glass of milky green. He waved the Tearjerker in front of the bartender's nose. "I paid for this," he said. He made to scoop the remains of Digger's candy off the table, but Digger had already done so. He opened the door for Digger, who went out, staring behind him with his deep little eyes. A few seconds later, just as the bartender had begun to curse once more, Wanbli darted in and out again, snatching up his wonderful fur coat.

Early the next day, the two friends left, quietly and discreetly, shuttling up to a large and expensive string liner.

The Gaudy Sky

FOUR

HE SAT among the stars with his knife in hand. He was not really looking at stars: not as he had been on the roof at Tawlin, or in the Sacred Sand Circle of Southbay School. No ship that ran along the minor strings had anything like a real window. Had there been such, the sight would have been incomprehensible to eyes, but the bubble dome was an excellent translation of what they would look like if massless directionality were more adapted to human experience.

That experience was brilliant and chilling to a man who had loved the night sky. It was as though Wanbli looked at his wife of many years (the wife he was not likely ever to have) and saw her for the first time: ancient, alien, potent and a werebitch besides.

So bright were they that the brilliance receded from the eye, leaving the universe stippled with black on white, black on parti-color, and streaked with smudges of dust and passion.

The passion was not directed at him.

He saluted the six directions, using the zenith of Six-sixty Pulsar, which was marked as a red dot against the dome, as his arbitrary north. The obsidian knife cut the star weave: black, black. He proclaimed himself of the real people, all the while knowing he had lost his reality—left it behind on Neunacht with the warm sand and the green sky. With Wacaan dignity and Hovart's building codes and with the green dusty sky of Neunacht that worked so much better than this dome at translating the stars into 'Indi.

From this cold glory he could not hide the fact that he had been a bit of a fool. He could not even blame it on Ake Tawlin: the crazy claim he had made. Confessing (no matter true or false) to having been one's illegitimate father did not automatically lead to flight off-world. Nor did overwork or mere boredom.

Wanbli had thrown away his future for the sake of these glaring, untranslatable stars.

The knife dove down for the last time; the ritual was over. He would not forget it again, nor his exercises. Fool or not, bound for victory or disaster, at least Wanbli could maintain his competence as a Paint.

He put himself inside himself: uncaring as the star bowl was uncaring. He allowed it to sweep through him, dark and light.

Next week he would lose Digger to the Institute of Probabilities. Well, good for him. There was a flyer who really knew his way, naive or not. No floundering among the suns for him. Chess player.

Wanbli felt he would have made a good chess player, had anyone taught him the game. It was all strategy, wasn't it? Couldn't be too different from the Third Eagle work. Maybe Digger could teach him. They certainly had nothing else to do.

Another few weeks and New Benares. Perhaps he should send a gram; let them know he was coming. That would be responsible behavior, but send a gram to whom? He knew no names. Nobody knew his. Not for the first time, he wondered how many people worked on shimmers, and how hard was it to break into the field.

It would be fine to work in a theatrical, playing any role, though of course adventurous roles were more natural to him. So often when Wanbli watched a good story he felt himself utterly dissolved within the action. In turn he was the hero, the villain, the hero's comic friend and even the heroine. It was dizzying, but it was natural. More natural to him than sparring, even. When Al Kyle sprang from the Mate's Chair to the top of the console, his stick whirling, Wanbli's own leg muscles twitched helplessly in the same motion. When Azima Helga cried, his own brown eyes blinked very fast. A good shimmer exhausted him.

No one else felt this way among the Paints of Hovart. Tawlin himself, though addicted to the shimmers, sat through them in complete, passive removal. It didn't seem to matter to him what was portrayed, as long as it had dangling anatomy.

No, this obsession with the shimmers was Wanbli's alone. That meant something.

Besides, he could handle a nerve stick ten times better than Kyle the actor, poor fellow. Wait till they saw him.

He let his eyes lift to the speckled bowl again and he was only half Wanbli of the Wacaan. The other half was Al Kyle being Grender Alzing, the mercenary. With his knife hand he stroked the beard a Wacaan does not grow. The stars were no longer malign.

"You look," she said, "like you've just seen God."

She was a very handsome woman: tall, dark, dressed in a shiny thing that threatened to slip off one shoulder and lie in a heap at her feet. Her voice was lazy. By her face, she was bored. So many people were bored. Wanbli put down the knife and rose to his feet.

". . . Or perhaps," she continued, looking him over with the same glance he was giving her, "you just are a god."

Wanbli felt utterly happy.

She was Ducelet, which was a lovely name, and more than that, she was the Elmira Ducelet. She seemed to think Wanbli should recognize that and so he was obligingly impressed.

Ducelet (never Ducie, she had to correct him) came from

Stanfor, a very old society. She enjoyed being the slightest bit degenerate and decayed, especially in bed. Wanbli raised no objections to this, though he was in truth a beans-and-potatoes sort of man in his amatory tastes. In a certain way, she reminded him of Ake Tawlin, but perhaps that was only the flavor of money.

Or perhaps again it was only wit trying to make up for the inadequacies of the body, for she certainly had no endurance once the hammock started shaking. That was nothing unusual; most of Wanbli's non-Wacaan sex partners had been ready to pull the pillow over their heads before he was fair warmed up. With the Elmira, however, this inadequacy was more a matter of principle than with most. She expected to be valued for the fact that her elbow joint was bigger around than her upper arm.

"You certainly are thin," said Wanbli, to be agreeable.

" 'Nothing extra' is our family motto." She was examining Wanbli's buttocks with a slothful eye. They just happened to be there, ready to be looked at. Wanbli turned his head an inch to the right and prodded his nose into her ever so slight protuberance of a belly. It just happened to be there. The bed adjusted around them with a noise of exasperation. "This is extra," he said. "It would be easy to get rid of too."

Ducelet swelled, all but her tum, and accused him of severity. She bit him on the buttock, too hard.

He slapped her away.

"I've got to sit on that." The Elmira laughed and laughed, past the point of reason. Wanbli was left with quite a set of tooth marks.

As I said, she was slightly degenerate.

These days Wanbli saw Digger rarely. The FTL liner (no shuttle, no boat, this) had too many distractions, and the Elmira Ducelet was only one of these. Wanbli was learning to play pong in the ball court, and was already handicapped over many of the passengers who had played for years. It was said that his colors against the white walls proved too great a distraction, and his opponents kept losing sight of the spinneret.

He almost always had an audience for his morning and evening salutes, and for his sets of forms as well. He never ate alone. The ship's recreational director told him that he had a job waiting, if he ever needed it.

On the fourth day (arbitrary reckoning) of his voyage he had a tiff with the Elmira, or rather she had a tiff all around him, and he was passed on to How Mundo, a very practical, nonpossessive woman of some years who traveled often on business. She had no wit in conversation, but she could go the course.

Sometimes Wanbli slept five or six decs at a stretch.

Digger's room was larger than the usual aboard an FTL liner of this expense, but it was not more plush. The walls were of brushed steel and the furniture covered in a heavy metallic, acid- and base-resistant weave. It had been a storage room originally, converted for passenger use by such foreigners as tended to be hard on their surroundings. It had the usual holo of what the stars might look like, were they visible at the speed traveled, but in this case the imitation was less than usually successful, for the frame of the "window" did not rest flat against a gently curved wall.

The unfriendliness of the space was partially overcome by the homely wealth of Digger's possessions. He had draped his numberless spools on wires stretching from the com knob to the vent knob, the holo and the lavabo door. They looked like so many drying fruit. His print books (and they were heavy, Wanbli had reason to remember) rose in piles on the three industrial-quality tables. Digger had left something crowning each pile, such as bound ream of paper or a dirty plate, so in the event of a gravity failure there would be something heavy holding it down.

A mathematician: not a physicist.

Digger was always at home. Usually his faxereader was brightly lighting his face. He was doing problems.

Wanbli sat down gingerly. The upholstery was unyielding to human anatomy, but still he felt more at home among this scholarly rubble than most Wacaan would have. He was also conscious of this intellectual ease and quite pleased by it. "What are you trying to prove today?" he asked, putting his head back and his hands behind it. "Squaring the circle?"

Digger shifted his little black eyes. "Is that a joke?"

Wanbli smirked and didn't deny it.

"It is young students who go about proving things. I am working from the other end. Please come look."

He went around to the front of the reader, being careful not to scrape against Digger. The screen, which was clotted with gibberish, cleared and then revealed an almost symmetrical shape in white against blue.

"A doily," said Wanbli. "My mother used to make them with string and a little hook."

"Much the same." Digger nodded his self-conscious nod.

"And you made this out of . . . numbers?"

The foreigner's hands made lotuses. It was a sort of laugh. "Someone did, many years ago. What I am doing is trying to stitch it, using these . . ." And with a few touches of his stylus he turned certain threads to pink. Pink with a few nodes of gold, ". . . into this."

The picture melted into a shape of much finer threads, almost beyond the resolution of the reader. Another touch caused the streaks of pink to shoot through this fabric: unevenly, and with nodes of green. "It should fit here," he added, pointing with his very clean claw. "But of course I can't force it."

"No, of course not," answered Wanbli. He knew that much. "Tell me, though. What will you have if you succeed in this? Something to improve people's lives?"

The screen cleared entirely. "A greater understanding of fractals," Digger peeped. "But I have misled you, Wanbli. This is not original work. I am merely reproducing an exercise."

Wanbli scooted away along the bench so he could relax. "Exercise. I've been getting a lot of it too, this trip." He yawned. "Nothing original on my part, either." He was thinking of Mundo and wondering if she expected him for lunch in her cabin, and if so, would he wind up getting anything to eat. Unlike her, he was not trying to lose weight and he was hungry.

Digger did not know about How Mundo or about the

Elmira, either. Wanbli would have found the necessary explanation tedious. "You have marvelous discipline," he said a bit shyly. "To exert yourself so constantly."

"This isn't discipline?" Wanbli looked pointedly at the piles and the spools and the scraps of unattended paper.

"Oh no," answered the Dayflower. "I merely sit on my butt and destroy the furniture."

Chess wasn't as much fun as Wanbli had hoped, and he didn't find there to be a great carryover between the workings of the board and the strategy of hand-to-hand. He tended to find his queen lost in the first ten moves. Wanbli kept on with it, however, even after he realized he was doing his friend no favor in burdening him with a beginning opponent. It was that matter of discipline.

The hour before the landing at Shasta, where the Institute of Probabilities was located, was very hectic, even though there wasn't much for Digger to do except strap books together. "I will leave everything here," he said, not for the first time. "It will look too . . . assuming if I come for the final interview with all my gear. I don't know that anyone has been rejected from matriculation at this point, but still . . ."

"I'll put it all in a heap right here by the door," said Wanbli, who had done most of the physical work of packing for Digger. "So you can dart in and out." Wanbli was riding on the high part of Digger's emotional stew, thankfully spared the undercurrents of anxiety.

Losing Digger already. It was as though he was losing another bit of home. But of course the Dayflower had never been to Neunacht in his fifteen years of life. It was only that Wanbli wasn't used to parting with friends so soon and so completely.

Such a big, grinding universe.

He stared at Digger, who stared back, his little deep eyes as wide as they could get. He was so excited his claws were out and his genitals in. "Hey," said Wanbli. "We should drink a toast before you go."

"You go ahead and order one," said Digger, settling uneasily into a chair. "I'm too excited for sugar."

"Order one?" Wanbli thought of his exchequer and of the very expensive fur coat he had not worn since leaving Icor. "Wait, why should I order one? I have our first drink together in my bag."

It took a few minutes for him to get back, which was just as well, as there was almost a dec to kill before touching Shasta. The Tearjerker had not been improved by its residence in polymer, but Wanbli raised the shampoo bottle to his lips and took a grand swallow, after which he breathed hard and capped the bottle. "There," he said. "After that sacrifice, your career will have to be spectacular."

"What about your career, Red?" He sat perched on the edge of his seat like a big and very heavy bird, his claws linked on his knees. "You are too bright a fellow to be drifting without goals."

"Bright?" echoed Wanbli. He was indeed beginning to drift and he wished he could catch his breath. "You mean colorful, I think. But don't worry about me. I have secret plans and I'll write to you about them. I can write, you know."

Digger smiled with a small display of ivory and then leaped up, certain he had forgotten to seal his faxereader, which was not at all the case.

Wanbli decided he liked the stars after all; his initial anomie had been only a result of too much too fast. He sat on his heels in the crystal dome, wearing only his half-thigh shorts, returning his own colors to the colors of the blazing display. If any other of the passengers—the Elmira Ducelet, Mundo, the hexaped that breathed out through its chest— came to enjoy the galaxy, they saw him so and went away again. Maybe it was the obsidian knife.

He had no close friends anymore, but then he had no boss, he was subject to no Clan Council and his digestion was good. For now, that was enough.

It was odd how reluctant he felt to tell anyone of his decision to be an actor in the shimmers. Perhaps it had something to do with certain phrases dropped by the Elmira, or with Comptroller Akavit's laugh. Acting seemed to be an ambiguous occupation, above a man's station or below his dignity. T'chishett knew nothing of that. Well, guard work was an ambiguous occupation too: a combination of hero, valet and thug. Wanbli was used to that.

The ship was spinning but the stars in the dome were not. The captain had chosen to project the Milky Way diagonally across it; more brilliance for your money, Wanbli decided. He would have liked some patches of black, for contrast.

And black did move between the stars, coming closer. It opened eyes at him and was a black man wearing black. "You have offended a very important person," he said, and unfolded his arms, revealing the pistol-grip nerve rod.

"I try not to do that."

It was a nasty, nasty gun, though its range was limited. It could kill, but it's foremost use was to make people hurt. Such tools were illegal in T'chishett, and only the T'chishetti themselves ever smuggled them in. The sadism of weakness, said the Wacaan. Wanbli's own nerve stick was not designed to be used as punishment, but it was the better weapon. No matter. The stick was three yards away, on the plush, sound-absorbing floor. Might as well not exist.

"You failed," answered the gap among the stars. "The Elmira has been made very unhappy by you."

Wanbli stared. "Ducie wouldn't send you to shoot me," he said, though not certain this was true.

"A woman like that doesn't have to command in words." The fellow's accent was definitely not Hindi.

"Now wait," began Wanbli, setting his toes to grip the flooring. First the left haunch, then the right. "I presume you find yourself . . . a close friend to Ducie. Right?"

"She is the Elmira." The man slipped the safety of the gun off. Wanbli was surprised he hadn't done this before. Not tremendously effective, to confront an enemy with the safety on. Perhaps things were not as tight as they had seemed.

"Well, think on it, flyer. Had Ducie not gotten rubbed wrong by me, you might never have had the opportunity to get to know her. That would have been a shame, right? So you have no reason to be down on me."

The gun leveled. Oh well, it had been a good try. Wanbli

reverted to Second Eagle training. With only his toes against the flooring for anchor, he leaped like a frog straight for the two dull stars that marked his attacker's position, black against black. It was the most difficult, slow sort of leap, but Wanbli was highly motivated to make it work. He spun in the air and hit his attacker upside down and facing away from him. Had his aim been perfect he would have been a few degrees more rotated, and the fellow would have taken his full force through Wanbli's bare feet to his bare face. Distances in the dome were deceptive, however, and he hit flat against the black man's body with the feet drubbing one-two immediately after.

Had the attacker's aim been perfect, Wanbli would have taken the interrupter shot right in the crotch. The man was not a gunman, however, or at least not under the circumstances of being hit with a full-body slam and thrown into a glass wall. The gun went off against the edge of Wanbli's thigh.

As they fell together onto the discreet black floor foam, Wanbli was howling. He called the attacker names that one did not in the least understand, and then both of them were scrabbling through the dark after the gun. The black man found it at the same moment that Wanbli found his feet and grabbed the head of the stooping man between his thighs. This hurt quite a bit.

"Just twitch," said Wanbli, "and I break your neck. Just a twitch."

It would have been difficult to snap a spine in this position, even if both legs were working with equal power, but Wanbli knew from experience that this was a terrible threat. Yet the man picked up the gun anyway. Wanbli kicked it out of his hand. Did this flyer really want to die? Still the man struggled, and Wanbli put his foot down on the wiggling neck. "Didn't you hear me say don't even twitch or I'd kill you?"

The man's mouth opened in surprise. One could see teeth. "No," he said aggrievedly. "I couldn't hear anything at all. You had your damn legs over my ears."

Wanbli lifted his foot. Gun in hand, he sat down to massage his aching thigh.

"I can't believe Ducie sent you after me. Unless she wants to be rid of you a lot."

The black man sighed and sat up. He was not dressed in assassin's black, Wanbli could now see, but instead in an almost glossy and very expensive fabric, patterned indigo upon black. It reminded Wanbli of damask. Like his mother.

"I told you, such a lady does not have to command directly."

"Well, if she commanded by chin points and whistles, still she meant to do you wrong. She knows I'm a Paint."

"Painted very gaudily too," answered the other. He rubbed his hands over his battered face and introduced himself as Reynaldo Errenthorp, which Wanbli thought was a name of great potential. He himself had often wished for more syllables, to increase his dignity.

Reynaldo started and gave a small shriek. "I'm bleeding. I'm bleeding like a broken hose!"

Wanbli looked closely, to where blood was only a slick surface against the dark. "It's not your face. It's your hand. It's sliced." His fingers fumbled carefully over the floor.

"My knife." He raised the obsidian tool in his hand: again, black over black. "You put your hand down on my ceremonial knife."

The black man whimpered and ran out into the light.

Wanbli arrested the bleeding with a spray from his first-aid kit. "At least it's clean. That knife was never used to cut anything but air. Until now. I'll have a hell of a time cleaning it again."

"I'm not carrying any . . . disease or anything." Reynaldo seemed inclined to resent things.

Wanbli smiled and slipped the knife (not wrapped, this time) into his suitcase. He sat on the bed next to Reynaldo. "No, I didn't think you were. It's a different sort of cleanness. My clan doesn't usually fight with such knives. They're sacred."

Reynaldo understood, or thought he did. He gave a man-of-the-world laugh, which slid into a giggle: slightly hysterical. He kept his eyes on the pink foam that hardened on his ebony hand.

"I'd give you a drink, but the only stuff I got is left in someone else's cabin. It wasn't very good anyway. Tasted like shampoo."

Reynaldo looked straight at Wanbli for the first time since entering his cabin. Visibly he took command of himself. "You're very good about this," he said. He was a tall, good-looking man. Not an athlete.

"Why not?" Wanbli gave a shrug that explained nothing but was very impressive. "All's you did is sting me a little. It's hard to kill a man with a gun like that."

"Oh, I didn't mean to kill you," said Reynaldo hurriedly. He added, with some diffidence, "She did suggest I go after you, you know."

Wanbli sighed and said nothing.

"I . . . I had begun to suspect she was finding me boring."

Now Wanbli grunted sympathetically. "Ducie can be . . . sort of perverted."

"Real bitch." They sighed together.

They went to dinner, waiting for the uncomfortable moment when ship's logic found the string. It was not the same string that had taken them to Stanfor. It was the third string Wanbli had traveled; travelers often counted their experiences by the number of minor strings.

Wanbli waved to How Mundo and to three other people, but he stayed in a private booth with Reynaldo. He liked to sound his new friends deeply.

Wonder of wonders, the black man came from New Benares. He was an importer of metal goods, but upon gentle probing he let it be known he had important contacts in the AT industry. Wanbli was on fire to pump him for information, so he asked about Ducelet instead.

"Why the Elmira?" Reynaldo raised his wineglass to his lips. As he now wore another outfit as black and glossy as the first, the stain of pink on his hand fluttered against darkness like a moth. "It is no silly, Johnny-come-lately aristocracy, Wacaan, sir."

"Call me . . . uh, Red. Wacaan is the name of the clan."

"It is a real title, inherited through living trade. Elmira

Stations and Planetary Satellites. They are the largest purveyer of turnkey cargo stations in the Short Arm. Their name in small, free-orbiters is more recent, but growing."

The transfer came and passed. Not a bad one, this time. Nothing like the slam of going FTL in a shuttle boat.

Wanbli wanted to ask what the wine was made of, but at the dinner booth, unlike in the star dome, Reynaldo was the stronger party. He drank wine like it was water, and although Wanbli wanted a taste, he did not want to pay for a whole glass out of his rapidly dwindling resources. He lowered his eyes and was abashed.

"We've bought a station. Neunacht. Us."

Reynaldo looked at him through the red of the glass. "Neunacht? I think I recognize the name. Warm place, isn't it?"

"Perfect," answered Wanbli.

"We been paying for it since my great-grandmommy's time. It's even a part of my clan's morning ritual. We invoke the moon and the moon's little sister, which is coming. Any year now, I guess."

The waiter came with steaming plates. Reynaldo asked for a fork in place of chopsticks. "That will make life different," he said reflectively. "Not necessarily for the better, either. Tourism. Loss of local handicrafts, local idiosyncrasies. Whole cultures disappear within a generation." He received his fork and tasted his fettuccine. It was passable. He was pleased to see that his dinner companion, despite all the bare skin and muscles, ate daintily. "I am surprised that with a station coming, you did not recognize the name of Elmira."

Wanbli looked up. He thought the fettuccine had too much grease in it. "We didn't get it from Elmira. It's coming from Cynthia Contractors."

Reynaldo stopped eating. His hand grasped the stem of his glass, but he did not raise it. "Cynthia . . . was bought out by Elmira ten years ago."

Equably Wanbli answered. "Well, then we're going to get it from Elmira. That doesn't change the fact that Ducie has behaved like a real whizzer."

Reynaldo blinked this away. "No. No, they bought the firm in receivership."

"Wherever." Wanbli whipped more greasy noodles over his chopsticks.

There was a waiter standing beside the table, hands folded behind his back. He stood silent for five seconds. This was beyond the level of service even of a large FTL liner. Wanbli glanced up and met very urgent eyes.

"Pardon me, sir, but didn't you board ship in the company of the nonhuman gentleman in cabin 287—uh—the Silver Suite?"

Wanbli made a series of connections in his head. "I'm not really responsible for damages, though. No relation."

The officer—not a waiter at all—winced noticeably. "We wouldn't think of holding you responsible, but we would be grateful if you would come with us. Me, I mean."

In the middle of dinner, thought Wanbli, but he went. Reynaldo, elegant despite his lacerated hand, followed unasked.

In the hall the smell of leather was almost overpowering, and there was another, worse, on top of it. "What in fortune did he leave behind?" Wanbli asked the officer, who opened the door.

What Digger had left behind was himself, stretched face-up from the doorway to the books on the overturned central table. With his tiny eyes shut tight and his lips everted he looked impossibly fierce and brutish. He had vomited.

"He's dead," said the officer.

Wanbli shook his head and rubbed his hands over his face. He backed into a corner and stared from an astonished Reynaldo to the official and back again, as though he expected either an attack or an explanation. "Are you sure? I mean . . . he was already gone. To his institute. I don't understand."

"He left a letter." The officer took it out of his pocket. "For you."

Wanbli took the sheet of paper. With surprise he noted that his hand was not shaking.

Friend Red,

They did not know I was Dayflower. They left me waiting for a dec and then the director came and told me he thought the institute was not appropriate for me. He said I would spend the rest of my life learning and never have a chance to put my study to use. He said he was certain I would eventually feel cheated. I don't think he told me the complete truth. I think it was they who felt cheated when they discovered I intended to use my life in the Institute. I had every intention of spending the rest of my life learning.

I am very disappointed. In them.

Please forgive me that I took your toiletry bottle without asking.

There was an illegible signature at the bottom, followed by a block-printed "Digger Whistle-two-hoots."

"The toiletry bottle?" asked the officer diffidently.

Wanbli found it under the table. It was empty. "It had booze in it; that's all."

Reynaldo spoke for the first time. "He intended to get drunk?"

"He intended to die. He told me many times it was poison to him. They eat sugar to get high." Wanbli was dry-eyed, but his throat was not behaving. He had lost friends before, and sometimes other friends had killed them. But never this. He looked down at his ugly friend, whose fall had scraped the binding off three books. "Are you sure? That he's not in a coma, or hibernating, or something?"

"Very sure. We've sent a fiddlegram to his people. No response yet."

There was silence. Reynaldo started to back out of the foul room and Wanbli could not blame him.

"Did you call the IP too?" Wanbli asked the officer, who was manfully trying not to gag. "I think they oughta know."

"Yes."

"And what did they say?" There was an un-Wacaan amount of anger in Wanbli's voice.

"I don't know. It wasn't I who called. I can find out of course?"

Wanbli took a deep breath. For some reason the smell didn't bother him. "I'll go myself. I want to see those people."

Both Reynaldo and the officer looked at Wanbli and then away. "I'm sorry," said the officer. "We transferred a little while ago; didn't you feel it? We couldn't go back now for any reason. Not if the captain himself died."

The response came from Digger's home county. They wanted him back and so the poor corpus was lifted by two men in heavy gloves and a small forklift and it went into cold storage. Wanbli kept a vigil in the empty room, with the cleaners working around him. No one suggested he leave.

> ". . . We are the big ones. We are the small.
> We live ten thousand years. We live a day.
> Our lives are a single learning.
> We are those who remain people.
> We are Wacaan."

He had not purified the black knife after all. He knew he did not have to, for no possible impurity could touch in this morning's ritual. Nor did it matter to him whether it was morning at Tawlin Estate by Hovart in T'chishett on Neunacht far away, where the dust made a green border to the blue living sky and the Paints killed each other on command: this sky was black and gaudy and the mathematician was dead.

Wanbli had found himself possessed of many books and spools as well as an expensive faxereader, upon the screen of which he did not know how to invoke Digger's bright lace.

Damasc.

> "I invoke the six directions upon this morning.
> I invoke the suns.
> I invoke all worlds and their little sisters that are
>   made by man.

They are all my own sisters.
I am of the people of the sky. I am Wacaan."

He had known he had an audience. He often had an audience; at one time he had played to it, but anymore he didn't give a good condemn. This presence had not felt threatening: not like Reynaldo that day. Only a few days ago.

It still might be that very elegant gentleman who often came by to smother the idle decs. Reynaldo liked having a friend among the exotic and deadly, and liked it all the more that that friend had a sorrow. It affected his own deep but conventional sentiments.

Wanbli finished the circle and laid down the obsidian knife. He had to urinate, of course, and as he rose he was a bit nonplussed to find that it was the Elmira standing at the gate of the dome.

"You're up early," he said.

"Haven't been to sleep yet," said Ducie. She looked haggard, but that might have been mere affectation.

Wanbli did not reply or move to squeeze past her or to set her aside. He stood silent and forced her to continue.

"I'm damn sorry about your friend."

He was slow in answering, feeling suddenly that he hadn't slept well. "How did you know? Reynaldo? The steward said they were trying to keep it a secret."

She was sucking on something: probably Pov-lacc. With her fashionably hollow cheeks it was very easy to notice. "Whole damn ship knows. It's gotten to damn twenty-five inhabited planets by now—that the foremost scientist among the Hemerocallis was rejected as a student by IP and killed himself.

"I hope those buggers find themselves with a public black eye stretching all along the Arm. I hope this leaves them in a hole. A cold, cold hole."

She spoke with more emotion than Wanbli had yet shown to anyone regarding Digger's death. Or regarding anything, for that matter. He was daunted momentarily, but consoled himself with the thought that it was better having her furious at someone other than him.

"He shouldn't have done it," was all he could think to say. "It wasn't worth it."

Ducie's eyes were militantly bright. It was undoubtedly Povlen. "It was a political protest."

"It was despair," he said softly, looking at the expensive drab floor. "I thought we were close. He . . . we still could have had a few good times. He didn't have to give up."

Ducie blinked at him as he went past her toward the nearest facility. "Could you . . . I mean wasn't that terribly dangerous or at least inconvenient? With his sandpaper skin . . ."

Wanbli laughed wholeheartedly. "Oh, lady! I meant good times out drinking." Then he remembered and the laugh fell off. "No, I don't mean that, either. Just had a few good times."

She was following him down the hall. Away from the uncompromising light of the dome her glamour reasserted itself. Wanbli remembered that he had liked looking at her clothes. "Hey! Ducie. Why did you sic Reynaldo on me like that? And him such a nice flyer too?"

Her giggles were childish. They took five years off her age and possibly she meant them to do so. "Oh, Red! You have no idea. He was such a bore, with his Elmira this and Elmira that. And the idea was so funny. You have to admit. You have to admit."

Wanbli turned as he came to the door. "I admit it. Now can you make Reynaldo admit it?"

Very gently (for she was the Elmira of the Stations) he closed the lavabo door against her. On a ship of this class they were sexually segregated.

The Steamy Sky

FIVE

WANBLI RODE in spins and spirals over the jungle surrounding the city of New Benares on the planet of the same name. Most new arrivals in his financial condition had to take the bus and he tried to be appreciative of his fortune, but Reynaldo was a wild driver.

"Good to feel warm again, het? Het?" shouted the black man. His aquiline nose and high forehead gave him a severe profile. Wanbli clutched his seat harness and showed his teeth in a grin, or at least he showed his teeth.

It was warm all right, even so far above the ground, but it was not the warmth of home. It was a wet warmth: twice as humid as Southbay. Five times as wet as Tawlin. The air fought against his lungs and he suspected he could feel an infection beginning there.

Downward was green with careless plants with their loose, sloppy leaves hanging over everything, smothering each other like people in a crowded city. Huge leaves, some almost a meter long, far too heavy to fold up at night or at dawn. But then they didn't want to. This limp foliage looked like lengths of fabric or plastic extrusions: nothing natural Wanbli had ever seen. Trees reached up into the sky and sometimes Reynaldo dove his machine among them chortling with glee. Wanbli thought he could make out other green things battening on the boles of the trees. Perhaps these would leap out into the car.

Wanbli, who had an extremely fine sense of balance, was very ill.

Upward also had its touches of green, as the ground gave reflection to the bellies of blooming clouds. Maybe it was about to rain. Wanbli hoped so, for then Reynaldo would have to come down.

It didn't rain. "Notice the buildings," Reynaldo shrieked over the wind noise of his latest precipitous dive.

"What buildings?" Wanbli had to try again. "What buildings?"

"You can't see them." The car swooped further, touching the damp canopy of the trees. A flock of birds, not darters but real birds with fluffy bodies and opaque wings, rose in angry protest, like Wanbli's stomach. "Unless they are part of a set, all buildings in the consortium have to be painted banana-leaf green. Makes things easier."

Wanbli closed his eyes.

Unexpectedly he felt the car touch down. "Het! Did you fall asleep?" asked Reynaldo, snapping his harness open and hopping nimbly over the low door of the open car.

"Something like that," answered Wanbli. He clenched and unclenched his fists. Silently he repeated the ritual to encourage the spirit to return to the endangered body. Choosing dignity over grace, he opened the door with the handle and stepped onto pavement. It was slimy.

"You're a cool character," said Reynaldo. He must have been very happy to be home. He trotted around and clapped Wanbli on the shoulder. "Some people are made nervous by my driving."

Wanbli took a belly breath of the strange air, hoping all would stay down. "I don't tend to be nervous."

". . . can believe that." Reynaldo led him away.

*   *   *

He lay by the pool, his belly against the domed tops of the paving stones. His cheek rested upon a flat stone of decorative unatite. He knew it was unatite because his host had told him so; it was pink and green in lacework. One of the by-products of Reynaldo's mining concerns.

It was much like Digger's doily.

Around him was the splash of water as Reynaldo's daughter played Naiad games. Scarlet fishes nibbled Wanbli's fingers, for he had both arms in the pool. The householders sat in chairs, one on each side of him.

"You know, Wanbli," Reynaldo began, after one of his ceremonial throat clearings, "I'm not sure about this station contract between Elmira and your people. After bankruptcy, the law is . . . very individual about what liabilities are to be covered."

"You're saying we have been paying for three generations for nothing?" Wanbli pulled his face over the stone.

Reynaldo was a black shape against moist blue sky. "I'm saying I don't know. It's not something to get perturbed about."

Perturbed? Wanbli laughed at the word, which he had usually heard used in the description of orbits. Planetary bodies. Ships. He imagined himself perturbed. His grin faded.

"I may never go home again," he said aloud, as though that were the answer to a question.

The heat was like a sweathouse. Wanbli became a ratchett in the sun. Only the girl made noise. She was half grown: all vertical.

"Don't stick your hand in the filter, Doas," Reynaldo's wife, Cyrene, called over the splashing. Cyrene was touching her wrists and elbows with enamel. She was not exactly a fashionable woman, being plump and comfortable and keeping a comfortable house, but she had a feeling for style.

Doas blew bubbles before answering. "It's not my hand, Mama. It's my hair. It gets caught and feels funny."

Cyrene did not look up. "The principle is the same, dear. When you break the field you let the refuse back into the pool. And for the same reason, don't swallow any of the water."

"For the same what reason?" Doas was being deliberately provocative. Wanbli knew it was for his benefit and he kept his eyes closed.

"Because the fish eliminate in it," answered her mother, unruffled. The girl sputtered and made three faces, one after the other, and then climbed out onto the moss of the bank. She sat there naked and dripping, regarding Wanbli peripherally. She was twelve years old: a simply conceived baby—no gene sculpture used or needed—natural average of her father's ebony and her mother's onion-soup coloring. Her long straight hair hung to her waist, dripping, and drops formed on her budding nipples. She had an undeniable gangly charm.

Wanbli kept his eyes closed.

"This is not a unified planet, though it possesses only one major industry." Reynaldo was making a large circle over the boundaries of Greenbunch Studio, dipping close enough so that the buildings could be discerned among the leaves. Wanbli was becoming used to this style of driving, though he noticed that not only was the paint scraped from under the vehicle but there were the marks of other, more decisive impacts on the chassis.

Not content with letting Wanbli run tame through the house, Reynaldo had devoted hours to showing him around his home city. Once again Wanbli wondered at the strength of friendship one could elicit from a man by the simple expedient of beating him up. Beating him up the right way, of course. Without humiliation.

"In the beginning they tried a Parliamentary Democracy, though I don't know how they chose *that* form. Perhaps because it made such good theater. It wilted, of course, because the only entities on the planet with any power are the three studios, and they were not about to be bound by the dictates of uninvolved people acting in a hall that was to them a cheap interior set."

Reynaldo dropped down into the center of a tree. Wanbli whipped his head down to his knees to prevent whiplash or worse, but the tree turned out to be made of flexible vinyl sheets that licked at his back as they descended. Camouflage again.

"They fought a war once. Greenbunch against the combined might of Myronics and UAT." They settled onto green paving. "Very expensive and played havoc with schedules. I was little more than a boy but I remember it clearly."

The parking yard was extensive and entirely invisible from above. Wanbli thought the T'chishetti could learn a lot from this place. Once stable in at least the vertical dimension, Wanbli began to perk up. "Did you fight?"

"I audited. It was a peacekeeping mission." There was a certain quiet pride in Reynaldo's voice. "In the end we pronounced the hostilities unfeasible."

Wanbli knew very little about organized warfare. He saw he would have to treat the black man with more respect.

This garden was familiar. Wanbli could not miss the lake in the middle: over an acre of shimmering water, crossed by a bamboo bridge. A fountain splashing and pumping. The colors of the lake bounced off the debris screen that covered the whole. At first Wanbli assumed that the pastel, soft-tissued flowers along the path were artificial, for none of them moved at his presence, not even when they were touched. The lake itself might have been a sheet of glass. (In T'chishett it would be easier to assemble that much glass than that much water.)

"Do you feel like you've been here before?"

"Many times," answered Wanbli. *"The Travels of Sito Moro, Kelvin* and of course *The Garden of Grief."*

Reynaldo looked a bit quizzical. "Those are all fairly old movies."

A great deal of money was represented in these rolling hills of grass and tasteful posies. The field itself, twice larger than all of Tawlin Manor—and Tawlin was shielded only over the windows—it must cost a man's left leg and privates too in energy.

"I can see why they reuse it so often," he said, to be saying something.

"Every child's daydream setting." Reynaldo gave a disapproving grunt. "Always the same too.

"Holo work is the death of art," he said, leading Wanbli over the bridge. There were other tourists walking toward them from the opposite shore. "With flat-screen work, the camera is the eye and the eye is always new. With shimmers, well, there it just is. Blop. See it. Walk around. There it still is, just the same."

"The same can be said for live acting," Wanbli offered, but it was the wrong thing to say, because Reynaldo turned and made a face. "Who said live acting was the be-all and end-all?" His expression cleared as he saw that Wanbli's gaze and attitude was pointed forward to the other end of the bridge. Wanbli had gone gray.

"What is it?"

"I . . . thought I saw someone I knew."

"Oh." Reynaldo led on. "Everyone does here. Is it Enric Paovo?"

The name drew only a twitch of a smile. "No. His name's Mimi—Aymimishett—and he doesn't want to be an actor. Or a thief or a tramp."

"A man of sound instincts." Reynaldo had to lean out over the rail to pass the group coming in the opposite way. Wanbli moved over, but he allowed the others to do the leaning. The man was not Aymimishett, of course. He was not even very red.

This morning, when Wanbli was scheduled to meet the friend of Reynaldo who might help him at Myronics, he completely lost the desire to be an actor in the shimmers. Perhaps it was the baby dream again. This time he had killed the baby and was awaiting punishment. Shortly after waking in a sweat, he had cut himself on the obsidian knife. Clumsy. Less excuse than Reynaldo had had. Cyrene and Reynaldo had had an argument after breakfast. Over the Elmira, though Wanbli had not revealed a word. Doas showed him her secret way out of the house when her parents went to it like that.

Stubbornly, Wanbli pushed his feelings into the shape of a good omen. All through his past, whenever he had had to make a decision in advance—to go someplace far, to leave a comfortable slot, to start a program as a beginner—he woke up with these cold-shower unenthusiasms. And usually the effort *had* been worthwhile. Ergo, this would be too. He decided to walk to the Myronics man's office.

"Show me terror," said the casting man, and when Wanbli responded, he burst out laughing. "I didn't say be terrified of me, mister. I want you to show me the language—theater language communication for terror."

Wanbli felt swallowed by the loose foam and leatherette of the lounge chair. Tilted back on his ass and helpless as a baby. He drew his legs up, crossed them and thought hard. He remembered *Hounds of Juno,* where all the old prospectors were savaged by the savage watchrobots. They had made a silly face: each of them. Wanbli made that face.

"Right," said the interviewer. "Now we're beginning to understand."

He was an individual of average brown, but with the blue-gray sheen Wanbli had first noticed in the woman aboard the shuttle that had taken him off-planet. A good effect, he considered, but it would require a completely different palette of tattoos—if these people ever wore tattoos.

"I've always wondered," Wanbli ventured to say. "I mean, that really isn't what a person looks like when he's afraid of something. It's more like he's going to vomit, or that he's eaten a mouthful too hot. When a flyer's really scared . . ."

"When a human being is really injured, he spouts blood all over. But if you drain your changer for a—a book, let's say—that's sold as a novel of suffering and transcendence, you don't expect to find the pages damp and red-stained. You want words. One step removed. It's the symbology that makes art out of life."

Wanbli tried to catch up with all this, sparking another giggle out of the Myronics man. "You don't have to understand, mister. Just do it."

"Oh, I will," said Wanbli, all readiness to please. He had come with no particular views on the nature of theater.

The man went back to his own cushy chair and threw

himself into it. He did not seem to feel the worse for being half swallowed by it. His head poked out the top and he drummed his fingers on a projecting knee.

"Your face isn't bad," he murmured. "Not even by our standards."

Wanbli said nothing. His face was not the focus of his vanity.

"The problem is your body."

Wanbli came half out of the chair; he didn't know how. "Problem? My body? What's wrong with it?"

The Myronics man seemed to enjoy this reaction: the outrage, the flush, the disbelief. He smiled and settled deeper in his own chair. But then he did not know what a Paint was.

"As far as the shape goes, and the general decorativeness, nothing at all. It's the color and those . . . markings."

"You only like certain colors?" Wanbli settled again so that this flabby office nester might not get any more enjoyment out of him. His opinion of the fellow's sophistication fell rapidly. A man who didn't like a good, bright red . . .

"My own personal opinion has nothing to do with it. It's all efficiency.

"You have all the brilliance of a turning leaf (in places where it gets cold enough for leaves to turn, of course). How many parts are written around fox-colored men with black and green feathers on their chests?"

"Not feathers: eagles." To Wanbli, a feather was a unit of coinage.

"And"—he drowned out Wanbli's protest—"if they were, why couldn't we take an actor we already have—with name recognition—and have him painted to fit?"

He seemed to be finished, so Wanbli cleared his throat. He got no further. ". . . And you needed to be told—told outright—how to show terror. Most shimmer-struck kids have got it down as second nature by the time they get here. And those are just the ordinary ones. A good actor doesn't even remember what the dumb brute of a human does to register emotion." He gave a whuff to show what he thought either of actors or of the dumb brute of a human.

Wanbli took the opportunity of silence to open his

mouth, but the other was faster. "So I don't think we need you at all."

Using his arms, Wanbli pulled himself out of the chair. It was like fighting with an intestine. This time he knew what would happen when he tried to speak, and it did.

"So goodbye," the Myronics man said.

Obediently Wanbli rose, but he did not go. He moved very fast past the man's many-shelved and -surfaced, kidney-shaped desk. He ducked under an antique air-conditioning unit with lapis lazuli knobs and a sterling-silver grill and reached one long red arm behind the man in his chair-nest. Two fingers slipped down gently into the man's eye sockets and pulled the head back over, where he held it. The man floundered toward the touch plate at the corner of his desk—the one that would call security—but only succeeded in knocking over a holo of himself shaking hands with Noren Myronics at the five-year ceremony. It was a thing he valued.

So was his neck.

Wanbli squatted down beside the chair, so that his head was almost at a level with the other's. The floundering arm he caught quite casually and locked with a folded wrist. The left arm was too far away and too unpracticed to do damage, and besides, Wanbli was hidden by the chair.

"You," he began slowly, speaking at his leisure, "are a difficult man to talk with."

His prisoner whimpered, but he talked over him. "I'm not used to being treated like this, and do you know why? Did Reynaldo tell you? No? Well, I suppose you really can't talk with your neck bent back like that.

"What I am is a professional killer. A real professional: we take vows. I don't always kill people, of course; sometimes I don't need to."

The truth was the circumstances had never been such that he had had to kill at all. Many Paints went their lives long and never had to kill.

"Now, that doesn't mean I will make a good actor. Not in itself. I have some good friends among my own clan who would make lousy actors." He had Aymimishett in mind, of course.

Wanbli shifted on the floor, working himself into a position of greater comfort. The man's neck stretched a little tauter. "But what it *does* mean is that I can move well. Also, I have a certain gift for getting into other people's heads. Like yours, here. If I had not realized you were working to get me angry at you, I probably would have fallen for it. As it is . . ."

"This can't . . . help you." The man in the chair got out these words with great effort.

"Oh, but it has already. You're listening to me. You don't like me, but you're listening. And you didn't like me before, either, so what's the loss?"

The Bermudas he was wearing were uncomfortable. He rarely wore so much, and especially not in a climate so hot. It just went to show him what you get for overdressing for the occasion.

After a few seconds of quiet meditation, Wanbli gave a sigh. "I think I've figured out your language. I could be wrong, and you could be just a nasty kind of flyer with a bad liver or something, but I suspect it's just a ranking problem.

"I'm going to give you a list of names, and you nod—no, not nod, just gurgle or something when you hear one you really like. All right? Now: Reynaldo Errenthorp—remember the flyer that introduced us? Remember him? Do you like that name?"

The man stared ahead, looking as blank and angry as a bird.

"Not Reynaldo. Not a big enough gun, I guess. Too bad. How about Mother Blanding. Does the name Blanding spark your eyes at all?" The mad-hawk eyes swiveled distrustfully. Wanbli was unsure, but he had another idea.

"How about this one, Popo: the Elmira Ducelet?"

The hawk eyes turned human and the great digestive chair squeaked and sucked beneath him. "You know the Elmira? Personally?"

"Very personally," answered Wanbli, and slowly, carefully, he let the man go.

"Let's talk about my career."

*   *   *

As a child reads his history spools and imagines the battle of Joveritz taking place by the back veranda swing, or Pyramus and Thisbe exchanging notes through the home airlock, so Wanbli's early imaginations took place on scenes constructed by Myronics or UAT—that is, when not on the aureate dust of Tawlin. For that reason, this day was a waking dream to him, doing endless interviews and exercises under the green canopy that concealed so much of New Benares.

"You can't see where the sun is," said Audry Hish in his ear. Audry was the staff manager of one particular branch of the Myronics tree. She had been leading him around. She was a graceful woman who appeared to be only a few years older than he was. Though her skin was a very rich brown, her eyes were light and flecked with green. Her face and manner were cool, and Wanbli thought her very exotic.

"I saw you looking up," she explained. "For shimmers, it's easier to film without direct sun, and as I said, it hides the passing of time."

She led him along the pavement among the smooth boles of the trees, some silver, some dark as her skin, some speckled rufous, like him. He stroked each tree wonderingly as they passed. Audry shot him a sharp look or two, but he decided to wait until she actually told him to stop.

The buildings were low and not much different from those of his home, except that the roofs were sharply pitched. Couldn't do much on a roof like that. They shone gray-black, like slate. Some of the buildings seemed to be made entirely of wood and Wanbli had to stare at these too. Such ostentation was almost embarrassing.

"You like the trees?" Audry's voice was as cool as the rest of her. She spoke slowly and with a definite accent, as though Hindi were not her native tongue. She seemed amused by him. Wanbli would have played for that amusement, if he had known what it was about him that amused her. As it was, he answered simply.

"They inspire awe, of course. But they also . . . clutter up the landscape."

"C . . . lutter?" Now he could laugh at her expression.

"Yes. I'm used to being able to see right to the edge, you know? To the horizon? Whereas anybody could be hiding behind these."

She looked long at him, as though he had said much more than he had said. She came up to his nose only, and had long, straight black hair. She turned again and walked before him, the ivory drape that covered her legs breathing in and out with her step. "I am from the forest. I find hiding places very useful. I don't think there are enough of them here."

He stood staring and then sprinted after her, her words echoing and echoing in his head. "I am from the forest. I find hiding places very useful. I am from the forest."

Someday he would understand what she meant by that. Someday he would know why that was so important.

It was easy to lose the dark of her skin and the pale of her wrap amid the dark and pale of the light spattered on the paving stones. She moved almost barefoot-quiet.

A car drove by from behind him, only a few inches above the ground. It was silent except for its whining turbine and it was moving fast. Wanbli got out of its way and then watched to be sure Audry Hish would also. She didn't miss a step. He caught up to her.

"That was Gregor Myronics," she told him.

"I thought Myronics was dead years ago. Or is it his nephew or son or something? Drives like to kill someone."

She nodded, still cool as cool. "There are many of them."

It looked like an obelisk toppling behind the trees: a tall, stiff, shining thing. It rose and toppled again.

"I thought they'd be finished spooling by now," she said, passing through a grove that waved lightly. The trees were whiter than her wrap.

It was a cheap spooling: only three cameras, set at 120 degree angles around a clearing in the woods. In that clearing seven people scuffled, danced and waved lances ineffectually through the air around the bulk and the high-raised head of a diplodocus. That was the obelisk thing.

"Another diplodocus attack," said Wanbli without thinking.

"Diplo movies are always change-ringers," answered Audry blandly. "And they're inexpensive as long as the hoomies remain star-struck."

One of the frantic cavemen (they were probably supposed to be time travelers, but at this point in the shimmer they looked like any cavemen) stumbled and fell under the descending foot of the dinosaur. A portly gentleman seated under the shadow of a birch made the ancient sign called "cutting the action" and the diplodocus shuffled backward, its foot extended in the air like that of a dancing elephant. The human bounced up and away, and by the motions of his mouth, Wanbli assumed he was apologizing.

The diplodocus pulled off his pachyderm feet—left, then right—exposing double-pawed legs: one hand, one hoof apiece. Carefully it removed its reptile head, revealing a face of great size and sensitivity. It kicked off its diplodocus feet. Otherwise, the hoomie was not in costume.

"They should write roles for them as they are," said Audry, as she led Wanbli down a mossy slope toward the crew. "What's wrong with a hoomie as hero?"

"Too big," answered Wanbli out of recent memory. "Not average enough. What could a hoomie play but itself?"

"I didn't expect it would play romance against Alo Baker." Audry sounded slightly aggrieved. She led him not to the director, but to a round, small man who sat on the grass and weeds of the far side of the dell, telling off the man who had stumbled. Not content with denigrating his coordination, he was enlarging upon the twin themes of the man's ancestry and probable descendants. Respectfully, Audry and Wanbli waited for the speaker's attention.

"Red, this is Pylos, our AR controller and technical authority. Pylos, this is Red, just in from Neunacht. He is the one about whom we called this morning."

The little man was bald. He had wrinkles and even scars, about which nothing had been done. Wanbli seemed to make a bad taste in his mouth. "So. You've come here to tell us how we ought to do things."

Wanbli opened his eyes wide and denied he had come with any such intent. Audry Hish seconded him in her very collected manner. "I think he seriously wants to be an actor."

The old man stood up. His head reached Wanbli's Adam's apple. "An actor, boy? Here we have fall guys, bad guys, bloody fatalities flailing in burning cars and the hundred soldiers swinging swords behind the hero. No actors. What do you want with us?"

"A chance to work." Wanbli bowed very low to the technical authority, not taking his eyes from the small, withered face. Pylos struck out while Wanbli's head hung before him, but Wanbli evaded without using a block. It was all very fast.

Pylos grunted. "One of those painted warriors, I see."

"I'm a Paint," Wanbli agreed and stood again in all his glory. Pylos regarded him for three seconds.

"Makeup!" he called.

It seemed all very fortunate that the stuntman had stumbled and twisted his ankle at the very moment Wanbli walked onto the set. It was like a scene from a shimmer itself: the new fellow being given his moment in the sun and saving the situation. Only Wanbli did not exactly save the situation. He was moving with great clumsiness, or at least the technical authority thought so, for he shouted corrections without end. Wanbli was either too far stage left or right or (most likely) downstage, allowing his body to obstruct the view of either the two speaking roles or the hoomie itself. He found the glimmer of his own limbs (which had been sprayed a neutral brown-beige much lighter than his own coloring) very distracting and the blank nakedness of his chest and abdomen was a shame and an embarrassment. But though the TA shouted and cursed he did not call "cut" and so perhaps Wanbli was not doing so badly.

Occasionally the speech director, a small woman dressed in the usual Myronics green, called for monologue, in which case one of the two "speaking roles" would say something. Jaime Lepp, the lead, had a poem he liked to repeat, which concerned a stately pleasure dome. It was always the same four lines, ending with "caverns measureless to man" but it was still poetry and ancient besides. It didn't much matter what he said, as all the dialogue would be inserted at the local distributors' level, in appropriate language and idiom. Certain shimmer-buffers, however, made it a point to know what the actors were mouthing, so it was not Myronics policy to allow obscene language. This made things difficult, local standards of obscenity being so various, and certain studios had published lists of safe orations and poems for the use of the mouth-moving actor. (Very little of Mother Goose had made it onto the list.) Myronics, however, left it up to the discretion of the actors and allowed them to defend their own obscenity lawsuits as well. This was known as artistic license.

The second lead, Cauppie (single names for romantic actresses were very in-fashion these last few years), did advertisements for wine and phercolognes, with which she brought in a tidy addition to her income. Pumping products under the dialogue was not considered such high art as Coleridge, but it gave one big backing in case of a suit.

Wanbli did not have a speaking role, so it would have been bad form for him to so much as breathe through his mouth. The afternoon passed quickly, with the three cameras darting around the circle, striking sparks from their polished rails. The cameraman herself sat on a small tower outside the dell, her hands waldoed into the scale model in her lap, pressing in and drawing back as though she worked bread dough. He felt her ghostly fingers moving over him, now including his spear and now his whole body (which was hop-hop-hopping and brandishing the silly weapon; what a farce), and now pulling in so that the entire arena would be filled with the gaping, peg-toothed mouth of the diplodocus. It looked so natural to the viewer. Surely Reynaldo was wrong about 3-D work being the death of art in theater.

They canned the death of the dinosaur and then they did the scene were it was first discovered and it picks up a spear carrier and chews him into bloody pulp. Wanbli hoped he would get chosen for that scene, but it was too much to ask, his first day on the set. It was a very pretty young time traveler-cavewoman who got to be crushed, and she seemed as conscious of the importance of her position as Mr. Myronics could have wished. She was killed twice, once with clothes on and once with them coming off.

The diplodocus head was not built for crushing anything, of course. There was a metal frame inside strong enough to support an average-sized human and the hoomie had no difficulty lifting her forty kilograms. The blood sacks were actually built into the diplodocus head, so that every time the hoomie worked the monster mouth the red ran out. Very clever, thought Wanbli, but the blood also made things slippery, so that the hoomie lost his grip and let her slide out sideways. She fell five feet and landed on her tailbone, cursing explosively, but her face was blocked by the shoulder of the diplodocus, so they got a "take."

Everyone seemed exhausted after all this running around except Wanbli, who was not even winded. He was a bit depressed, however, knowing he had not pleased Pylos. He had done his best, too.

The hoomie seemed as weary as anyone, and small wonder. He lay on his belly, his four legs curled lamb-fashion under him. The long arms which extended from his front elbows were busy lighting a large cigar. His large-eyed face bore the pressure marks of the diplodocus mask as he puffed the cigar alight.

Wanbli leaned back against the hoomie's haunch, along with two or three of the other stuntmen. The smell of burning leaves reminded him of Hovart Clan sweathouse, though there they had never used tobacco. He had heard somewhere that the herb was poisonous. Maybe not to an alien.

Audry Hish was still there, looking impossibly cool and uninvolved. Perhaps watching the shooting was part of her job. Perhaps it was also her job to smile at the new recruits and ask them if they liked their first day's work. He hoped it was not just part of her job.

"Aren't you a little nervous about Estamp here?" She waved behind him, at the thirty-meter-long shape of the hoomie.

Wanbli put his hand on the warm leather leg. "This flyer? No, funny to say, I'm not. And when I first met a

Dayflower—and they're only two meters and a bit—I was panicked. I think it's just that our friend here is too big to be thought of as a danger. It would be like . . . like being afraid of a mesa, or a promontory."

Estamp's talking end had been conversing with a group consisting of Lepp, Cauppie and the speech director. He must have had magnificent hearing, because Wanbli found himself in a spreading cloud of tobacco smoke, looking up at two large eyes in a puckery face that hung above his own. "If this"—and he tapped his thigh with his chin—"is a promontory, then I supposed this end must be the headland. Eh?"

"Don't drive him away, Stampie, we just got him," said Audry. To Wanbli she added, "Hoomies have two brains, Wanbli. The one in their middles and the one they keep specially for punning."

Limping down the dell came the man whose accident had brought Wanbli unexpectedly into the action. He was livid with anger and Wanbli rose from his seat on Estamp's foothill, adopting a loose but ready stance. It was not Wanbli that was the focus of the man's rage.

"Lookit. Audry, lookit, right there. In front of everyone. I told you there would be trouble if they were allowed to burn incense before a shooting. And look what happened to me. How can you doubt now?"

Wanbli saw Audry wince and draw her composure more firmly over her. "There wasn't any incense burned, Jermonico. Not anywhere near the set. I made sure of that especially, after our talk yesterday."

"Then what do you call that?" Jermonico pointed a quivering finger at Estamp's beautifully shaped but very large lips, where the smoking tube of tobacco was almost hidden.

"I call that a cigar," said Audry resignedly. "A very stinky one. And besides, this is after the shooting, not before."

"The principle remains the same," said Jermonico. "It's a form of incense, and incense on a set means a death."

"But you're not dead," interjected Wanbli. He was very interested.

"That's because it's only a *form* of incense." Jermonico was grinding his jaws out of resentment.

" 'Sometimes a cigar is only a cigar,' " said Estamp, puffing away.

"See? He's still doing it!" The human stuntman pointed at the hoomie stuntman and hopped in rage on his single good leg.

"Well, why not, Jerry? Your ankle is already sprained. Might as well be hung for a sheep as a lamb. Want a cigar?"

Audry shot the hoomie a withering glance as two other actors joined in the conversation. One of them was the young woman who had been crushed by the diplodocus. It was she who spoke. "I hate to be an I-told-you-so, Audry darling, but if you had just let us cleanse and dedicate this set in the normal way with our smudge sticks this morning, accidents of this nature would not be so likely to happen. Not to mention what I've done to my coccyx. Unconfined energies need to be tuned."

Jermonico almost climbed up Wanbli in an effort to be seen. "You are playing with demons, Kate, and you will all wind up the worse for it. If you call spirits, don't you think they'll come?"

"Anyone for a little fire and brimstone?" Estamp blew a more-than-mortal-sized cloud of smoke that set everyone in the argument to coughing.

Wanbli whispered into Audry's ear, "Maybe I can help you find a hiding place in the forest."

It seemed impossible to Wanbli that he had ever made his living killing people on command, or at least being ready to kill people. This mockery of violence that was his new occupation put it all into an alien perspective. At the same time, his exile put his home and people into an impossible sweetness of memory.

How could he go back to that? How could he not return home, and immediately?

But of course, he *couldn't* return. He was an outlaw, a traitor, and now out of money besides.

* * *

Audry made absentminded music with her spoon against the side of her tall glass. "No, he's not like that with everyone. With most new arrivals he's more the benevolent-uncle sort. I'd have to say he doesn't like you."

Wanbli's stomach sank. He scraped his uncomfortable beaded shirt against the back of the ornate restaurant chair. "I suppose he knows I got the referral through influence."

Audry glanced up at him, cool and distant. Cool and distant, but at the same time not uncaring. "Everyone here got her job through influence. Except me, of course. No one with influence would want my job. And it wasn't anything you said—I was there. It seemed to me that Pylos just didn't like your looks, Wanbli. Perhaps it's racial antipathy."

It was a wonderful restaurant, and Wanbli had managed to snag a table in the corner where he could put himself against two walls and watch everything. This didn't give Audry such a view, but she wasn't a Paint and probably wouldn't care about the angles.

She did have a nice body, though. Best he had seen since Vynur. Since home.

"He *did* seem to know your people. What did he call you: painted warriors? Is that an organization of some kind?"

He nodded, wondering what was in that tall green glass of hers. He could smell the fruitiness of it across the table. "We're . . . uh, bodyguards. From the Wacaan clan on Neunacht. But how he should know I don't know."

"Perhaps you have a bad reputation." As she spoke, she sipped: a pretty sight. He did not know which was more inviting, the frosted green glass or the heavy, red-brown lips that puckered around it. He decided the lips had the advantage, just as Audry said, "Do you want some? I hadn't thought of suggesting it to you; it's so much a lady's drink. It's called 'spring equinox.'"

Wanbli put his mouth right over the spot her lips had made in the ice frosting of the glass. He hoped she would notice this gallantry. It was sweet, light, flowery. It almost destroyed him.

"O Protectors! And you drink this down like lemonade!"

He finished choking and handed the glass back across the table. "What is it you were asking about . . . our reputation? Do we have a bad reputation?"

Audry Hish put the drink down and looked across the table at the new stuntman—at his bright beaded shirt, his flushed cheeks, his heavy gasping and his watery eyes—and she answered, "Never mind, Red. It was a silly question."

He would certainly have invited her home, had he had a home and not merely a guest room in Reynaldo and Cyrene's house. He wished very hard that she would invite him to her house, but she did not. Perhaps she lived with her parents.

As it was, she drove him back to the door of the villa, remarking that for a penniless bodyguard and aspirant toward the Arena, he seemed to have fallen on his feet. Wanbli wished he might have found the proper smooth and witty way to explain that he had made friends with Reynaldo by beating him up, but the wit wouldn't come and the time was soon past. He was waving and she was driving off in her little green groundcar. He hadn't touched those perfect, heavy, red-brown lips once, not even with his finger.

Reynaldo wanted to hear all about it: the interviews, the first shooting, the hoomie's terrible jokes. Wanbli wanted to talk about Audry.

He asked Reynaldo, who was older and with a child besides, whether he believed in love of a man for a woman the way the shimmers had it: love that destroyed reason, that overturned dignity and swamped the vessel of the soul.

They were in Reynaldo's den, which had been walled and paved in bricks, regardless of expense. The black man laughed and curled his toes in his slippers. That was exactly the sort of love he had for his wife, he said, and in proof of it, if he didn't tell her so once a week, she would see to it that all reason in the house was destroyed, his dignity spun like a top and the vessel of his soul sunk without salvage.

Sunk without salvage: he repeated the line twice, liking it. Wanbli laughed with great appreciation and knew he had extended his welcome at the house by at least another seven days.

* * *

s dreams were very scrambled that night. Estamp, the
omie, wore Tawlin's eyes in its puckery face. Someone
e Audry (but not Audry herself) was telling Wanbli that
was arrested and being deported to Icor. He said it didn't
atter, as long as she would come along, but she would not.
e was in the ship and there was a repeated bumping. It
as a body bumping the hull. It had been released too close
d caught in an antenna. Wanbli expected it to be Digger,
cause Digger was dead, but he looked out the window
d it was the stiff form of Aymimishett, going thump-
ump against the metal scales of the ship. Aymimishett
ying, "I don't want to be an actor, or a tramp or a thief."
I don't want to be an actor.

ew Benares had two moons, just like Neunacht: ordinary,
w-density moons, one of which chased the other continu-
ly across the sky, passing it once every fifty-five of the
cal days. The moon that chased was called Dogmoon, and
was spotted. The other, white moon was called Rabbit.
abbit's orbit was eccentric.

For one entire pursuit Wanbli worked the sweatshops of
lyronics, bathed in neutral beige paint and following after
udry Hish with an eccentric dedication. Audry was al-
ays kind and usually cool, though more than once she
lowed him to kiss her heavy, berry-colored lips. (This kiss
ecame, for Wanbli, more than a salute among friends.
issing Audry was a religious observance; afterward, he
ight not remember the touch, but he would remember the
we that went along with it.) He spent hours in the commis-
ry, waiting for her to come to lunch. He walked the
outes she drove, so that he might wave ever so casually as
he passed. They had late, weary little dates after his long
ay's shooting was over, and her longer evening of schedul-
g the next day's activities. He visited her nunnish two-
oom apartment but did not so much as touch the fabric of
er exotic tropical dresses.

Wanbli was learning a great deal about the nature of ro-
nance.

Audry's title was Active-Roles Manager, which meant

she kept up the large multicolored stunt-schedule charts
making maximum use of those actors whose job was to
perform the acts other actors could not or would not do: to
run around and get hurt. In flat production a lot of tricks
could be worked—blows sent ten centimeters off target—
blows which looked deadly and merely struck air, focus on
a face while a man was supposedly being knifed in the stomach—but in AT work everything but disembowelment had
to be shot as it was to appear.

It was Audry's job to make sure that all the crew had
work (except those carrying injuries which would appear
obvious in shimmer, of course) and that one stuntperson
wasn't exposed to unusual risk: made to jump off the roof of
a building three days running, let's say. The others would
be jealous of both screen time and hazard pay. It was also
Audry's job to visit the hospital regularly.

The largest part of her work, however, was in reconciling
the beliefs of the Active-Roles crew one with another.

All athletes are superstitious. Boxers, hand-to-hand fighters, duelists and wrestlers are the worst of the lot. Those
whose fighting skills are an outgrowth of a basic religious or
philosophical stance, such as karatekas, Dominicans or
Registered Xenophobes, grow completely intransigent, and
the intransigence of an RX is not compatible with that of
the Hounds of Christ.

So: incense or no incense, bows to the east or to the west
or to the south (Audry had no one in the charts listed as
north-bowing), sets purified by sexual activity or by absti-
nence of same, on-location chow breaks or red, white, or
purely liquid food, offerings of sun vegetables or root vegetables, according to which moon was leading . . .

It would not have been so bad if each athlete had been
content to control his own consumption, emission or intro-
mission. It was instances such as Tweet Lashva's complaint
that Eliot Edwards's sexual continence was destroying the
quality of the neural field around the set: this interchange
ran half through one evening and into the night, with Eliot
countering that Tweet was a gland-drugged whore and was
only angry that he had refused her. Audry was inclined to
take Eliot's side in the matter, but it led to Tweet's with-

drawal from the project, and that was its own problem. There were not so many women who would allow to be done to them what *was* done to them by the Myronics Active-Roles Division. Small men in padded bras did not look the same falling from high places.

Audry herself was from the city of Old New Benares, where she had a retired mother and a younger sister in school, both of whom she was helping financially. Though the customs of ONB favored serial monogamy, Audry was by no means as unapproachable as Wanbli believed. It was only that the oddities of her crew had put her off involvement for a while, and then she was always tired.

Wanbli would wake up in his little dormotel cubby (not too different from what he was used to at Tawlin, but uglier), perform his now heretical ritual in dim light in the parking space that was his, though he had no vehicle to fill it, and then void against one of the ever-present tree boles. They seemed created expressly to fulfill this function. He did his own workout after breakfast, wherever he thought people might come to watch. The gravity was a bit heavy for Wanbli, the air a bit too damp. It was a place for passions as well as infections to grow. He ached plaintively for Audry's heavy lips and touched no woman at all.

Less and less did he want to be doing what he was doing on New Benares, but then no one seemed to want to be doing what they were doing. The stunts wanted to be serious actors, the actors wanted to be Bright Lights, the Lights wanted to direct, the directors wanted to produce and the producers talked about nothing except the expense of their children's genetic surgery. No one admitted to being what he seemed to be except those lucky few such as Reynaldo, who had jobs of real work. Or such as Audry, who was not as lucky but knew damn well what she was about.

But the less exciting the career became, the more comfortable it was as a job. It was such a routine, with the juice stands always on the same corner under the same green weather, and the shops for rolls and mashes for breakfast and the commissary for lunch, and on location shoots they fed him supper too.

He was good at what he did, having a gift for choreography, and when Pylos said, "One, you fire; two, you take three steps, fall on your stomach with your head facing west, roll three times and drop the gun so its shadow covered your face," that was how he did it: fire, three steps, fall west, three rolls and lose the gun. He only had to be told once.

One would think that this prompt and intelligent obedience would have won his superior's heart in time. Wanbli did think so, and so he kept trying. But Pylos, the Master Martial Artist and Technical Authority for all Myronics, did not like him. After he found Wanbli on the grass behind the commissary doing forms in the air and mugging for the crowd, he liked him even less.

Some days the Active-Roles wore pink body paint, some days biscuit brown and some days shiny blue-black. Often they were covered up completely in clothing, layer upon layer of it under the tropical sun. In the beginning Wanbli tried to keep straight the plots of the ATs which he touched with his small presence, but he gave up. There was no one around him who did know, to explain, and then there were so many jobs. In one shimmer, which the AR crew shot for almost eight working days, the baddies were all red-skinned and still Wanbli had to slather up, because they wanted *their* red, which had a tad more pink to it, and not his. Audry explained it all to him and he carried the paint pots for her and never, never complained about anything (not like those others) but he was like an old wolf in a collar; he never got used to covering his eagles.

"Red, how would you feel about going to Bakersfield?"

Audry was driving the crew bus back to Central Garage for the evening. Wanbli always had the little seat beside the driver's; it had been weeks since anyone disputed it with him. That day he had done nothing but tumble off one wall and have two collapsible bayonets thrust through his middle. Both had worked perfectly, so he was very fresh.

He didn't know if her question was business or whether she was really asking him out. Before his hopes could soar too high, he asked, "Are we shooting in Bakersfield? Where's that?"

She raised to her lips the straw of a traveler's flask bag, keeping half her attention on the road. Wanbli was slightly surprised to note that the flask was filled with the green liquid that had gagged him on their first date. The things people could get down their throats.

"Yes, we're shooting in Bakersfield, or at least six of us are. Most ARs don't like to go, though. It's a desert climate. We're shooting a remake of *Hounds of Juna.* This time with more groping and less red blood. Fashions."

At the word "desert" Wanbli glowed like a candle and when those perfect lips so coolly spoke about groping he came close to saying, "Oh, sleep with me, darling Audry: Audry of the berry-colored lips and infinite black eyes. Touch your body to mine and we will make every night and every day beautiful and worth living, though all around us are moss-headed, numb-bodied fools!"

He came close to saying it, but the same wistfulness that had sparked this poetry in him inhibited him from saying it at all. What he did say was "I'd do anything to get back to the desert, Audry. I gather you're going?"

" 'Where the sheep are, there find the shepherd.' Just six of us—and Pylos, of course. It's all hand-to-hand: fists and feet against the evil creatures of the mine owners. Warrior stuff. That's your strong point, Wanbli, isn't it?"

"It was," he said. He was staring out the window. Audry gave him a deep, round-eyed look and sucked on her straw.

It was a desert, all right, but not Wanbli's desert. The arid regions of Neunacht were native and lived in a light, almost playfully delicate balance. There were usually spots of blue and rose in the corners of one's eyes, and the sky was a good green. Bakersfield was one of the inevitable consequences of Terraforming: even such mild Terraforming as New Benares had undergone. Audry called it a "cusp" point. It had large sliding piles of sand which moved under the wind and very few plants, either native or introduced. The sky was more white than blue and the air tended to leave painful crusts in a person's nostrils. Yet it was a desert. Wanbli, aware that his color had been fading from ferrous to earthenware, stripped to his breechclout and tramped around the landing station. Anytime he left the pavement, his bare feet sank out of sight into the sand.

"You, Red, come here and help for once." Pylos had only now come down the ramp of the big airvan. His old man's eyes wrinkled painfully in the glare.

Pylos was short, partly through stooping, and a trifle thick through the middle. Wanbli was not misled by these things; most of his teachers had been old, a few of them had had bad posture and at least one had been far fatter than Pylos. All his teachers had decked young Wanbli whenever he needed to be decked, even his instructor of botany. They were terrible old people, and Pylos walked with the same rolling confidence. The rumor was that he had learned all there was to know about hand-to-hand in the NB war twenty years before and had been putting it together in new combinations since. Wanbli ran to his order.

There had been talk of introducing a giant mechanical hound into this remake, but Estamp wasn't excited about the climate of Bakersfield and it would have been very expensive to transport him. The hounds—really loader robots in fancy dress—had been shipped down the week before and were lined up at the edge of the field. The AR crew had been warned that the units' gleaming two-meter plastic jaws were extremely fragile. The name roles would be carted in on the days their desert scenes (not many) were to be shot and taken back almost immediately, so there were only a vanload of ARs, the engineer's wagon and one other ship on the field. Not Myronics'. At the sight of this strange vehicle Pylos cursed and sent Audry over to intimidate them.

Audry, instead of stripping for the heat, had changed into a long garment that hid her body completely and tended to float. One length of the gauze went over her mouth and nose, filtering the grit from the air, and the glimpse of her black doe eyes against the white (when he knew those lips were in there somewhere) brought Wanbli close to hiccups. It had been a long time.

After ten minutes she came back. "I couldn't budge

them, boss. They had indefinite clearance signed by a nephew. I did warn them about stepping out into the shooting, though. They seemed to think it amusing."

Pylos had been filling a glass at the electrolytes dispenser. Slowly he turned to her. It seemed he was amused by the intruders' amusement. "Maybe I can be less entertaining, child." He always called Audry "child." Wanbli didn't think that meant Pylos thought she was one. Just the reverse.

Audry glanced obliquely at him. "It's a Patish troop," she said.

"Patish?" he repeated. "Well, damn." Pylos went out the door, but did not proceed toward the other vessel.

Wanbli pressed past Eliot Edwards, who was reverently libating the interior of the van with electrolyte fluid, to Audry's side. The floating gauze tickled his leg. "Why is that important—Patish, I mean?"

"They're nonhuman," she replied, and brushed by him like a breeze. He was left oddly embarrassed.

"I knew that much," he called after her, but she didn't answer.

They trooped after Pylos, heavily laden, to where the scene setter had laid out the arena and piled an artificial dune to conceal the refueling station. Wanbli was uncontestedly the strongest AR, and he pulled the water wagon on its great balloon tires. As they passed in the shadow of the foreign lander, someone came out and watched.

Tall and willowy, it was dressed much like Audry against the sand, but hadn't the shoulders to be mistaken for the narrowest human female. It looked straight at Wanbli and its eyes were so very much like hers—round, black and soft-edged—that he stopped in his tracks and the wagon almost ran him over. Then the figure turned its gaze on someone else and the fur of the muzzle became apparent, richly brown and glossy as mud. A pink tongue extruded from the end of the face and wrapped three times around the muzzle before licking in. Wanbli found himself hurrying to catch up.

* * *

Pylos called them all together. They gathered in the shadow of a rock, limbs outstretched to touch as little of themselves as possible. Wanbli was drinking not electrofluid but water, slowly and constantly, from a canteen.

"Listen, you wamanas. I've got two days with you and that's all. I ought to ride you—this is an expensive blink—but I'm involved in seven different shimmers at one time. Two days for blocking out action and after that you're on your own."

Each of the ARs tried to hide his or her elation. Only Audry succeeded. Audry was different. Wanbli tried to pass along his canteen, but Eliot tasted it and refused.

"This shimmer is half fighting, half sex and half scenes of sand boats cutting a wake. Each of you four fellows has two scenes apiece, as well as the usual group flounders. You, Tersea, get to be both the women who catch the liner, as well as backing the heroine. You, Red, get to back Kyle." This was said flat-voiced, with Pylos not looking at Wanbli at all, but still it raised a murmur.

Backing Al Kyle in his remake of *Hounds of Juna* was about as high as an AR could go. Jaime Lepp, at Wanbli's right, gave him a good-natured dig in the ribs. "It's just a matter of . . . what worked out," said Pylos, flipping through his reader with his thumb. (What worked out had been determined by Kyle himself, who had taken one look at Wanbli's physique and declared dictatorially that no one but this barbarian would get any of his shirt-off scenes.)

Wanbli looked unmoved. He was unmoved, his theatrical ambitions dead, his hopes all pinned on the cool, blue-brown, heavy-lipped source of peace squatted in her white gauze one meter away from him.

He could take her away, back to the ever-spreading trees. A cabin in the wilderness. A place of hiding. A deer carried home over his shoulders. She would rush out in excitement to meet him, with a long skirt and a spatula in her hand. Perhaps it was a paintbrush and a painter's smock: he didn't yet know Audry's proclivities that well and his fantasy was adaptable.

"When's the last time you did any real fighting?" Wanbli

132

was dragged back to Pylos's dry question. His unprepared memory flashed back to Tawlin—to the attack by Heydoc and Susie. " 'Bout seven ten'ys ago," he said.

All the ARs sat very still and gazed at Wanbli. Nobody tittered. No one raised a doubt. Behind Pylos's weathered eyes something moved briefly. "In a bar?"

Wanbli didn't hear the contempt in the question, though he was usually open to nuance. Just now he was so far away, with Audry and the dead deer. "Oh. If you count that, it's a little more recently. Say six ten'ys."

Mail came, and much to Wanbli's surprise there was a gram for him. A printed letter. He giggled to think how much energy Reynaldo was putting into his friendship with a penniless alien AR. He must have worked up this printdoc the very minute Wanbli told him he was going up to Bakersfield. Probably a joke. He ripped it open without reading the return.

Clan Council
Hovart
T'chishett K1K4
Neunacht BR 2-98

Wanbli Elf Darter Son of Damasc Branch-of-Flame:
You are to remain in place until contacted by council again.
Important business.
Mychael Irradiate

Mychael was head of HCC.

What kind of message was this? Not "you are cursed," "stand accused" or even "change your shamed name," but only "wait." Wanbli, holding the single sheet of print, felt cursed, accused and shamed. If it had ordered him to kill himself, it would have been less of a shock.

Audry was at his elbow. "Bad news?" she asked. Not uncaring.

"It's . . . from home," he said. He mumbled.

"Has someone died?"

Wanbli shivered, just exactly as if someone had died. "No. It's about . . . the station. Something about the space station we're buying," he said. It was the first thing that came into his mind.

"I throw a punch, you bounce back from it. Simple law of reaction." Pylos picked up Jaime Lepp off the ground and added, "Back, remember, not straight down. We'll run this again."

Wanbli, with the other ARs, stood watching. Jaime Lepp had not been drinking enough water, was Wanbli's observation. Most people strange to the desert made that mistake. Eliot, for example, poured water over the rag on his head instead of downing it. Not so effective.

But there was more to Lepp's difficulty than that. Pylos wasn't easy to understand. In his mind, Wanbli ran the move over and over. He was the avatar of Al Kyle: M'boten, the wrecked adventurer, lover of orphaned Lizza of Juna. Jaime was an unnamed company inspector. Nasty. M'boten catches Nasty about to tie up Lizza and her little brother and throws a single punch to the jaw that sends Jaime—Nasty, that is—airborne for six feet. Wanbli imagined himself on the practice stand of Tawlin, both punching and being punched. "It doesn't feel right," he said, not loudly. He suspected the guy would go straight down.

They were doing it again. Jaime was a great faller; that was his specialty. He lost his balance like no other man in the AR crew, and could hop invisibly backward at the brush of a fist with more than a dancer's timing. As Pylos's bony hand launched toward his head he went back.

Not fast enough. Pylos moved at full speed and all heard the clack of teeth hitting teeth as Jaime went over backward. All stared at the man blinking up at the dazzling sun. His mouth moved. He seemed to be tasting blood.

"That looked better," said Pylos, breathing hard. He smiled slowly at Lepp. "Amazing what being really hit does for verisimilitude."

Jaime got up, looking away. He was obviously angry, but his eyes were wide and set. Wanbli knew him to be a gymnast: no fighter at all. Not used to being hit. He put his finger to his mouth and it came away pink.

Pylos watched this with an expression on his face which was half worried and half pleased about something. "All right. It's a little scene, children. A tiny scene. Let's do it and get it spooled before . . . before the bruise comes up."

Wanbli winced but stepped into the circle. The cameras lengthened their noses, focusing close to the spot of loose sand where Jaime waited, brushing sand off the silver glitter of his Juna Corporation kilt and greaves.

M'boten was wearing a torn shirt and tartan trousers (a real man's clothes). His hair fell in his face and so did some very convincing shadows, so that no one could tell that this was not the aging, blue-eyed Al Kyle. He allowed the three camera people and two set directors to place him properly.

"Let's take it in one, Red," called Pylos. "Do what I did."

Wanbli turned his face, which leaped free of the shadows, looking harsh. His eyes glinted garnet, looking very odd against the pale dye of his face. "Hit him, you mean?"

"That's the only way we're going to get it out of him, don't you think? Or does the thought of hitting somebody give you problems, Paint?"

Being hit wasn't much of a much to Wanbli, as long as it didn't alter his face or send him to the dentist. He glanced back at Jaime to find that one didn't agree. The man had an expressive monkey face, better suited for a character actor than an AR, really, and it showed fear bordering on dread. Fear of Wanbli.

Not since childhood had Wanbli had to strike at anyone who was afraid of him. He was unprepared. He tried to whisper something reassuring to Lepp: to tell him that it wouldn't be that bad, that if he moved smartly he wouldn't catch it at all. Then the little "beep" sounded and he had to move.

It was a big, blustering, syrup-slow punch with nothing behind it, but so spooked was the AR that he ducked down and sideways, terribly inefficiently. He caught the edge of Wanbli's hand on his cheekbones and fell sitting on the sand.

He cursed in Polish.

Pylos cursed in good Hindi and waltzed in as the cameras snapped off together. He kicked Lepp out of the way.

"I told you to hit him, to knock him back. Now we've got to do it all over again. Is this kindness? To him, to me? To us all?

"Or can you throw a controlled punch at all? I want to see a real punch out of you, not this nonsense."

Wanbli saw Jaime edging out of the circle. He wanted to tell the man to go drink something. There was Audry, hiding in the shade of a camera. Always hiding. No expression in her black-brown eyes, on her berry-brown lips.

"Do you hear me!" The bellow brought Wanbli back. Pylos was slightly berrylike in color himself. The top of his head came up to Wanbli's nose. "Yes," said Wanbli. "You want it again."

"I want to see you throw one. If you can." Pylos pointed at his own face and took one step backward, supremely confident, almost sneering.

Wanbli knew his last punch had been laughable. He wasn't proud of it. He felt much better about punching at the technical authority, who was an old teacher and could deck him: no offense in the world involved. He threw at Pylos's jaw a back-knuckle strike, fast and loose as a rubber band: just a warm-up.

He stared down at the TA, who had gone six feet airborne and landed flat on his back in the sand, just outside the focal circle of the arena. "That's the move, all right," admitted Wanbli. "But I really don't think it would work that way. I think the flyer would just go down."

Pylos didn't answer or open his eyes.

Wanbli felt the sting on his knuckles where they had made solid contact with the flat of Pylos's jaw. He took two steps forward. What was the old teacher—the old TA—the old viper—trying to prove this way? Was he waiting for Wanbli to kneel beside him, so he could lash out and destroy his diaphragm, or his throat or his genitals? Very nervously, Wanbli bent knees beside Pylos and put his hand to the old man's neck.

"I . . . don't feel a pulse," he said. "What kind of hospitals do they . . ."

Audry was beside him, still swathed in white. She opened Pylos's eyes and looked at the pupils. She reached into his mouth and pulled at the tongue. She looked up.

"Go away, Red," she said very softly. "Go someplace else very quickly."

He stood on the landing strip among scurrying engineers and drivers who did not know yet. The sun was white and deadly—not his sun at all. Around him rose the humpty shape of the vans and the freighters of Myronics. Beyond that, only the artificial desert.

Go someplace else. Hah.

How did it happen? A back-knuckle. A stinger. Not the blow to knock a man out. Not a blow to kill. Protectors, had he killed his first man out there, and by accident? Sweat rolled down Wanbli's shoulder blades and he was very cold. Calling the discipline of his Third Eagle training, he stopped pacing. Slowed his breathing. Closed his eyes. Turning his soaring fears into a giant darter and beat that to the ground.

He rehearsed what he would tell them when they asked for an explanation for the defunct TA. "I hit him on the jaw: a light stinger. It shouldn't have done any harm. He must have had a weakness in his neck. Besides, he asked for it."

No, no, you never, ever said, "He asked for it." That was not Third Eagle, but First Eagle stuff. It turned the whole world against you. It led to forced personality restructuring.

But he had. He had said . . . what? Wanbli screwed up his sweaty face with concentration. To the best of his recall, Pylos had said, "I want to see you throw one. If you can." And then he pointed at himself.

It had been at himself, hadn't it? Wanbli squeezed his head between his hands. He sat down on a metal drum, which made him stand up again, fast. Everyone would admit Pylos had wanted Wanbli to strike at him. Please, everyone, admit that. Jaime would stand behind him, certainly. Even though he'd hit him. And Audry, of course.

Go somewhere else. He wished he could. Wanbli had lost every trace of interest in the art of acting.

The air conditioning of the crew van gave Wanbli a fit of shivers. It was empty of people. There was his pack, with his few possessions in it. He would squat here until they came for him. At least he would show dignity.

He leaned back against the fabric of the pack and it crackled. He glanced in to see the white glimmer of the letter he had received that morning from Hovart Clan Council, and which the recent extremities had driven from his mind.

He thought: they are not going to restructure me. They are going to kill me. Some quiet emissary will arrive from Hovart or more likely South Bay itself, find me on trial for murder and very neatly dust me to save clan honor.

As had been done to the maniac who broke Tag. Not a Wacaan anymore. Wanbli himself had said that to Tawlin. Glibly.

But then he never had been a Wacaan, according to Tawlin. Well, now he was willing to believe that. Wanbli sat still and hoped they would come for him soon.

The footsteps were very light and rapid. The shadow in the van's doorway was small. The person who stood before Wanbli was a young boy in shorts with fat, dimpled knees.

"They've got him on a stretcher," he said. "Silver sheet over him." The boy had fog-gray eyes and a lisp.

"He's dead?" Wanbli was surprised how collected he sounded.

"Looks that way." The boy, like a cricket, rubbed one leg against the other. He wasn't sweating much. Time passed.

"You going to sit there?"

Wanbli glanced up into a pink, chubby face. "What should I do, flyer?"

Very airily the boy said, "Oh, I think I'd go away if I was you."

"Did Audry send you?"

This question received only a giggle.

"Go where? There is nothing around here but sand. It's not even a desert, just . . . sand."

The boy hopped in place, as little boys do. "There's another ship, you know. Not *their* ship. *Our* ship."

Wanbli, remembering, opened his mouth but said nothing.

"We," announced the little boy, "are the carriers of culture. The fulfillers of dreams. We are free people."

Wanbli stared straight across at the boy's face. "What has all that to do with me?"

He must have been older than he looked, this little fat-faced boy. He said, "Come across and be one of us. It is"— his fog-colored eyes shifted up and down—"your destiny."

SIX

IT WAS AS THOUGH he were on the liner again, back in the days when he carried a heavy changer and was on his way. Wanbli sat in the lounge where the boy had left him, amid the daises, padded platforms and piled cushions: common-denominator furniture, suitable for any traveling race, except the hoomie. Wanbli shivered, for it was chilly in here after the desert. Except the hoomie.

From his pack he took the wonderful fur jacket, which had not seen use since the planet of its purchase. It smelled musty already. He put it over his shoulders.

His blunderbuzz fell out at his feet. Indecisively he regarded it, touched it, took it out of its holster.

It was disturbing how much he wanted to put it on. He asked himself if he thought he could buzz his way out of his problems. (It was a rhetorical question.) Going from little error to big error, from honest mistake to murder. Ending up in a bloodbath—no doubt suicide. He'd seen enough shimmers to know how it went.

140

Just a few minutes ago he'd been resigned. Not happy, but resigned. Now, because some hatchling had an idea, he was cowering under the aegis of perfect strangers. He remembered the Patish, and its tongue. Perfectly strange. Why would the creatures feel bound to protect him? How could they, against Myronics Security, which was a good-sized army, or even against the less imposing civil authorities of New Benares? It didn't make sense for strangers to try.

Running away was not the act of an innocent man. He had convicted himself before all eyes. Perhaps even Audry's.

But she had said, "Go away. Go somewhere else . . ."

There was someone in the doorway. Wanbli had heard nothing, but there was someone in the doorway. He gave a spring sideways and came rolling down a set of padded stairs which existed to serve the seating requirements of six different races. This it did moderately well. Rolling down would not have suited any of them, but Wanbli did not lose his blunderbuzz. He came to rest with the rise of the two bottom steps in between himself and the open doorway.

It was empty again.

A voice spoke around the corner. It was thin and lisping, as the boy had lisped, but Wanbli recognized it as Doych, a language of which he only knew a hundred words. He shouted back that information.

"I am telling you that you do not need that gun. I am the owner of the ship and it was I who sent Pascal to invite you here."

Wanbli stood up. He was not full of trust, but that hardly mattered. He could not hold off all comers indefinitely, from behind a universal chair. He was not a frightened beast. He put the blunderbuzz down on the second stair.

The Patish came out. If it was the same creature he had seen that morning, it had taken off its robe, wimple and drapeau. It was a four-limbed biped, but a greater proportion of its length was body than would be normal in a human being. It had fur which grew in multiple rosettes or cowlicks around its body. Its sex was not obvious. It was less than five feet tall.

"I'm sorry," said Wanbli. "You moved very quietly. I was startled."

It approached within three meters and stopped there. "I understand better than you might think, sir. With your reflexes, you might almost be Patish. Humans usually move like the slow-turning seasons."

Wanbli had to smile.

"You might wonder why you have been invited here, at such an odd and unusual moment in your life. Or perhaps I assume too much, and it is no strange thing for you to break a man's neck."

The smile went out, but slowly. "Is he dead, then?"

The Patish's tongue extruded. He used it to scratch between his hairless fingers. He sighed, very humanlike. "I see no reason to doubt it. They have removed his form from the arena and there is a great deal of expostulating going on. The woman in the *bawghaa* sits still and strokes her face with her hand repeatedly. The other athletes shake their heads. The man with the pale hair raises his arms and slaps his sides; he is depressed. So is she."

Wanbli digested all this. He could see Audry behind his closed eyes. He leaned against the universal chair. "You watch very closely. Not to be ungrateful, owner, but what is it all to you?"

Now the Patish approached closer. It sat itself on the lowest step and gazed up at Wanbli, looking like all beasts and not a beast at all. "People of all races interest me. People in crises interest me profoundly," it said.

"And I interest you?"

The head leaned closer. Wanbli hoped the tongue would not come out. "Yes. You do. Don't I interest you?"

Wanbli felt his blood speed with embarrassment. He put a lock on his expression. Neutrally he replied, "Of course. I wonder why you would hide me."

The impossible, embarrassing face withdrew. "I think there's more to it than that," it whispered, its muzzle turned toward Wanbli's scattered pack. "But the answer to that is simple. We of the High Culture are always recruiting." It forestalled Wanbli's question by adding, ". . . recruiting artists."

Wanbli sat down where he was, on the carpet. "I'm what's called a Martial Artist. Is that part of your High Culture?"

The Patish had double-cusped, pointed teeth, which it now displayed. Wanbli suspected he was seeing what was supposed to be a human translation of Patish emotion.

"The High Culture is expressed in the relationship of one being with another, with as little material artifact intervening as is possible. Not to denigrate crafts such as painting and sculpture, which have meant so much to your species, but the material element becomes a great crutch. With the arts of individual combat, there is nothing but the delicious interplay between individual and individual.

"So yes, my friend, an artist of battle is a high artist." Then the creature barked, just like a dog, and it said, "It may not be commercial, but it is certainly art!"

It seemed to sober suddenly, and its tongue wound left and then right. "One hopes to achieve both . . ."

A delicate chime interrupted. The Patish lifted its head to listen. Something that was not human spoke a message, in a language of whines and rumbles.

It showed its double teeth again. "Two small ships are approaching in formation. What might that mean, my dear sir?"

Wanbli did not move. "You know as well as I that Myronics Security travels in pairs."

"But, sir, I do not know that. We are not natives of this very hot and vulgar planet. We have nothing to do with the sort of cheap showmanship of the shimmers. This is a deep-space vessel and we light but for a moment 'like snow upon the desert's dusty face' and we have no intention of remaining long enough to melt.

"The question is, shall we leave you to the tedious business of explaining to these parochials how the practice of your art happened to be fatal to that nip-farthing old man . . ."

"That what kind of old man?"

The Patish groomed a rosette under his chin. "He was cheap. A skinflint, grasping . . . The idioms are endless." As Wanbli continued to stare, it added, "He visited us yesterday evening, sir. Professional capacity. It is not that we landed in this howling wilderness with any thought of finding an audience, but yet it is not in the real artist to refuse."

Enlightenment grew behind Wanbli's impassive countenance. "You flyers are . . . prostitutes."

The tail of the Patish swelled visibly. It was not just the pelt, but the tail itself thickening like a sausage. "Sir, if you ever use that word again you will go out the door. Even if we are in space."

Wanbli did not reply to that. "Who else was here last night?"

"Do you go or stay?"

He felt completely unable to decide. It was a frightening feeling. To run out on Audry was not the act of a brave man. To remain at the landing with her as witness to his arrest and prosecution, though . . . That would be no gift to her.

Likely the studios had heard from Hovart Clan Council already. Even if this thing with Pylos had never happened.

He was going down in flames. It was all over with him. These people were whores. Once he had entertained the idea of being a sex toy as preferable to a Paint's way of life. That was when he was also hot to act in the shimmers. That was someone else.

He opened his mouth and answered the Patish, but afterward he had no idea of what he had said. He sat with his head on his knees beside the universal chair in the empty lounge and after a dec or so he felt the shudder of engines around him.

My dear Miss Hish, he began, and then sat back to stare at the blank screen. Wanbli knew how to compose a polite print document, but he didn't find it easy. The blank screen had a tendency to glare at him.

How long the time has been since I have seen you. Twenty days, really.

I eagerly inquire of your health and that of your aged relative.

That was the important part, all right, but it didn't look right to have nothing else down there. Looked more like he was expecting to inherit money or something. Perhaps it was only necessary to pad. After the first, undeniably true sentence, he added: *Life is not the same here without you.* No, both sentences ought not to end in "you." It was like beginning all one's lines with "I." *Life is not the same.*

Indeed it was not. Wanbli, gazing unfocused above the faxereader, could hear Covazh, Nem Patish's scion, down the hall serving a customer. Covazh was young and athletic and had a trick of hissing once it'd got going. Perhaps it was only the air in its lungs; the client was human and Patish did not do well in human standard temperature and humidity.

His fingers hovered over the key wheel but did not spin out *Oh, Audry, all the time I was with you I guarded my chastity.* That was not one of the few sentiments he had been taught would fit into a polite print document, though it was true, and he would have liked to use it, having just learned the word "chastity."

Come to think of it, he was guarding his chastity still, if he remembered the definition correctly. No one came to a Patish establishment for any act as ordinary as copulation. It was all "pheromonal catharses" and "ephemeral opuses" and the occasional individual who wanted someone to tickle him or to tickle.

I am doing very well, he wrote. *I am appalled by everything around me,* he wrote and then blinked both lines out.

Humans who wanted to be tickled to orgasm requested a Patish; that was one of their specialties. Those who wanted the dominant role (and there were a few, especially in this city of Poos, where the flagship facility of Nem Patish was located) always wanted to tickle another human. Wanbli was the perfect whore for the business, because he was not at all ticklish and yet he could act. How odd, after New Benares and Pylos and all, to find he had been right; he could act.

Nem wanted him to have surgical implants, to make his performance less dependent upon mood. Bracing and plumbing, the operation was popularly called. Little Pascal had had the implants at the age of six and now entertained himself by shooting his penis out to strike marbles on his bed, like a biological billiard game. But Pascal had not yet reached puberty; it was all the same to him. Wanbli had so far avoided the issue by claiming he didn't want to be off work that long. Truth was, he'd kill the Patish first.

The only operation he wanted was one which was forbidden to the men of his people. But the Patish did not at all understand his desire to have his valves opened, or at least put under his control. They refused to tinker with a working sterility device.

The print document letter, in final form, read:

Dear Miss Hish,
How long it has been since I had the pleasure of seeing you. I have taken your advice and sought my position in life elsewhere, but I am not yet convinced that it has been the right decision. I do miss you a great deal, and hope you can find the time to renew our sundered correspondence.

You must write and tell me how things are with Mummy and your little sister. Have I missed any interesting messages?

And do you still work for that funny little old man?
Your workaday friend,

Wanbli considered the signature for a long time and finally put down *Feathers.*

There were no feathers to be seen, really. During the flight from New Benares to Poos City, Wanbli had had them painted over with an enduring red body stain. The gold had been hard to obscure.

Poos City, on Morion, was the first important place Wanbli had visited. (New Benares, for all its superficial glamour, was basically parochial.) On Poos, Wanbli learned the truth of Ake Tawlin's repeated assertion that he was poor. All of Neunacht was dirt poor compared with Poos. Wu and Fabricant gave the city twenty-five lines and recommended most prominently the Hall of the Seven Sentients.

This had been the Hall of the Six Sentients until the

hoomies had sued to have both of their brains recognized as one. A mistake, some thought. People will always judge others by their own standards.

Wanbli visited the Hall and spent hours in contemplation of the Dayflower display, emerging sadder than when he had gone in. He did not enter the Patish rooms at all. He also became acquainted with the extensive public gardens of Poos, where under the green canopy the Neo-Mithraists kept their intoxicating beds of violets and the little carnivorous native clowr made tall topiary columns: mauve over Lincoln green. He was fascinated not with the plants but with the heavy, black garden soil, so different from the porous gold of Tawlin. He suspected the humus carried disease, but then his mind was on disease; either the body dyes or the numberless inoculations necessary to his new occupation had given him a rash and a permanent sniffle.

The slums of Poos were more famous than its gardens, though not recommended in W&F. The prosperity of Poos was reflected even in these crowded streets, as the original housefronts had been extended out the front and back in cheap foam in a myriad of styles. It seemed that only the ferocity of the drivers, both surface and pneumo, kept the streets from being built over entirely.

One day, under both sun and streetlighting, Wanbli was attacked by a young woman with a stiletto. Not expecting trouble (for in general no one messed with a man who looked and walked like him), he might have been injured, had she not begun the attack with a highly sexual embrace.

Wanbli was tired of being clutched by strangers and so he spun her off with a simple wristlock and the knife clattered to the paving stones. So had the woman, twitching and muttering.

Wanbli had hauled her to the nearest clinic: the one with a fountain and the nonrepresentational portrait of Galen on the façade, only to be told that it was only withdrawal from addictive substances. Such withdrawal, complete with shudders and bowel incontinence, was the woman's inalienable right and if Wanbli didn't want to be in violation of Poos's law, he would put her back where he had found her.

He sat her on the steps of the clinic instead, and then,

without expression, he tugged his crotch band aside and peed into the fountain. His inalienable right.

Wanbli was becoming morose.

The answer to his letter came as promptly as could reasonably be expected:

Dear Feathers,
    Things are much the same here—you'd be as bored as ever. My funny old boss is spitting acid. He claims he was assaulted by an unscrupulous rookie AR millions in shooting delays. So humorous.

                                            Audry

There it was. Wanbli was ten seconds overjoyed that Pylos was alive. He was ten minutes furious that the old man would blame him. For the next dec and indeed the whole day he was slightly sad that Audry hadn't written more. But deep-space grams were terribly expensive and he doubted she made that much. He had no time to dwell on the matter then, because he was busy with an anniversary party.

Every year, on the Morion autumnal equinox, Gerald Deec and his wife, Mamba, came to Nem's Arrangeurs to celebrate their anniversary in a re-creation of their wedding night: he relived it as exactly as memory could recall with a female arrangeur who resembled his wife at thirty years as exactly as Nem's could manage. She did the same, with the aid of a human man who looked as she would have preferred her bridegroom to look. Wanbli, cast in the role of Deec, Esq., wondered why they bothered with an exact replay. Surely in the subsequent twenty years they had both honed their marital skills. But it was not an onerous way to pass a day and there was no tickling involved at all. Madame Mamba tipped generously.

When next he was free, Wanbli sent his second doc.

Dear Audry,
   You were there and so was Jaime and three others.
Tell them he lies.

Time passed and time passed and time passed. There was no reply.

"So you're all subtracters?" asked Pascal, with what might have been a sly grin on an older face. Wanbli glanced down at the boy distrustfully.

"Subtracters. You know. Strike men. Professional eliminators." Pascal played with the single earring in his right ear, spinning the spiky wheel of it.

"No." This small misunderstanding was somehow bothersome. Maybe it was the headache he always seemed to have these days. "We are bodyguards. Our job is to keep the employer alive, not . . ."

"But those other two. You just finished saying that they took a job on *your* boss."

Wanbli took a delaying breath. "When the employer requests, and when a Paint is convinced that another T'chishetti is a positive danger to the estate, then the Wacaan can move. Under no other circumstances."

"Yeah, yeah, yeah," said the boy, being obnoxious as only an eight-year-old can be. He had been so all morning. "Call it what you want."

Pascal was chewing bubble, with just a taste of Pov in it. He was on a roll.

"Thank you. I will," answered Wanbli dryly.

The boy snickered and bounced roughly off an old woman in a turban. Wanbli, following, apologized to her.

"I can tell you're behind me," Pascal called, crossing the street against the signal. "You still stink from yesterday."

Yesterday had been fully booked by foreigners, with pheromonal accompaniment. Wanbli had scrubbed for twenty minutes afterward. He had even used vinegar. He wasn't ready to hear this out of the eight-year-old.

His feet stopped. He let the boy forge ahead in the crowd. Without Wanbli's red-eyed two meters of height warning the Seechuk Straightaway pedestrians to give way, it became more and more difficult for Pascal to make progress. At last he turned and noticed that Wanbli had deserted him. He came back, breasting the traffic flow.

"You were told to stick by me!"

Wanbli grinned. "Were you told to be a little turd?"

The boy blinked. He rubbed the back of his pudgy little hand over his rosebud mouth. His little tongue made a tube and he whistled through it. Like a Patish.

"Who do you think old Nemmish will believe when I tell it you walked out on a pickup?"

A pneumo shot by, popping ears all around it, followed by a police automatic remora. Wanbli swallowed and pulled on one ear before answering. "I don't know, but I'm willing to find out, flyer." Then his eyes squeezed at the corners as he asked, "What are we picking up for him anyway that he needs two of us?"

Pascal sighed. "Not him: it. Patish don't like to be called him. Or her. And it's just a package. Nothing special." He trotted on again.

Wanbli knew very well that the Patish had a separate pronoun which meant "individual whose gender is none of the public's business," but they reserved that for their own languages, which they did not teach to foreigners.

They gave nothing away.

In later years his memories of Poos City would reduce themselves to two: disillusionment and the pinky-peach glare of the light strips.

The lights of Poos ran along the first-story cornices of all buildings. They were mostly filter-banded mercury vapor strips engineered to give as useful and pleasant an illumination to the various sentient races moving through the commercial capital as was possible. They had been pressed into a series of spirals, in an artistic style now a generation out of date.

What was designed for all races was generally accepted as good for none—the lights made Wanbli squint worse than the setting sun of T'chishett—but they were a trademark of Poos City and they were left shining night and day, from

broad Seechuk to the ticky-tacky alleys of the Wallow up-
town, driving the shadows of seven races away.

Pascal ducked into the recessed doorway of a small building with a double storefront. The right side had had its
windows etched with Gothic arches containing an arrangement of spiral galaxies around a rather blotchily done blue-
and-white planet. In the center arch was a full-body picture
of a human male, looking very dashing and exotic in ancient jodhpur trousers and a shirt with buttons. Above the
window the sign read MAN THE EXPLORER and in smaller
letters FATHER TO CIVILIZATION.

There had been attempts to break the window. Paint had
been splashed. Across the figure's genital region had been
scratched the words: "One more nutty religion for old Poos
City."

Wanbli put his eye to the polymer, but it was filthy and
the place behind seemed an empty room.

Meanwhile Pascal had opened the door to the other shop,
a travel agency, where the display in the window was of a
lake with a large white bird sitting on it, and an equally
white Palladian revival palace in the background. "See
Nashua itself through out convenient Securi-Tour System:
The Heart of Empire."

Nashua called itself an empire, but Wanbli had never seen
any evidence of that. But then he *was* provincial. Now he
curled his lip at the Imperial Palace but the bird puzzled
him. It was big and bulky and didn't look at all like the sort
of thing that could balance itself atop the surface tension
like a dipper bug. It looked like it should sink.

It was a swan, that's what it was. He remembered the
name as the door shut behind him.

One entire wall was a destination board: a holo of twi-
light over Poos City, with the orangy sun of Morion setting
behind the Civic Center, the seven (six original plus one)
identical spires of the Hall painting black vertical lines to
the left of it. A woman in a traditional Poos peach suit
stood in front of it, with a pointer.

"Gideon," said her customer, an older man with a
scrubbed face. "Gideon," repeated the agent, and she
touched the pointer to one star in the picture's sky. "Let's

go to Gideon, then." The starry blackness became shot through with the lightning network of the minor strings which stitched together this portion of the galaxy. There were many of them, and from the angle of the holo (the angle of Poos) they looked reminiscent of a certain doily of mathematics, seen on a faxereader screen many days ago. Fractals, Digger had said. Behind all—behind even the mass of the galaxy that dusted the holo's background—were the glimmers of other star nests, cut through by the blazing line of the major string which had formed the birth of minor strings and galaxies alike.

Wanbli didn't know what connection fractals had with the minor strings (the strings of travel). He wondered if Digger had understood it all. To learn that would be a sort of gift to the dead Dayflower. The sort of gift a mathematician would appreciate.

One of the strings, touched by the travel agent's magic wand, developed an embolism which sped brightly along it, connecting and passing itself, bing, bang, pop, to other systems. Wanbli looked away to keep his balance.

Pascal was leading him down the central aisle, ignoring the woman, the holo, the picture displays and the artifacts of several cultures and races which lined the three inoperative walls. There was another door behind this front room. The boy palmed it open.

Behind him Wanbli heard the voice of the woman. "Here you are. Gideon Metropolitan. That was a departure on the seventeenth, wasn't it?"

As Wanbli followed Pascal, he heard the man reply, "I don't think that's Gideon, ma'am. Looks like Gibbonsville to me."

This room was empty but for two files, a desk and numerous spool racks. In the right wall was set a door without plaque or knob. Pascal beat on it with his open hand and after a millidec it slid open.

The light was gray through the filthy window but within it was quite comfortable. Wanbli glanced past the two men at the table to the figure in jodhpur trousers etched black into the window.

"Well, if it isn't the oldest little boy on Morion. How's your whizzin, sprout?" It was a third man who spoke: he who had opened the door. He was dark and thin. He wore a large pink pearl in his lapel.

"I keep it clean," answered Pascal composedly. "And this is Red. He's new with us."

The two at the table had cards in their hands. Two other hands lay fan-folded, face down. Wanbli looked casually around the room, but no fourth party was visible.

Pascal stalked to the table and leaned against it. His attitude was pure swagger. He tabbed open his jacket, which was blue, puffy and decorated with racing cars. From an inside pocket he took a box and he emptied it onto the table. Ampoules of glass gleamed yellow in the poor light. "Straight from Shimmertown: uncut."

Across from him sat a large pale man with very short hair. He gazed from his cards to the ampoules and back again. His fellow, also large, was fashionably hairless. He leaned back in his chair and swiveled slowly out from the table, his eyes lowered.

"Aces and kings," said the large pale man. "All the rest are mine." He seemed to be talking to the table, but as he swept in the cards, the ampoules went with them.

Pascal glared at the tabletop, which was almost at eye level for him. "Not yours until you pay for it."

Bristlehead started to stand. His opposite number was up already. "The baby whore has delusions of some kind. Tell him what he can do with them, Walter. I'll take care of muscles."

Wanbli woke himself from his puzzlement and took a step forward. All the men were out of their chairs now. The one with the pearl stood only arm's distance from Pascal. He smiled, half apologetically. "Nem owes us, cub. This one's on him."

Bristlehead had his hand in his pocket. The three men almost hid little Pascal from view.

This was a bad setup; Wanbli would never have let it evolve to this had he known. Why hadn't the boy told him this could be a fighting matter and what in torment was being played here?

Wanbli decided to focus first on the man with his hand in his pocket. If Pascal could only survive for two seconds on his own . . .

"On us, is it? Wait till you see what's on you." The boy's hand flashed to his ear.

Thin-dark hopped back as the boy slashed. The man's hands had gone to protect his crotch, but the boy's target was just to the side of that. There was a shriek as white slacks went red with arterial blood.

Wanbli had no time to look. His man had a gun—worse, a slicer. He grabbed Bristles' wrist, pointing down with all his strength, and as the flyer pulled back Wanbli used his left arm to break the elbow. He let his hand continue the arc of that movement until it ended against the large, thick neck.

Fashionably Hairless had knocked Pascal forward and was kicking him. The boy grabbed at the leg. Wanbli leaped over the body of the bleeding man with a thrust kick aimed at Hairless's head, but already the man had fallen backward, hamstrung by the golden razor earring.

Pascal was cursing. He had blood spattered over his face: not his. He went to the big man Wanbli had brought down, stepping on and over his enemies as uncaring as a cat. He took the ampoules out of the man's pocket and put them back in his own.

The man with the severed artery was howling and pressing against himself. The other was clawing at the table.

"Pascal. What about number four?" The boy squatted above Bristles, razor in hand, indecisive. Wanbli grabbed him, one hand on the back of the collar, the other on the hand that held the weapon. "What about the other flyer?"

At last he got Pascal's attention. "There are four hands of cards. Where's the fourth player?"

Pascal peered vaguely at the table, at the blood on the floor, at Wanbli. At last he said, "Bridge. Dummy."

Wanbli almost hit him. The boy wriggled out of his grasp. "No, I'm not insulting you. That's a dummy hand. They're playing bridge with a dummy. Don't you know anything?"

Wanbli still paced the room, looking for hidden opponents. "Bridge? Never heard of it."

The boy called Wanbli a terrible name as he slapped open the side door. Wanbli caught him in the storeroom, but he resisted all temptation and only wiped Pascal's face with a sheet of spool cleaner. No sound came through the sliding door at all.

As they hurried through the front office the travel agent was saying, "It's a good thing you caught that for me, Mr. Arbiezen. We didn't want to go to Gibbonsville at all, did we?"

"I really wish you were easier to hide!" Pascal's small being was wholly scornful, looking up at Wanbli. They had come fast and far, with the boy half carried, and were now strolling through a very nice residential neighborhood of Poos City, not far from Nem's.

"Me? You little fart. I have never had any reason to hide, before this deal." Wanbli wasted very little energy in outrage. He pushed Pascal on ahead. "What was it anyway? The drug, I mean."

"What's it to you?"

Wanbli pushed much harder.

"All right, all right. It's multendorf. Multendorf HS, to be exact."

Wanbli hadn't expected to hear that. He had expected it was simply smuggled Povlen, or some opiate. "Multendorf homo sap.? Protectors, Pascal. That's suicide. That's hell."

Pascal snorted and shrugged in his puffy jacket. "I didn't exactly offer you any." He brushed ineffectually at an ocher stain and walked on.

Wanbli followed, trying to think. "Wait, Pascal. Before we get back I've got to know. Are you doing this on your own, or is this part of Nem's thing too?"

Pascal stopped very suddenly. "How would an eight-year-old child be doing drug running on his own? I'm Nem's man."

Wanbli went on ahead. "You're Nem's idiot is what you are."

"Why?" The boy had to run to catch up. "It trusts me. I'm in a position . . . a position of responsibility."

Now it was Wanbli's turn to express scorn. "And do you

think you'll get something out of it? You don't see him using his own cub for nasty jobs like this, do you?"

"Not him, it," the boy answered weakly. "And . . . and that's because Covazh is too young. Too dependent. I'm better at dealing." His breathing was ragged, for Wanbli was setting a very fast pace.

"Hey, Red, Red. Don't cut up with me, huh? Hey. I don't feel so good."

Wanbli glanced down again at the boy, the bloodstain, the stem of the broken earring hanging from his ear. "I don't wonder at that," he said, and tweaked the boy's ear. He was considering what an eight-year-old Wacaan would have made of such a situation. They weren't expected to handle life and death at the age of eight.

But now Pascal was grinning. It was white, and tight, but it was a grin. "You know we really did them, didn't we? We did them all, the cheaters."

"You mean you did," Wanbli corrected him, and he watched the boy's tongue, curled at the corners, sneak in and out through his lips. "You're still not going to be a Patish, flyer. No matter what you do for them. For it." He ruffled the silky hair. "You could be something better."

"Oh, turn it down," said Pascal, with a taste of his usual scorn. He showed Wanbli a way through the yards and gardens to their own back door.

Wanbli heard him running ahead down the hall, his small feet pattering as he shouted, "Rachel, Kouamie—wait till you hear! I need a new earring, Rachel." An eight-year-old boy.

"You got a letter, Red," said Nem. He extended the sealed foil envelope across his desk. Wanbli took it and stuffed it into his purse. "Why didn't you tell me you were dealing drugs, Nem?"

The Patish folded his hands upon the polished wood desktop and blinked his soft eyes at the human a meter and a half away. The desk was of a kidney shape, and unconventionally he had placed it with the hollow side toward visitors. Though its top was always polished and empty, Nem made great use of that desk. "Why is it your business what I do?" it asked blandly, adding, "Please, Red. Sit down. I hate to be hovered over."

Wanbli did not sit. "It is my business because it put me into a very bad situation right now. The boy was almost killed."

Nem showed his double-teeth pleasantly. "I gather the boy did very well. Didn't he take out two of three attackers?"

"Yes. Leaving the one with the slicer. But beside that danger, trading in multendorf is a maximum-penalty crime almost everywhere. By Mo, I'm guilty and I don't even know what the maximum penalty is here in Poos."

"That's simply said. It's death," said Nem, working his tongue. "But you notice you have not been caught, Red. No one in my employ has ever had trouble with the police. Or is likely to." The Patish hissed and slapped the table. "Would you *please* sit down; you are too damn tall to hang over me like that!"

Wanbli glanced at the heavy black chair placed in the hollow of the desk and stepped backward. "I'll slouch."

Nem let his sleek head hang forward. Absentmindedly he stroked the rosettes against the direction of the hair. "Oh, suit yourself, human."

"But as for the trading, I can only ask you if you have ever known an artist who did not have to do something else occasionally to support its art?"

Wanbli laughed with real appreciation. He leaned against the wall. "I might think you really believed in that if I hadn't been working here five ten'ys already. Pascal *does* believe it. You've sold the boy inside and out. Probably because he's too young to really know what sex is."

"And what is it, Red?" The Patish drummed its nails on the desk. "What is sex really, if not a high art?"

Wanbli smirked his superior smirk for just a moment, and then it faded. "What we do has an old established name."

It occurred to him suddenly that all this furor was for nothing, for he could walk out of Nem's Arrangeurs at any moment. He could go anywhere. He could go home, for instance.

It was an astonishing idea: to go home to Hovart, where the sun rose green and set pink and they knew what good zoning was. To go home and be—he thought hard—not a Paint anymore, but something else. Wanbli laughed out loud. The little furry alien with the spit curls seemed suddenly irrelevant, harmless, like a stuffed toy.

But he had one more point to press with Nem. "You know, you're not treating the boy right, flyer. You've made him think that he's one of you in spite of being a human."

"And he's not?" Nem's tongue became agitated.

"Is he in line to own the business? Or is he just destined to get used up someday, on a job like this one?"

Used up. Just like a Paint. Raised like a son but not a son: trained, sent out and used up. The analogy seemed so perfect and so unexpected that it swept over Wanbli with religious intensity. A great understanding. No wonder he felt so protective of the little pup.

Nem spat with outrage and stood as tall is it could. "Since you're such a strong supporter of the boy, Red, perhaps it will please you to know that it was his hand that injected the multendorf into the air currents you have been breathing." The rosettes on his cheeks stood up in Patish emotion. "It was really not necessary for you to sit in the chair."

"Multendorf?" Wanbli raised his eyes to the empty white ceiling. He glanced from one wall to another. "It must not have worked, flyer. I feel fine."

"I'll bet you do." The Patish watched and watched as Wanbli stood in place, looking fit, relaxed and progressively more glazed.

He felt absolutely wonderful, truth to tell. Like victory and wide vistas and all pain in the past. It didn't feel like a drug, it felt like fulfillment. He bit down on his thumb until he drew blood and tasted it. "I see," he said evenly.

"And now you're not angry at us anymore, are you, Red?" whispered the Patish.

"Oh, not at all." Wanbli smiled: not a smirk.

"And you see how foolish it was of you to get upset?"

"I've always known it's foolish to let go temper." Wanbli turned toward the door. "Big waste."

"Then sit down and we'll talk about it." Now Nem moved around the desk.

Wanbli had his hand on the plaque. "Sorry, Nem, but what I have to do now is head home."

The Patish was in front of him. "But, Red, you don't want to oppose all of us: Kouamie, Covazh, Pascal, Rachel . . . myself? You don't want to fight?"

Wanbli ruffled the pelty head as he had Pascal's. "No, I really don't. Luckily I won't have to, Nem. Not with you flyers. I'm still Wacaan, you know. Or maybe you don't." Wanbli moved his employer aside. He opened the door.

"Red!" Nem shouted and as Wanbli glanced back at him that tongue shot out over a meter through the air, right at his left eye. Wanbli's body parried without bothering his mind about it and he found himself grasping the end of the thing in his hand. Liquid shot out in a thin stream, hitting the wall, which smoked. Wanbli was much amused; he did not let go of the thing as, with his heel, he kept off the eighteen claws Nem put into the battle. Feet were pounding down the hall, so Wanbli ended the scuffle with a slap under the Patish's long jawbone. Teeth clicked against teeth and Nem grabbed his tongue with both hands as he watched Wanbli running down the corridor.

It was Kouamie and Ivian, answering Nem's silent alarm. Kouamie was a Patish, though not of Nem's family. Wanbli didn't wait, but twisted its arm so that tongue and all claws were facing away from him, and made as though to throw the Patish at Ivian, who was human and who put her hands in the air in the universal gesture of the noncombatant.

"You got a letter," she hissed as he darted by. He grinned back at her, exalted afresh by this small gesture of companionship. "Thanks, I got it."

His room was just around a corner, where from old habits his pack stood, sorted and ready. It was a much bulkier weight than it had been when he left Tawlin: full of clothing.

The door into the car yard was not locked, but when he palmed it open there was Pascal, eight-year-old Pascal, standing with legs braced holding a slicer aimed at his midsection.

"You won't," said Wanbli gently.

"I will," shouted the boy.

"Then that's too bad." Very calmly Wanbli walked through, shoving past the barrel of the gun. Pascal kicked at him nastily, but he did not shoot.

"You . . . you whore," the boy shouted, and then he threw the slicer down on the steps and ran back down the hall crying.

Wanbli felt such detached sympathy for Pascal that he almost went back.

He went to the Hall of the Seven Sentients, this time to the Patish display, which he had missed. It was very interesting, and would have told him about that tongue. Stomach acid, very concentrated. Fully in the bloom of the multendorf, Wanbli sat on a bench before the exhibit of Patish family life and he opened his letter.

The foil came open in two sheets, one of which was blank except for the New Benares dateline and the words ENC. 1. Wanbli interpreted this to mean the letter was forwarded through the only person in New Benares to know his location: Audry. And that she had nothing to say.

Except for the multendorf, that might have hurt.

The inside missive was a full-page (unusual profligacy in a long-distance printgram document) and without greeting. It went:

> *You were really a fool to pop off like that. I know all about that money you came into—what a farce, 'Bli. You get rich because someone tries to kill me. Can't really blame you for cutting loose—feathers were made to fly. But your stone-faces in the clan aren't going to forget it. They want their paints under their thumbs. Shit, but you're so much like me.*
>
> *They stuck me with two—only two—paints, no brain nor imagination between them. Both men. Can't learn to operate the machines at all.*
>
> *Listen. The reason I'm writing is on behalf of all of us who pay too much taxes. What has happened to the Cynthia Conglom? Do they intend to honor our con-*

tract? No answers! No answers! You're out there—do something. Seventy-eight years of payments and do we have a station or no? Check the Elmira reps on NB.

You are not hard to trace, you barefoot dongberry. Pursue this matter if you want to come home unscalped.

That business about your mother wasn't serious, if that's what burnt your synapses.

Over the signature was Ake Tawlin's official seal. Wanbli folded the foil (it could not crease) and put it back in his purse.

He had a very clear memory of Reynaldo's hesitant remarks concerning Elmira: remarks that would one day, he had known, become very important. Wanbli stared unseeing at the holo of the pink undeveloped Patish baby in its parent's external pouch. Now was that day. He had used up goal after goal, distraction after distraction, and here it was.

A poor society on a poor planet. Not even the merchant princes of T'chishett were what he would call wealthy, not after seeing New Benares and Poos City. Poor, backward and without opportunities: that was all of Neunacht. Sniping at each other and full of self-importance. Hell, no one out in the big worlds knew who they were.

How Wanbli pitied the whole place. How he loved it. He had seen nothing as beautiful as Tawlin on three planets. No one as fine and honest as old Aymimishett. Wanbli rocked gently back and forth, overcome by the memory of Mimi. Of all the poor, thickheaded, hopeful peoples of Neunacht, the poorest, most thickheaded and most hopeful must be the Wacaan.

> "I invoke the moon, my little sister,
>   And the other who is my little sister to come."

Poor simps. The Councils had invested as much in the station as anyone. And written some very silly ritual. Now if he made it past Nem's people, Myronics Security and the unknown drug runners, it would be up to Wanbli to let all the people of Neunacht down.

No Sky at All

SEVEN

THE PORTS of Poos are illustrious, as are the taverns attached to them. That into which Wanbli walked was lined in wood, every stick of which came from off-planet, and every stick of which had been brought by the Merchant Guildsmen of Poos and donated, in exchange for a drink. The result had no unity of design, but it was mentioned in Wu and Fabricant: Wanbli read the page hung framed on the wall beside the bar.

The multendorf had not yet let him down. Perhaps when it did he would die, and save many people some problems. Or maybe there would be no ill effect at all. Right now he was content: filled with the glory and the inevitability of going home.

His changer did not read impressively. He had had only two pay periods at Nem's. The tips made up more than the pay, but still, it would not get him home. He would have to make himself useful.

Useful. That was a stunner. How could he, with his peculiar assortment of skills (or lack of them) be useful on a string-going vessel? He scratched his Third Eagle, wondering.

He remembered the social organizer on the liner out who had offered him a job. She might have been joking; a Wacaan warrior looking for a job as a steward seemed such an unlikely eventuality back in those days. And Wanbli suspected that he wasn't, perhaps, as much the life of the party as once he had been.

"How can I help?" asked the bartender, who was a sharp-featured human female of some years. The question was entirely too appropriate to be real. Seeing him start and stare, she repeated herself in Ang, of which he knew nothing.

He replied in 'Indi that he would have whatever was going. It didn't matter what he ordered, after all. Unless it was fruit juice, he couldn't drink the stuff.

The dark brown substance she poured him looked really vile. It was a small, heavy glass, which seemed to concentrate its deadliness. Wanbli carried it to a table and sat down to think, and to watch the travelers pass the time.

How distant, how compassionate he felt, gazing at the worried faces, the thoughtful faces, the tired, blank faces around him. There in the corner was a Dayflower, swathed in a metal-mesh drape to protect the chair and table under him. Wanbli, for a misty moment, thought the fellow was playing chess, but it was cards actually, with two truckers and a very well dressed woman in leather lace. A business-being, probably. Why shouldn't the Dayflower people engage in business; there was plenty of time to buy and sell, given thirty-five years. Were they playing that ominous and exotic game of bridge? No, he decided, for there was no dummy. Besides, they were too high-class.

Wanbli was good at the card games of his people: hi-lo, piscine, rummy. He had played hi-lo with the other arrangeurs at Nem's; all bets on the smallest digit of the changer. But now he wouldn't want to play, for his was the detachment of the departed spirit, and as such he had gone beyond win, lose and "gin."

He picked up his glass and swirled the brown liquid.

Dreamily he held it to his nose, waiting for the sting. It came, but for once it did not choke him; it was not unpleasant. It felt like mint, but not cold like mint. He dared a sip, which tasted unpleasant but felt very good. Wanbli stared cross-eyed at the glass in surprise, then remembered that his body was running with natural painkillers, all at an unnatural level. He tried it again, amazed at the effect.

A group of six came in, dressed alike in very dreary tan, just different enough from the truckers' khaki to mark them. As they sat down at the table beside him, a number of other groups, including the four cardplayers, got up and moved. The lady in laces stalked out of the bar entirely, clattering in her high wooden clogs.

Wanbli could not see anything special about the newcomers, except that their coloring was a bit extreme. Two had hair as pale as their uniforms and blue eyes. Two were black. One looked like Ake Tawlin, but even shorter. Wanbli, however, knew he had no right to call another individual's color extreme. He had met no one as red as he since leaving home.

He pulled at the drink again, and grinned so that the glass clinked against his front teeth. "If the multendorf doesn't kill me," he whispered to himself, "this will have been a very educational experience." He sighed. "If it does kill me, it still will have been very educational."

"What was that?" The accent was flat and guttural.

Leaning over the back of a stool toward him was one of the tan party—a pale one. He had thick eyelids and almost no eyelashes and a very sharp nose between rosy cheeks. Wanbli thought he looked less human than the average Patish. He didn't judge the man for that; he just noticed it.

He understood the mistake. "Oh, I was talking to my drink."

The Dayflower was now following the woman out of the bar. "You know," Wanbli said to the very pale man, "I had a friend once who used this stuff—alcohol—to kill himself. Very sad."

The almost invisible eyebrows rose. "Many do."

Wanbli nodded and put his glass down. "Yes, I guess. It

was the last time I went to a bar. He was a Dayflower, like that one. He used my drink to commit suicide."

The man's eyes, like his nose, became sharper. He spared a small smile. "That wasn't considerate of him."

Wanbli glanced over to see that the others at the table were looking at him. "I'm sure he didn't mean to be inconsiderate. It was just that he was a mathematician," he said.

The other pale one—a woman—spoke in a language Wanbli did not recognize. She seemed to be speaking to him. Or at him.

"Greta says that here at least is one man who doesn't mind talking with us."

Wanbli met his interlocutor's eyes. These were the color of sky with just a wisp of cloud. "Why should I mind talking with you?"

His lips were thin and pink, and he hardly moved them to talk. Wanbli thought the man's face looked like a neat case of white leather over a framework. A football, perhaps, or a fancy shoe. So even and rounded, without the jutting framework of nose and cheekbone of a Wacaan face, or the pudgy, dimpled cheeks of the T'chishetti. He could clearly see the pink-white scalp under its cap of sand-colored hair, as the man turned to translate Wanbli's question for his fellows.

The diversity among humans was endless. Wanbli, sparkling and tingling with well-being, was glad to be one among them.

The group showed their teeth companionably and one of them laughed. The pale man turned back to Wanbli and said in careful Hindi. "We are revivalists."

Every few years there would be a revival somewhere in Southbay. Last time, just as Wanbli was training for his Third Eagle, it had spread so far and taken so aggressively a Wacaan separatist flavor that Council had had to interfere. Wanbli's own religious sensibilities did not incline toward group fervor, and he had become heartily sick of hearing "The Womb of the Father" sung off-key.

This, of course, would not be a Wacaan revival and could only be more interesting. He scooted his chair toward them all and waited receptively.

But the sand-haired man did not elaborate. Instead he bought Wanbli another drink.

Two of them spoke Hindi, and two more had enough understanding to follow Wanbli as he talked. Or at least they nodded at appropriate times. He was telling his own story: not about Nem's, or the fiasco on New Benares, but the part that had turned out to be important. He told them how the Wacaan had come to Neunacht full of ideals of the pure warrior life and been outcompeted by just about everybody. It was not written that way in the local history books, of course, but that's the way it was. How he had learned to resent his peculiar bondage to the T'chishetti, who seemed to possess the world, and how he had discovered, quite recently, that the T'chishetti resented it too. How could that happen? he asked the tan people. How could there be an unbreakable arrangement that suited nobody who was involved? The table agreed that it was very strange but that such things happened.

Then he told them how all the clans of Neunacht had been paying for generations toward a commercial station that would open up the economy of the planet enormously and make it possible for them all to live the way they wanted. The pale man, who was leaning very close to Wanbli for purposes of translation, hazarded that maybe it would not do all that: people are often disappointed.

They would be very disappointed, admitted Wanbli, because the station was not coming. The corporation providing it had recently reorganized and was not going to fulfill, and he had to take that message home. He bore an immense and dark responsibility.

The other Hindi speaker—the one who was even shorter than the T'chishetti—did not accept this. "You are only one man," he said, pointing a finger. His name was Lin and his was a very dignified manner. "You cannot take responsibility for an entire colony."

Wanbli sat back. The multendorf had not left him, but he was feeling a little muscle sore. Also a little light-headed. "I used to be just one man," he answered. "But now I think I'm either no one at all or everyone. You see?"

The ones who only understood a little bit of Hindi nodded forcefully.

There were more drinks and the revivalists began to talk about themselves. They said some very strange things. Edward, the pale man, said he had been born three hundred and nineteen years ago. Earth years, not standard. Lin was fifty years older.

It was either the translation or the drinks, decided Wanbli. Human people fell apart after about one hundred years: no way out of it. Or perhaps there was a religious meaning to the figures. He did not press or contradict them.

They admitted that revivalists were very unpopular in places. They traveled in groups because alone they were often beat up or even found murdered. Sometimes even large parties were attacked by mobs of locals. Wanbli thought this was a shame, especially when he discovered that none of the party had any idea of self-defense beyond that of carrying a gun, and so he explained to them what a Paint was (he did this very nicely, without boasting, because he was merely concerned for them) and he offered to see them back to their ship.

It was dark when they all left the tavern, and the airs of Poos were bracing. Wanbli was beginning to need bracing. There was a long walk, some confusion, and Wanbli was left with a memory of thumbing his stick—which he had not put to use once since training classes—and of having put some very noisy flyer down on his tail on the sidewalk. All very frustrating and incomplete. Then he was inside again.

The multendorf let him down.

When the door burped open, Wanbli was curled in the hammock, an afghan wrapped around his feet. He opened his eyes. It was very unpleasant.

"That was the longest, worst hangover I have ever witnessed," said the woman in the doorway. She was wearing a tan uniform which ought to have been familiar. "We had to put you into one of the revival units or I think you'd have died. You were in there for twenty-four hours, which is many times what it takes to put life back into a frozen body. Your metabolism did not want to stabilize at all."

Wanbli had to stop and think what an hour was. It was an archaic way of dividing up time: not in units of ten. Or perhaps that was shillings he was thinking of. He decided sitting up would be preferable to thinking. He unstrapped, and wrapped the woolly afghan around his shoulders.

"You also ran down the battery in the scrubber once we got you in here," she added, gesturing to the corner of the room, where the squat canister unit sat, all its lights dim. "I have no idea what you found to vomit after all that time, but there it was."

That explained why he felt so very light, and also the taste in his mouth. Still, the level of ache in his body had reduced itself to manageable levels, and when he put his feet to the floor nothing terrible happened.

It seemed pointless to try to convince the woman that it was no hangover he had suffered. She might only think him a multendorf junkie instead. "I'm sorry to have troubled you," he said. "I'm not sure myself what went wrong with me."

She was a woman of middle age, slightly heavy. She pulled up on the knees of her trousers and settled down on the lower lip of the round sphincter doorway.

Round sphincter doorways were very antique. This one looked like an original. "You weren't any real trouble," she said, "because we didn't dare do anything for you after pulling you from the unit—not with you half out of your head, and after the performance you gave on Morion night before last."

There was that single memory again: dropping the flyer on his tail. Wanbli squinted horribly. "What exactly did I do? Was I . . . out of line?"

The woman looked like she might snicker, but only for a moment. "Not out of line in our book. You wiped up a gang of locals armed with paving blocks, and you had only your hands and a stick. I'm told you could have done without the stick too. This was outside the Flotsam and Jetsam. They don't like revivalists on Poos, you know."

"I heard that before." Wanbli felt no particular elation at the news of this victory. Crowd control was not a heroic action, especially with a nerve stick.

"And we're very grateful. Only we didn't know what you might do, half delirious as you were."

Wanbli let the afghan fall from his shoulders. He noticed that he had sweated away most of the body paint. His eagles were returning. He felt fuddled. "I don't think I'd do much. I'm not really hair-trigger or anything. I don't kill people on reflex."

He raised his head and tried to make sense out of the humming walls, the firmly built-in furnishings, the lack of pressure on his sit-bones. "This is a ship?"

"Of course it's a ship." He could see the question hadn't made the woman happy. By her stance and attitude, she was obviously a person of authority. Once, Wanbli would have exerted himself to be attractive to a woman in authority. Not so long ago.

"And it's moving?" he continued, regardless of the fact that she thought him a bore.

She sighed and stood very straight. He could see the bones of her shoulders through her jacket. "Mister, don't give me any—guff—about wanting to be put back on Morion. You were damn enthusiastic to come with us, before you came down from your spree, and we don't have the money to waste . . ."

Wambli spread out his hands in protest. The afghan slid entirely off him and floated to the floor in the two-thirds earth gravity: standard ship weight on most nonluxury deep-space vessels. Authority or no, she appreciated Wanbli's build. Her change in expression was better for Wanbli's spirits than a dose of painkiller. "I don't want to be put back. It's true I don't remember much, but I'm happy. Happy," he repeated. "I only want to know where and why, and if you're too busy right now, even that can wait."

Evidently she was placated. She lowered herself onto the dead canister of the cleaner and put her hands on her knees. "Where you are is in a dormitory of the Earth colony ship *Condor,* which left from Peru in the year 2038 toward star M781-31. Their destination was the big moon of the seventh planet of the system, which they had reason to suppose was of Earth type."

Wanbli did some figuring on his changer. "That was two-hundred eighty years ago. Years of some kind. We didn't even have fiddle flight then. We hadn't caught the strings."

Again she was irritated. "I told you—they told you we were revivalists."

Wanbli rubbed his aching shoulders and tried not to look stupid. "So who are you trying to revive: the ghosts of the crew?"

"I thought you were just that ignorant, but Pierce said . . ." She got off the cleaner and hopped to the hammock. As she landed next to Wanbli, he bounced a little. It was unpleasant.

"I am one of the crew of the *Condor*. Don't I . . . look a little odd—exotic—to you?"

It was Wanbli's turn to frown. "You look a lot more normal than most I've seen in that uniform. For example, the pink guy without lips . . . I mean no offense to him, but *that's* exotic."

She chortled with one brown hand over her brown face. "I'll have to tell Pierce you said so. But the truth is that *I* am one of the ghosts of the *Condor*. I'm one of those colonists.

"I was a sleeper."

Wanbli rocked back in the hammock, setting up waves. "Protectors!" Diffidently he reached to touch her hand, as one might touch a strange beast, or a saint. "You've been asleep for hundreds of years? Since before my home was even settled?" She didn't bother to answer.

"So you finally got to your planet and . . . then what?"

"We never arrived." The woman took her hand out from under his. "We would have been traveling for two hundred more years, but the revivalists snagged the *Condor*."

Wanbli forgot his headache in fascination. "So you never even got there?"

"It was just as well. Bigmoon, we now know, has an average surface temperature of 210 centigrade. Small error." She rose again, moving in ship weight very buoyantly.

"I'll have them send you in some grub."

Wanbli wilted at the thought.

* * *

They were a community of four traveling ships and one ancient mammoth without fiddleheads, which orbited loosely around the planetless star B-333. In age they were between fifteen and fifty; there were no children at all, and no officially recognized pairings. Not all the crew of the *Condor* spoke Hindi, and those that did had a peculiar range of accents. Their own common language was Old Ang, which he applied himself to learn, waking and sleeping. Their custom was military in its scheduling and neatness. They did not force this life upon Wanbli, but he did his best to fit in.

Individualism was the watchword of that small assortment of planets in communication which was called—arrogantly—galactic civilization. Or perhaps the watchword was better expressed as Caveat Emptor, but whatever the drive of the individual society, it wasn't denial and sacrifice. The fiddlehead drive had put self-sacrifice out of fashion.

Here, however, were the revivalists, all of whom had been born more than three hundred years ago, in days when the smallest journey took longer than a human lifetime. Each of these ship-bleached ancients had chosen to journey: had chosen to sleep, to die, on the chance that they might someday wake up again.

Frugal in thought and action, they were not what Wanbli had grown used to meeting on the commercial liners, on the green-painted lots of New Benares and still less under the peachy lights of Poos. They bore no resemblance to the willfully bored Truckers' Guild.

But they were not strange to him, for he was a Wacaan of Neunacht. He had met such pride and such poverty in Hovart and most of all in the homeland of Southbay Extension.

"You flyers," he said to Edward over the screen of the readwriter, "have a lot going for you. You can pace yourselves, you can do without—I've never eaten plainer—and you can all work together for your common goal, whatever that is. You have it all snapped together except for two things. You don't know how to fight and you don't know how to have fun."

"We don't usually talk out loud in the library," Edward answered mildly. He hardly moved his thin-lipped mouth.

Wanbli sighed and waved the screen dark. He took the very pale man by the wrist and led—no, pulled—him out through the antique sphincter door. Edward dropped his spool on the table by the door; one was not allowed to remove library books from the room, even when being abducted.

"I said, you flyers don't know either how to fight or . . ."

"I know what you said, Red; I heard you." Edward was half a head shorter than Wanbli. He dusted off his impeccable khakis with both hands. "And as far as hand-to-hand fighting goes, it isn't really as necessary in the interstellar community as it was among primitive humans. Destruction has been perfected on such a massive scale that it makes a simple punch look . . ."

"That's a fallacy," said Wanbli earnestly. "A very common fallacy. The fact that one big corporation or government can vaporize another big corporation or government doesn't touch the fact of whether one single man can stand up to what comes against him. Against himself, for that matter." His tone was touched by doubt as he asked, "Hey, if you believe there's no use to fighting, why'd you start taking boxing lessons from me? I mean, if you don't put any value in what I do, what am I doing here? I mean, charity is all well and good and I'm grateful, but . . ." Wanbli, full of inchoate conviction, became lost in his own syntax and fell silent.

"Good conditioning," answered Edward. "Obviously your workouts are very good for the cardiovascular system." His colorless eyes glanced briefly, covertly, at Wanbli's arm, which was still raised with the force of gesture. "And the muscular system, of course." He gave Wanbli a wintry smile—Edward's smile—and returned to the library and his spool.

The truth was that the *Condor*'s crew was very bad at the lessons Wanbli was teaching. They had discipline and they had machines which delivered stimulus to increase the size of the muscle mass, but they had no instinct. They moved slowly and what they learned in pieces stayed in pieces in their performance. Their punches were short and heavy and their kicks—well, frequently they fell backward when they kicked. Perhaps it was the light gravity.

Of them all (and they were so regular in attendance, every other day depending upon their work shifts) only Coordinator Khafiya, she who had greeted Wanbli upon his own unpleasant awakening, had any degree of grace. She was the oldest on board the *Condor,* and one of the oldest to have been revived from sleep. Perhaps it was contact with the soil of a planet that made a fighter. Perhaps it was having to scrap as a child.

Edward was the one who fell most often, but he also got up again and wasted no time in frustration. He alone had the idea that a punch was meant to land on somebody and to hurt. Wanbli had a little hope for Edward, but as with the rest of the crew, the very white man's greatest pleasure in the lessons seemed to be in testing his changing muscle/fat/connective ratios and his blood and lung volumes. They all kept charts.

As though, thought Wanbli, the weight of one's flesh had anything to do with being a warrior.

He waited by the door to Central, which was in the belly of the ship. He practiced forms, for he was still not used to weighing a hundred and twenty pounds and he tended to slam himself into the wall. When the Captain came out, he had just done so, making quite a noise. It was embarrassing.

The Captain was a gray man, but not an old one. Though Wanbli had been presented to him, the Captain had never seen fit to attend one of the self-defense classes. He raised his neat gray hairline. "Trouble with the gravity, kid?"

"Only at top speed," answered Wanbli. He slid off the wall bench where he had landed and straightened his breechclout.

"And are you having no other problems in adjustment to shipboard life?" The Captain was trying to be gracious, in his ponderous way. "I am told you have made a positive difference in the condition of my crew. The average m.f.c.

ratio is four points to the left in the three weeks you have been with us, and even bone density has shown improvement, which is surprising in such a short time. That is to be commended."

"Thanks, Captain Brezhner, but what I really hope I'm doing is making it harder for people to pick on you folks when you down-planet."

Even Brezhner's eyes were gray. They flickered as he replied, "I don't think you really have to worry about that, Red. You don't have to . . . feel quite so protective. We can defend ourselves when we really need to."

Wanbli didn't want to argue the point. "What I really wanted to ask you, Captain, is when the *Condor* will be swinging by B2-98. I came aboard because Eddie told me that eventually I'd get home this way."

Captain Brezhner sat himself on the wall bench. "Yes. Edward Pierce. You know, he broke our tradition seriously in inviting a stranger aboard. It took a ship meeting and hours of discussion before we could reach consensus. I think it was the fact that you were so sick, and taken off our revival equipment seemed likely to die, that caused the argument to turn in your favor."

"I'm very grateful, of course . . ."

The Captain waved that away. "Gratitude, in this case, runs in both directions. Our function in society being what it is, we don't find many friends. Fewer who will wade into a . . . a shindig like that on Poos for us. But I'm merely explaining that we have no precedent for what we should do for you now.

"We are chasing down a ship, you see."

Wanbli sat down beside him. "I didn't know that. Nobody in the gym said a thing about that." (What *was* their "function in society" anyway?)

"Well, we are always chasing down a ship, of course. We are revivalists. This one is heading for a two-planet of an M class star, 71-88. I don't know what that is in your modern Brawliens catalogue . . ."

"I wouldn't either."

"But we ought to make contact within ten or eleven days, and after that it will be up to the Coordinator's staff to decide our next move. Likely we'll be able to work a side trip to your string station."

"Uh, we don't have a station. Ships have to plow all the way in." Wanbli felt an obscure sort of shame creep over him. Shame and a new realization of what it meant for a planet to be so poor as Neunacht. The *Condor* could not take him home.

Captain Brezhner was standing. "Well, we'll work something out," he said vaguely and stepped through the next sphincter. It closed awry and Wanbli came behind him and preened the cartilaginous veins smooth again.

Sphincter doors had never worked right.

The *Condor* did not have a starwatch or even a flat screen to the "outside." It had been equipped, after much money and more tinkering, with a simple fiddlestring and the noise of the fiddlehead engine permeated the largely ferrous hull, but the revivalists had not been motivated to the extra expense of a visual space map.

Wanbli thought it odd they should be so uninterested, since all the crew were planet-born: Earth-born, in fact. Truckers (one understood) had no sense of the stars as lights in the heavens, but most people born under a sky like to look up.

But it may have been the expense: starwatches were luxury items and the revivalists measured the grams of their dinners. Or it might have been that they were tired of the whole starry picture: none of them had intended to finish their lives wandering in a pod of steel. Wanbli sat with his eyes closed and performed his heretical ritual, invoking the Protectors and the soul of dead Digger, imagining sometimes the invisible glory around him and sometimes the homely sky over Tawlin.

> "We are the outlaws and the presidents,
> Teachers, saints and whores to worlds,
> Defenders and betrayers at one stroke,
> We are Wacaan."

The dream came back again for the first time since New Benares: looking for the lost baby, throwing it off the Pontiac table, waking in a sweat. This time the face of the infant bore no resemblance to Ake Tawlin's. This time he was sure that Damasc, his mother, had been at the bottom to catch it, but when he reached the bottom there was neither mother-ghost nor dream-baby, but only the Rall aircar, which he had been certain he'd driven off and sold.

He was peeling potatoes in the *Condor*'s galley. Potatoes were heavy and so an expensive item in the diet, but they had picked up potatoes on Poos. They were always peeled by hand and since his arrival among the crew, it was Wanbli who peeled them. It was something he could do.

Edward Pierce sat across the table from him and watched, proprietarily. Wanbli was, after all, the lipless man's protégé. "I can't believe you people let yourselves be used that way. They send you out to kill your own people?"

Wanbli rinsed the finished potato in the spray cleaner, which wasted much less water than a tub. He liked potatoes; he didn't even mind peeling them, except that the purple juice tended to stain the hands. "It isn't that simple," he answered. "We kill our own only when they make it impossible for us to fulfill our missions."

"That's *their* mission, to prevent you." Edward pulled on his long, thin white nose. It was a strange sight, for the nose was quite flexible. Wanbli tried not to stare.

"Besides," continued Edward, "these 'missions' consist of killing someone anyway. You shouldn't do that, just upon some bigwig's order."

Wanbli resisted asking what a bigwig was. His Old Ang was only tottering. "A person must be willing to kill as he is willing to die. Otherwise there is no life at all."

"I don't buy it." Edward Pierce wore a smirk that was much like the one Wanbli used to have, back before when. "Hey, what did you do to yourself now?"

Wanbli was holding his hand under the spray cleaner, which ran pinky-purple. "I just cut my finger."

"Well, don't get blood in the potatoes. We're all vegetarians here."

179

"I noticed that," said Wanbli dryly.

Suddenly Edward broke out in giggles. "Oh, it's so funny to hear you talking with a strong Indian accent, Red. All singsongy, up and down and up in the nose like that."

Wanbli thought Old Ang sounded like two dogs barking for a fight, but did not say so. "I'm a 'Indi speaker, so what should I sound like?"

"Well." Edward tried to calm himself. Wanbli started another potato, regardless of stray corpuscles. "Like an Indian, of course. Not that kind of Indian. A redman, Red. American Indian. You look like one, except . . ."

Wanbli waited as the revivalist evaluated him. "Except that you are too red. And your hair is wrong; it should be black. And your eyes are just plain weird."

Wanbli did not know what "plain weird" could be, but he knew he was not being complimented. "Were there a lot of people who looked like you back on Earth?" he asked the pale man.

"Me? I'm one pencil out of a dozen-pack. In Maryland, anyway. Fairer than most, maybe." Edward pulled on his nose again, turning it blue.

"But you'll have a chance to see how much you look like an Indian when we snag this ship. If we find it." He picked up a potato, played with it, stuck fingernail crescent moons into its skin. "It's supposed to have Indians on it."

"If you find it? Do you miss often?" Wanbli was getting very interested in this chase, as the atmosphere aboard ship became tense with expectation. "The snagging, I mean."

Edward picked a peeler off the table and began work on one of Wanbli's load, neatly and slowly, as he did everything. "Not often. If we do it's because the old records are wrong, or there was a deflection, or malfunction. Usually the latter.

"We can't afford to miss."

Wanbli nodded. "All those people, alive and helpless, waiting for you."

The revivalist dropped both peeler and potato. His glare held both anger and fright. "There is no one alive aboard that ship!"

Wanbli was daunted. He must have misunderstood. "You

said I would see people who looked like me. Sleepers from
. . . Maryland or somewhere."

Very forcefully Edward nodded. "Yes. Sleepers. People
who let themselves be put down. No brain activity. No heat.
So much cordwood. You do know what cordwood is?" He
repeated the word in Hindi.

"Wood to burn, I think. It has always seemed wrong to
me to burn something as beautiful and rare as wood."

Edward got his composure and his smirk back. He
picked up his potato. "You only think it's rare because you
come from a desert."

Wanbli didn't use a peeler, but a knife, and went through
potatoes much faster than Edward. "Not just that. Remember the Flotsam and Jetsam, where we met? All those little
bits of wood, very . . . precious." He used the Hindi
word.

"That's freight cost that made it expensive. You could
have paneled the whole place in local lumber for less than
they paid out in drinks for the donations. It's shipping that
makes everything expensive." Edward was working on an
eye, which he cut out with surgical precision, dropping it
into the spray cleaner. "Especially people. You have no idea
how expensive a useless thing like a person is."

Wanbli smiled a sad smile, not a smirk at all. "Yes, I do.
It has cost me a great deal to run nowhere as long as I
have."

Edward Pierce touched Wanbli's arm in companionable
fashion. His fingers were wet and slimy, so he used the back
of the hand. "Tell me, Red. How many men have you killed
in your life? Do you remember?"

Wanbli sat up straight, both hands under the spray
cleaner. The cut finger was still oozing a little blood. "Unless one or two of the thugs I met in Poos City has died
since, I haven't had to kill anyone."

Edward's blue eyes rolled. His face was white astonishment. "Nobody? After all this talk about living and dying,
you haven't killed anyone at all?" He began to giggle again.

Wanbli tried to maintain his dignity. "I haven't had to. I
may have cut off a Patish's tongue for him, though. That
must be worse than death to them."

The revivalists were out-of-time, but they were not wholly ignorant. "A Patish? You cut off his tongue?"

"I held it out and slammed his jaw closed on it." Wanbli had difficulty escaping the contagion of giggles. "You see, he was trying to . . ." He didn't know the Old Ang for the phrase "dust me" so he continued: "Burn me in the eye with it. Or perhaps take out my throat, so I did the obvious thing. Is it . . . is it as humorous as that?" At this point he decided that yes, it was as humorous as that and gave up knife, potato and spray cleaner.

They gave way to hysteria, just the two of them, for sixty seconds and then Edward put both hands to his face, cleared his throat, checked the wall clock and rose from the table.

"I love it," he said, and walked out.

Wanbli stared after him. It was possible he liked that strange, clumsy, cold and very white man. If he liked anyone. If he still could like anyone.

Four days later Wanbli surprised himself by going to bed with Coordinator Khafiya. It was her idea and he responded through politeness, thinking he would probably prove impotent. He had never in his life been impotent and as it turned out he was not so now, and had a reasonably good time. Almost like before he had been celibate and then a whore. He fell asleep with the Coordinator curled up in front of him and his nose at the base of her neck.

The capture of the sleeper ship *Commitment* was only exciting in theory. For Wanbli, it turned out to be only a matter of waiting for someone on tracker duty to give him reports. He did not even have to cancel his classes.

There was nothing to look at, but when traction had been achieved, a bell rang in the halls and the crew set up a mild sort of cheer.

Next day Captain Brezhner called him into Central and allowed him to look at the only visual display on the ship, which suffered from exaggerated contrast and was off-color. The *Commitment* was tubular, with bumps on either end. It could have been anything, hanging there in space: an air pump, a bottle, a New Year scepter. It did not look especially big.

"Not a particularly good catch," said the Captain. "The materials are common and the technology too obsolete for resale, unless to an antiques fancier. But it is sizable, and a lot of something that's already out in space is better than a lot of something that needs to be lifted."

Wanbli was already used to the revivalists' custom of evaluating everything in terms of cost and he didn't know how to ask politely how it was that the crew of the *Condor* had any say in the disposal of the *Commitment*'s equipment.

When Edward came to ask him if he wanted to be with the evaluation party, Wanbli almost said no, for two reasons. First, his mind was turned strongly toward home and what he would say to the clans concerning their station that so likely was not coming. Secondly, it did not seem that the revivalist actually wanted him along. He didn't look at him, and in his voice was no enthusiasm. But then why would he ask?

Wanbli said yes, because both of these sound reasons faded before the chance to be part of something so historic as the recovery of a sleeper ship.

"There's no need for pressure suits, Red. Just your warmest woollies." Edward grinned at Wanbli's ignorance. "If we all had to go in suited, we wouldn't dare bring along an . . . untrained person. The reason we waited so long to go in was to stabilize enough to run a tube. We only have to walk. The difficulty for you will be lack of gravity."

Indeed, it was a difficulty. It meant shoes again. Wanbli shoved his feet into the magnetic-soled cloth shoes, which were the same color as the khaki uniform which made his neck itch. Then, because the pressure against his toes and instep was intolerable, he took his knife and cut slits in the fabric over the spots that chafed worst.

He met Edward with Greta and approximately ten other revivalists at a port in the hull he had never yet seen opened. Only Edward Pierce was vacuum-suited. "You look like an old man with bunions," said Edward, pointing at the damaged shoes, as one bland-faced crew member started the workings of the sphincter.

"I feel like an old man," Wanbli said.

Nobody spoke for a while.

"I certainly hope this is the right carrier." It was interesting to note that Greta, who had no Hindi, was also not native in Old Ang. Her voice had peculiar inflections.

"You're the research leader. You should know," answered another. The sphincter dilated halfway, stuck, and was finally pounded with a closed fist until the blockage jarred loose. The tube tunnel was ferrous and lights shone from the walls. (A person might as well be underground.) One after another, the revivalists stepped through, lifting their weighty boots over the slight sill.

Wanbli came last. He glanced sourly down at the outfolded sphincter. "First Father and Mother created doors to slide naturally. These things never have worked . . ." And then he ran out of gravity.

He thought it was an FTL transition. The Captain had forgotten they were out there and boosted them unprepared. But transitions, however unsettling, were momentary. The gravity changes he had endured on short-haul and shuttle craft had been gradual and never had they lost weight altogether. Wanbli thought his heart might stop.

They were all laughing at him, even the four who were holding the now floating stretcher. If he was falling they were all falling too and no one minded but him. Edward Pierce, composing his white, rubbery face, came back to him. Each of his steps sounded like a gong. "Forgot to warn you. The boundary of the ship field has to be very sharp, or else we'd come home buried in dirt and rubble. It's always a plunge off the edge."

"I'm all right now," said Wanbli, but the tight treble in his voice betrayed him. Greta sputtered.

"You were worse, first time," said Edward, poking her in the stomach. "You were much worse and you'd been warned."

"That's why I'm laughing." Her reply was somewhat defensive. Again they began walking down the tube.

It was bouncing, Wanbli's feet decided. The entire tube

was bouncing and stretching and would soon split and spill them all into space. He told his feet they could not know they were bouncing, in the middle of all this terror and confusion. He was only grateful he had held his bowel and bladder. He didn't think the lavatories on the *Commitment* would be working.

It was not a long walk. They passed a swelling around the wall of the tube—another sphincter door—and then the gray, pitted shell of the *Commitment* appeared before them. The tube covered a rectangular hatch.

Not a sphincter, thought Wanbli.

"Seal seems intact," murmured Edward through his suit speaker, with no particular enthusiasm. Perhaps that was the result of poor amplification or perhaps it was only Edward.

"Connection party already reported that," said Greta.

Wanbli could see the man's peculiar thin-lipped mouth draw up. "What do they know? Get back now. I'm going to close the door and feed air if it needs it."

Obediently they all stepped back over the last sphincter. This one closed without difficulty. "It really was a bad idea," said Wanbli to the person next to him, who turned out to be Greta. She glared in alarm and he added, "The sphincter doors, I mean. Rarely work right."

"If they were that bad we would not be alive in the *Condor*."

Wanbli hadn't planned to start an argument, standing here in an umbilical cord in black space. As he tried to explain he had only been teasing, the floor began to bounce and shake. Really, this time.

"He is forcing hot air," said Greta. "To make it habitable."

"I don't feel any wind." Wanbli thought it was just as well. A strong wind in his face, combined with the feeling of falling, might be more than he could take.

"The air moves between the two shells of the tube. It produces . . ." She sought in her Old Ang vocabulary. "Turbulence."

As the swaying increased, the revivalists clung to one another for support. Wanbli sank down and squatted over his metal-clad heels. The disturbance went on for minutes and by the time the tube was quiet, Wanbli had adjusted to the lack of gravity. At least for a while.

Edward popped the sphincter and they all stepped through. The hatch was open and there was light inside.

"It's old, but it's mint," said Edward. Wanbli did not understand the use of the word "mint," except that it was frosty cold all around. He clanged down into a very large chamber: a slice in the body of the ship. There were hand-holds all over the walls, both the curved sections and the flat. Great square boxes were bolted to the flat walls, and the curved expanses were broken by panels of controls with little lights and toggles. Machinery had been locked into tracks, neatly in lines like the parking yards of New Benares. That tall thing had to be a crane. Yes, it had a cable running along its treelike neck.

Very primitive, everything.

"God, this ship went out a century before I was born," said one of the revivalists, who was holding the opposite end of the carrier from that which Greta carried.

"It went out fifty years before I was born," she replied. "What of it?"

"Just that it must have been one of the first."

Edward returned to them. He had his helmet under his arm. "Not one of the first; it's not small enough for that. A civilian effort, of course. But not too long after the first. There might be antique value here. It's just a matter of finding someone who wants it.

"Here, Red. I want you to come with me." He took Wanbli's wrist in his flexible-gloved hand. Wanbli had to notice how similar was the glove to Edward's own skin. "Don't touch the walls at all; everything but the air is still damn cold in here."

Wanbli followed along the curve of a wall, going clank, clank, clank. They passed through another rectangular hatchway into a room which had very different angles from the one they had left. For a moment Wanbli's innards protested and he almost reached for a deadly-cold handrail, but he controlled himself and then his body decided which wall to call the floor.

Edward watched. "Very good. It hadn't occurred to me that you hadn't been weightless before. You seem to have traveled."

"Travel as long as you like," answered Wanbli, glad his voice was near normal again, "but they'll never put you through this on a liner. Only certain truckers ever have to be weightless."

"Have to be? I like it. The truckers and us too, don't forget, Red. All the sleepers were trained in null-grav."

"Well, you're special," answered Wanbli, and meant it. He looked around him.

The room was a pie wedge, a quarter-circle, one-fourth the size of the one they had left. It had more light than the freight room behind them, and one entire wall filled with instrumentation. In the center of one wall—the one which seemed most "floor" to Wanbli—rose a black square not much smaller than the dormitory at Tawlin, and on it sat four boxes, dwarfed by their setting, of black plastic and glass. The other walls of the room held many similar boxes. Wanbli did not have to be told what they were. He stepped forward, fascinated, forgetting the frozen walls, forgetting that he was falling.

"There are four slots in the reviver, to handle four coffins at a time," said Edward, guiding Wanbli's hand away from an injudicious attempt to touch the black dais. "And four coffins were placed there in the beginning. It was the responsibility of whoever of these four made it through to haul all the rest in and out. No task at all in null-grav."

Wanbli found the stairs and climbed up to the top. The coffin closest to him had little winking lights. "Have those been blinking like that for all these hundred years?"

"No, they just started when I turned on the heat. Now they've got to adjust for that."

Wanbli stood beside the waist-high coffin. The glass was covered with frost. "That just happened too. Here, I want you to see this." Edward took his insulated, gloved hand and scraped across the layer of ice. Painted on the glass was a decoration, which Wanbli recognized as part of the map of the six directions. Under it was a stylized seashell in swirly purple and silver. Edward brushed closer to one end, and there under his hand was the face of a man.

He was big-boned, young, with a large nose. Wanbli thought he saw him move, but it might have been the weightlessness playing tricks again. "Is . . . is the machine waking him up now?"

Edward Pierce snorted and rubbed his nose against the shoulder of his suit. "No. I doubt this prehistoric behemoth ever would resurrect a man. Few of them ever worked when needed, you know."

Edward gave Wanbli a sharp glance, but Wanbli was still staring down, his mouth open. "You see what I mean, Red? Doesn't he look like you?"

Now Wanbli's mouth was open for another reason. "Like me? No! Not at all. Not in the mouth, the chin, the nose, the ears . . . I can't see the eyes but I doubt they're Wacaan garnet. He's not one little bit like me."

"Well, he's red at least. That isn't a common color."

Again Wanbli peered down. "I wouldn't call that red."

Edward cleared the glass again and gave the sleeper another look. His laugh was staccato. "Far as I'm concerned, you might be brothers." He left the coffin and walked to another. In the middle of the dais was a spot with no ferrous component, and Edward, striking his boot against it, started to float into the air. Wanbli brought him back.

The second coffin contained a much slighter individual, young, with dark skin. His symbol was the crossbars of Christianity. There had always been Christians on Neunacht, especially among the clans that specialized in medical work, but Wanbli had only become really familiar with the crossbars in Poos City. Many prostitutes were (or became) Christian. It was a tradition.

The third coffin held another russet-colored man: this one with a long, lean-boned face. Under the four directions on the glass he had a very familiar shape. "Eagles!" cried Wanbli. "Not our eagles, but clearly the same thing."

"Uh-huh. Feathers." Edward nodded forcefully, as though he'd proved a point. "But this one"—and he knocked against the glass—"is dust already."

Wanbli glanced down below the glass, to find that the tiny lamps were not lit. "He's dead?"

Edward sighed. "They're all dead. This one, however, is beyond revival." The pale man's eyes unfocused and his thin eyebrows drew down. He looked beyond Wanbli, beyond the ship, in what might be religious fervor. It occurred to Wanbli that if Edward believed the sleepers to be dead in their present state, then he must believe he himself to be dead. Or to have been dead. Did that explain anything? Were the revivalists clumsy because they had been dead? Plodding because they had been dead?

But Edward did not look dull at all at this moment. His white, rubbery face was intense and his metallic eyes bright.

"Did he die—become unrevivable—when we blew in the air and heat? Was that what did it?"

Edward looked away. "He died when he lay down in the box. This talk of when he became unrevivable doesn't make any sense." He went on.

The fourth coffin held a man not much darker than Edward, with a square face. His lights blinked merrily. His sign was a circle with many radii.

"According to Greta, there were a few Pan-ethnic Socialists on this ship." He straightened. "Notice how all the rest of them"—and the gloved hand swept over the ranks of glass boxes. Wanbli began to count them by rows: ten, twenty, forty . . .

". . . depended on one or more of these four to revive them. If something happened to them, that was it. Later years, each box had its own revival capacity. Or we thought they did."

And you? Wanbli wanted to ask. What had Edward thought, lying down to die in a box? Had he really thought it death at the time? It didn't seem the moment to ask.

The others of the party were in the room with them now. They pulled gloves from their belts and began to release the coffins from their moorings. They didn't bother to scrape clean the glass to look first.

Wanbli, who had not brought the gloves and who was afraid to make a mistake anyway, wandered up and down the aisles and looked at faces. Here was a young man, slightly overweight and very dark, with the same Christian cross over his chest. A nice, simple religious symbol, thought Wanbli. Compared to some. Next to him was a strapping and beautiful young woman, under the four directions. Another girl was next to her, more delicate but still appealing.

"Eddie," he said, scuffling loudly down to where Edward supervised the loading of the first coffin: that of the big-boned man on the dais. "All of the first awakeners were male, yet there's as many women here as men."

". . . no, it's not perfect, but it's as close as we're going to find to the right equipment in this year of Our Lord," Edward answered a question from one of the four carriers. Pallbearers, thought Wanbli suddenly, and shivered.

Edward turned and heard Wanbli's words retroactively. "Yes, the supervisors were all men. So?"

"And the women let that happen?"

"Evidently," Edward pushed him gently away; the first coffin was moving to the door.

"Protectors!" Wanbli moved back, but not too far. It was a strange sight, the man in his glass bier, sharp-nosed in profile, wafted like a flower among six hands. "The women of our clan are brittle as bombs—always thinking they've been left out of something. It could never happen that way with us."

"Things change," said Edward calmly, "and then they change again. Many times." The revivalist sighed for the second time, and then he turned on a wrist player and music filled the air. It was a sound that went up and down and in and out, but the melody was fragmented and the whole effect busy and dry. Wanbli's ears were not trained to it. He was scandalized that Edward would trivialize the moment so.

The loading was fast, for they were practiced and there were two gurneys always in play. Wanbli slid his fur parka sleeve down his wrists to cover his hands and he began to help with the work.

He helped to carry out a young woman with strong bones and a very proud face. Four directions again, this time with the sign of a horse. That image Wanbli recognized, for

Myronics had kept a large stable. He wondered if she would prove to be an Old Ang speaker. Or 'Indi, of course. Even if she spoke Doych he'd be able to share a few words with her. After toting two men, one circle and one cross, he picked up another woman, beautiful in the opposite way, all tiny and looking lost in the seven-foot coffin. Crossbars over her.

In the end there were nine coffins left, including the one on the dais printed with eagles. "You're not going to even try with them?"

"No. Believe me, they're dust." Edward's glance slid away from Wanbli, but then, that was Edward.

"You can go back now, Red. That was a lot of walking, and the job is now Greta's and her crew."

Wanbli had trouble hearing him over the music. "You're staying."

"I have to. I'm in command."

Wanbli stuck his chilled hands in his pockets and turned to go, but he stopped again. "That . . . music you're playing. Does that make it easier? Sorting the dead from the . . . I mean the sleepers from the unrevivable."

The distance was back behind the revivalist's eyes, as it had been at the tavern that first night. "It makes a long job shorter," he said. His yellow hairline lifted. "Don't you enjoy Mozart?"

Wanbli snorted. "I didn't know it was something that could be enjoyed. Sounds sort of like a headache."

"We are different," said Edward, cold and gentle.

EIGHT

WANBLI WANTED to be present for the wakening of the sleepers (as who would not), but he also dreaded it. The revival would also be a disappointment for them and a loss of hope. They had planned to be a handful of humans on a hospitable new planet, and in actuality they would finish their lives as scavengers in a metal house, with no patch of ground to call their own.

This wasn't too different a fate from that of his own people, who had wanted to be self-sufficient and had found themselves watchdogs on a very short chain. Still, the Wacaan had the sky above their heads.

How ironic: the poor soil-scrabblers alone could see the stars. Wanbli rapped a rhythm against the echoing wall of his quarters.

No one but the truckers lived this way by choice.

He waited to hear that the revival was complete. He wondered which of the passive, unapproachable sleepers would make it, and which were already dead: perhaps these three hundred years. The big-boned man with the shell on his coffin, the splendid-looking woman, the delicate woman. The youngsters with black skin and the crossbars . . .

He remembered the face of the third man, out there on the black funeral dais, whom they would not even attempt to save. This did not ring right to Wanbli; they should at least try.

The revivalists picked this time to have a general meeting. They were all up at the gym, which was also the assembly room, recreation room and place to store anything outsized they encountered in their scavenging. Wanbli was thus denied the solace of working out. Only two crew members were absent from the meeting: the Captain and one of the astrogators were down in Central, communicating by short scan only. Meetings were not under the Captain's authority anyway; they were Coordinator Khafiya's affair.

Wanbli lay back in his hammock, Old Ang story tapes plugged into his ears. Studying the language had become much more entertaining once he'd reached this level.

This one was about a young woman orphaned by outlaw parents on an automatic mining station. She and her younger brother lived among the surly group of fugitives and criminals who had hidden in this out-of-the-way spot, outwitting the mechanical guardians of the station and stealing refined ore and equipment. Goulas, the King of Fences, wanted to make her his love slave, and the Company Investigator, discovering their pitiful lair in the sands, demanded she submit to him in exchange for her brother's life. At this moment there wandered in a reckless, laughing desperado . . .

Wanbli realized he was listening to a version of *Hounds of Juna*. He flung the ball of the speaker field across the room in disgust. How he hated that movie.

Edward popped through the doorway, the receding sphincter plates withdrawing around him like an alio releasing its ratchett. "Didn't you hear me?"

Wanbli pointed to the ball, which was still rolling across the floor.

"Well, you are asked to attend the meeting for a few minutes," said the revivalist, and then he about-faced and hurried for the door again. The sphincter was slow; Edward pushed the membranes roughly aside and stepped over.

It was an odd sort of asking, when the asker didn't stay for the answer. Wanbli decided the invitation was obligatory and he followed Edward warily out. The door was half open, its flaps folded out of order. Wanbli let it be.

They were sitting on the floor. The gym had not been emptied of its apparatus, and crew members occupied the seats of the mass-building machines and sat in rows on the rolled mats, like birds on the tree branches on New Benares. It was like Hovart Clan meeting, except these lacked the Paints' gift of arrogant lounging. Their khaki uniforms were neat and their faces intent.

Edward Pierce led Wanbli to where Khafiya was sitting on the bench press, a portable screen propped on the handgrips. The screen made silver snow, tuned to nothing at the moment. Khafiya granted Wanbli a thin smile: one that did not admit she had ever fallen asleep curled under the weight of his arm.

"He had his head in a speaker," said Edward. Someone in the room giggled. Khafiya did not respond to the humor of it.

"We have an important question to ask you, Red."

He tried to look attentive.

"Is there any chance you will want to stay among us? Not just as a way of getting home, but permanently." Her eyes flickered over him. She did not smile, she was not welcoming, nor yet rejecting. She only asked.

Wanbli felt in a bind. He liked these people, hopeless as they were in many ways, and did not want to offend. Also, he needed them to get as far as he could toward Neunacht. He called upon his training for words that would walk the tightrope.

"I have an urgent message for my people. I must go home."

Khafiya's face didn't lighten. "Messages may be sent printdoc."

Wanbli tried to imagine a printdoc that said all he had to say to the Wacaan. To all of T'chishett. To Neunacht. *Your station not coming. Money wasted. Your way of life is mistaken. Stop it at once.*

"A message won't do," he said with more assurance. "I have to be there."

She nodded. "I just had to know. Thank you." She turned her attention to the screen.

Evidently he was to go now, not knowing what it was all about. There was Edward, waving him away from the Coordinator. He went, feeling foolish.

Edward had no explanation, either. The pale man was gazing past Wanbli at the crew. He was muttering to himself, counting, pulling his nose.

Wanbli strode off, his steps filled with natural Paint swagger. Between the gathering and the wall of the gym, he stopped. He folded his hands on his chest and leaned against a traction machine, watching.

This was the place of his own power aboard the ship, if he had one at all. This room was where he was teacher. Perhaps for that reason, or because they thought he had been told to remain, or perhaps just because of the garnet glint in his eyes, the few who noticed him did not challenge.

"So. What does that give us?" Evidently she was continuing a conversation interrupted by his visit. "On the *Condor* we can take two . . ."

"Three," interjected Edward Pierce. His voice was joking but slightly edged.

Khafiya pushed hair from her face and turned to him. "You always do that to us, Ed. Two is more realistic: one for security and one in line for Central."

"Three," he said again. "One will refuse membership and demand to be set down on the nearest planet. One in three always does."

"Then we'll have another opening for the next catch. We don't exactly need two more mouths, you know."

"Three," said Edward.

Khafiya waved it aside. "Well, we'll vote on it. Now the *Albatross* refuses any recruits this time . . ."

"Damn gooney bird has said that for four years!" The words came out of the ship's announcement system. They sounded like Captain Brezhner. Coordinator Khafiya was no whit intimidated. "They haven't had deaths or defections for four years, Brezhner. What should they say?"

She returned to her screen. "The *Hope* is down seven; they won't refuse us, especially since their last chase ended in an explosion. But for the same reason, they don't want to feed a full crew. They'll take two for now.

"I still haven't heard from the *White Cockade.*"

"Went down at the battle of Culloden," shouted a young woman Wanbli recognized as an Outsider. The Outsiders patrolled the hull, fully suited. It was a dangerous occupation and the three Outsiders (Edward Pierce was another) were granted a lot of leeway. Wanbli heard the spreading laughter and wondered what the joke was.

"I've got 'em." It was Brezhner's voice above their heads again. "They're on right now; I'll put 'em through to your blackboard."

Khafiya glanced down at the screen and played with the focus. Over the amplifiers came a voice in heavily accented Old Ang. "Coordinator. Sorry to be late in getting back to you."

"Too busy chasing?"

"Don't we wish so. No, we have been arguing the point at issue here. I did not want to get back to you before we had browbeat a consensus."

"Which is?" All the crew of the *Condor* shifted and leaned toward the voice.

"Send us a beautiful young lady. One."

"Come off it," said the Coordinator. "We're in full meeting here and have a lot to decide."

The voice rumbled. "We are serious. We are full crew, but down by two women. We need a female person, and I wish we could take two, but since we can't, we would like the one to be beautiful."

There was a snicker through the gym. "I can promise you young," said Khafiya. "They're all young this catch."

The voice rumbled again. It was laughter. "Then she is certain to be beautiful. Young women always are."

Wanbli thought of the splendid young woman in the coffin, and of the delicate, flowerlike one, and of the pretty black girl who was hardly more than a child. It seemed they were auctioning people off here. Except the goal seemed to be to obtain as few as possible and give as many as possible to other bidders.

"You're a walking fossil, DeLorca," said Khafiya to the screen before her.

"So are we all," answered the voice. "Send me one female." The connection was broken with an audible pop.

Khafiya took a collecting breath. "So much for the WC." There was more laughter, incomprehensible to Wanbli.

"Now for the *Big Ball* itself. I had their response yesterday. Home will take three. Only three."

There was silence and a swaying. Then someone spoke out: "Three? One, two, three?"

Khafiya shrugged and locked eyes with the questioner. "We can't continue to use them as a dumping ground. The *Ball*'s almost a closed system."

She bent back to her screen again and touched the controls, perhaps randomly.

"What about their destination—uh, Roseland is its present name. Will they pay us to deliver the first settlers to their doorstep?"

Greta spoke up. "M-1447: Roseland denies all responsibility. They claim they never heard of the *Commitment*."

Khafiya did not look too surprised. "Why can't all societies be as nice as Colomblank and take in their own strays?" She chewed a nail for a few seconds.

"So we go to the secondary markets. Kalliope, what's the nearest open colony to our present position? Isn't it Mauli? They had absolutely no limits, last I recall."

A very thin woman with black hair and a long nose cleared her throat. "G506 Mauli star is only forty klicks, that is, light-years, away. But as of last month Mauli Corporation underwent a merger with the second planet of its binary."

Khafiya winced. "War?"

The dark-haired woman did not reply to that. "They're not up to taking anyone now."

"Well, what else, for God's sake? We're not in uninhabited space!"

Kalliope looked down at her hands, seeming to wish she

had something to hold. A shield. "There's Houton Center, of course. Out into the Halo." This statement raised a murmur.

"Houton is at least a thousand light-years away," said the Coordinator, flat. "Not on any convenient string. We can't make it with the stores we have."

Researcher Kalliope twisted her hair around her hands. "Actually, Coordinator, we'd be better off if we *were* in uninhabited space. These urban areas all have growth limits."

Khafiya leaned on the handlebar of a triceps puller and let Kalliope sit down. "Okay, that's hopeless. What about tertiary markets? Did anyone research that? Sandy. Okay, spill it."

The man's hair was nothing at all like sand, Wanbli thought. It was more like rusty wire. He was a burly, belligerent student and easy to knock flat. He stood up now, brushing nonexistent dust from his trousers. "Coordinator, there's a small market for parts back on Morion. Nothing financially significant. And it's only eyes and ganglia. Houton again . . . but that's not feasible, as you say. It's too bad we're in the traffic lanes."

He scratched his wiry head and looked around at his fellows. He almost noticed Wanbli, who had faded behind the spine tractor. "Poonas is only eighty klicks away, and they'll take anything certified obtained legally for ritual use, but they pay in goods or local scrip only, and we're carrying such a midden heap of trinkets now . . ."

"Forget Poonas," said Khafiya, looking sullen.

"Then that leaves agricultural use only: stock meals and fertilizer, and that doesn't pay the cost of shuttling down." Sandy took from his pocket a tissue and honked away. "It's really too bad we're in the traffic lanes."

All the revivalists glanced at one another and shook their heads, as at some improbably bad bottom line to a column of figures.

"All right." Khafiya's voice rang with more authority. "It's spoilage, obviously. Time for the vote."

For a moment Wanbli believed that he had misunderstood. That they had been talking of cargo all along. The coffins, perhaps, and not their sleeping contents. Then he saw Edward Pierce's face clearly and he knew he had made no mistake.

"I move," began Khafiya, "that we declare all the cargo spoiled except for seven, to be chosen by the assembly." There was a large response.

"Eight!" called Edward as Wanbli edged out the door. Groans of irritation were the last sounds of the meeting that he heard.

He was in shock—the kind of shock in which one discovers suddenly that one has been mistaken: the whipped cream was actually depilatory cream, the second-story flooring was cardboard all the time. These clumsy, inhibited but kindhearted relics of the past were actually monsters that would convert clean flesh to fertilizer for profit.

Wanbli left the meeting with no thought but to put distance between himself and the hideous, foreordained voting. In his head was a humming that was more than the resonance of the fiddlehead engine fooling the speed of light. His fingers shook against his thighs, and in an empty passageway he leaned against the wall. It was neither hot nor cold, like them.

Perhaps they were right, and that long sleep was death. And they were so many zombies, deciding which corpses in a shipwreck to consume and which to add to their own meaningless ranks. In that case there was no tragedy here, but only horror. With the side of his head pressed against the neutral fabric of the wall, Wanbli closed his eyes and he saw not one face from the ranked coffins, but all of them superimposed upon one another. The crossbars, the seashell, the horse, the eagles . . .

These were not dead. Perhaps the crew of the *Condor* had convinced themselves into death, but the sleepers in Medical were as alive as so many seed pods shot into the desert air to float on trembling wind-wings and to wait.

There were forty-three crew members in that meeting. Wanbli stood and considered running back there to tell them how grievously they were mistaken, to stop them before they committed a huge murder. But Wanbli kept his reason; he knew what they would reply. They would tell him that he could not be expected to understand. They would show him once again the bottom line and say they could not afford it. They would repeat again the bizarre axiom by which they regulated their career: a sleeper is not in any sense alive.

Wanbli found he was at the door to Medical. It was locked, as he expected. He wandered away from it, back to his own metal cubby and his own pack. When he came out again he was wearing one and leaning on the other. This time his use of the nerve stick as a staff was not part of an act or image. He needed the support, and in that way, like an old man, he returned to the door of Medical.

He would wait for them here and stun them as they approached their murder. That would only be a delay, of course. Even if he could overpower the crew entirely he couldn't drive the ship. And it was going to get him killed. He slammed his angry hand against the vanes of the sphincter and cursed his own helplessness.

Someone called out from inside, asking him if the meeting was over. Complaining his audio was bad.

So this was where the other missing crew member waited for the outcome. Of course. Someone had to watch the bodies.

Wanbli froze in place, his hand raised for a moment, and then he answered in urgent-toned gibberish. His body and some nonverbal part of his brain became engaged in a planning the rest of him could only observe.

The sphincter stretched. It was Guillermo, small, slight, with a shade of green to his brown skin. Medical attendant. He blinked at Wanbli and puckered his forehead. "I couldn't hear you through the door," he said.

"The mongrel thing stuck again," said Wanbli, waving the personal key he wore on his wrist. "Wouldn't open to my code: just shuddered in place. I hate these shithole doors." He stepped into Medical, enveloped in an intimidating cloud of ill temper. Guillermo took two steps back.

"But they do close automatically in case of depressurization," the attendant said to the taller man. "They never stick then."

"How do you know? You been depressurized lately? They only have to stick once." Wanbli looked down at Guillermo without favor. He was Wanbli's most hopeless student, and the one who created the fat/muscle/connective ratio charts that obsessed all the other revivalists. It was easy for Wanbli to glare at him.

"They're about to vote now," Wanbli answered his original question. "But it's going to be a difficult consensus."

This was a safe thing to say. Clan Council meetings had taught him that all consensus was difficult and arrived at only after much browbeating of minority opinion. A good number of Third Eagle techniques had been developed from strategies recognized from Wacaan clan meetings.

"Why?" Guillermo's face expressed honest surprise. Perhaps that was another aspect of the revivalist's zombie nature. They agreed with each other. Wanbli snorted.

"Why? Because . . . Eddie Pierce, of course."

Guillermo's wonderment became sly understanding. He let out a long appreciative sound. "So, then what are you . . ."

Wanbli had stepped over to where the coffins of the *Commitment* lay in rows, touching. The rounded glass of the lids made the whole assemblage resemble the faceted eye of a darter. The coffin of the splendid young woman was in the outside corner; it had been Wanbli's whim to make sure of that, in unloading the day before.

"We need to revive one right away, before the end of the meeting," he told Guillermo, and he began to haul on the top handle.

Guillermo was at his side, both hands on Wanbli's arm, restraining him. "You have to what? No, we don't do it that way. Until the vote . . ."

Then the plan that the rest of Wanbli had devised became clear to his conscious mind. "Not me, flyer. *We.* That's why I was sent here. It's a sop to DeLorca of the *White Cockade.* Didn't you hear him? He blasted his message all over the ship!"

Guillermo faded back and let him pull. "I heard, but hearing meetings is not like being there. I didn't understand there was anything special . . ." He came in from the other side with a neat wheeled forklift that eased the coffin up and toward a row of hatches in the rear wall of Medical. The hatch opened to reveal a long concavity with gel walls and drains. It looked much like a ship's lavabo turned on its side. Wanbli did not remember being inside one. The forklift deposited the coffin into the declivity and Guillermo sealed the hatch. Ten seconds later the hatch opened again and spit out the coffin, its seal broken.

At first Wanbli thought this meant the machine had rejected the splendid woman: that she was dead in the real sense as well as that of the revivalists. But the shell was empty; it had left her inside.

He heard himself saying, "Don't you have to set anything? According to the person you put in there?"

The medical attendant made fussy little sounds. "Not for the body, no. Humans are pretty uniform and the reviver adjusts by its own readings, It's the mechanism of the box we have to adjust for and that I did yesterday. I set them all. It's as well to be ready." His glance slipped from complacency to startled amusement as he watched Wanbli. "Red! Why, *por Dios,* are you taking your clothes off right now?"

"I'm not, really," answered Wanbli, who had pulled separate the opening of his one-piece khaki, just over the navel. "It's just that you're right. It's as well to be ready, and I wasn't. I'm going to need this." He pulled out the woven waistband of his breechclout, which he wore from habit under the uniform of the revivalists.

Guillermo did not understand yet, and so in meek astonishment he had to suffer his lock bracelet to be pulled off his arm, that very arm being twisted back behind him, tied by the wrist to his other arm and then his legs, bent back at the knees, added to the package. He had gotten around to resisting by the time this had been accomplished, but only uttered a few loud queries and exclamations before Wanbli had found a roll of support wrap and used it to plug the unfortunate's mouth. By now Guillermo was quite alarmed and rolled his eyes with much emotion.

"I'm not going to hurt you, Gilly," said Wanbli jovially as he threw the wrap's paper wrappings into the trash re-

202

ceptacle. "But I don't have much luck arguing with you flyers, so I played a little trick on you. It'll all work out."

Guillermo made noises through his nose, disagreeing heartily.

Wanbli returned to the doorway of Medical and looked thoughtfully at the sphincter. He'd made a study of door sphincters during his stay on the *Condor*. Now he opened the thing halfway and yanked at the vanes, jamming them in groups of two so they could interleave, but not smoothly. Then he palmed the hand press and watched the thing close, grind against itself and come to its final rest in a knot.

"Can't believe they work that well in pressure loss, either," he said, either to Guillermo or to himself.

The medical attendant's office was only a chair and a flat desk attached to the wall. A portable screen, similar to Coordinator Khafiya's, sat gently mumbling on top of it. Wanbli increased the volume.

". . . more we have thirty votes for reviving eight and thirteen for the original figure of seven." Khafiya sounded dispirited through the speaker.

"I will never pass seven, not if we're here all day and night," Edward Pierce was shouting. He, on the other hand, seemed to be enjoying himself. "Come on, people. One more isn't going to hurt anyone."

"Well, I ain't gonna goddamn eat just a goddamn little less than ever," he was answered by someone very angry. "I eat too goddamn little as it is."

"No, you don't, Sandy. You could go down another eleven percent in fat and be the better for it."

There was laughter, but tense, tired laughter.

Wanbli left the volume high and started to work.

There were a dozen hatches in the wall. Using the little forklift, which was very nimble, he filled each one with a coffin. Only nine spilled the coffin back to him, so he had to reach back in and pull out the three and place them ready beneath the units that seemed to be working.

The vote was running thirty-seven for eight, five for seven and one temporarily abstaining when the first of the revival units uttered a very sweet chime and Wanbli wheeled a gurney over to the hatch.

The woman was shivering, but she did not feel cold to Wanbli's tentative fingers. Her eyes were open, and though they had no shade of Wacaan garnet in them, they were very pretty eyes.

"Is this still the clinic?" she asked in perfectly understandable Old Ang. "Was it called off again?"

She sounded in accent exactly like Edward Pierce.

Wanbli crouched beside the gurney. "No, it was not called off." He pressed her face toward his. She almost focused on his eyes. "Please listen closely to me. You have been traveling for three hundred years. Your destination is not . . . what you thought it was. You would not have survived the landing. You would not have wakened anyway. Your ship has been snagged out of its flight by a group of— uh—people who want the hardware. They are planning to toss almost all of you out into space, still sleeping. I've locked us in here, but the others will be arriving any minute. We have to prevent their stopping us before you're all awake. We have to take over."

She looked at him with serious brown eyes. "I think I had a dream," she said, and fell asleep under his hand.

Wanbli made a sound of disappointment. He lifted the woman off the gurney, laid her on the floor and ran back to the forklift.

"What's the matter, Guillermo; you go off-line?" The voice was Khafiya's. She was rapping against the vanes of the jammed door. "Meeting's over at last," she shouted. "It's time to choose."

Wanbli had thirty-four sleeping people lying in the corner of the room, all around the medical attendant. They slept a natural sleep, occasionally turning and flopping arms in each other's faces. Two of them were talking in their sleep. Six more had been placed back in their coffins, cooling moment by moment.

It had not occurred to him that the first thing a sleeper would do upon reviving would be to fall asleep like a person starved of all rest.

Nine more sleepers were "in the oven." Wanbli had doffed his khakis and was glistening with sweat from as hard a work as he had ever attempted. His eagles shone bright, and because he had donated his waistband to Guillermo, he was naked. All the sleepers were naked too. He had turned up the heat.

He didn't answer and he heard the sphincter door rasping: attempting to open. It didn't budge. "Door's stuck," said the Coordinator without surprise.

Two more hatches opened and Wanbli was busy with the helpless contents. One was brown and one pale. Both had made it.

He had placed both in the nursery with the others when he heard Khafiya calling, "We're going to have to burn it open, Will. Stand back."

Wanbli trotted to the door and stood not in front but beside it. His sweaty shoulder slipped against the wall. He was warmed up well now and too alert to feel doubts. "I wouldn't do that, Khafiya. I've got Gilly here strapped to the door with tape."

The medical attendant made loud whining noises in negation, but these only served to heighten the effect.

There was a peculiar silence.

"Red? Is that you?" This was Edward.

Wanbli collected himself and stood straight. "I am Wanbli Elf Darter of the Clan of Wacaan, and I stand between these people and the death you would bring them. Here I will remain until your death, or my death, or the . . ." He didn't know the Old Ang for "cessation." ". . . end of the threat which you pose to them."

This time the response came quickly. "Oh, Jesus, you misbegotten fool!" It was Khafiya. "You're making a theater tragedy out of nothing!"

"You didn't think it was nothing back there in the meeting. I could see your faces. It is only that you are willing to kill them to avoid expense."

Three chimes sounded in quick succession, followed by three more, and Wanbli left the door to remove the six living sleepers. Roughly he hauled out the ones for whom the sleep had been final and dragged them out of the way. Then he filled the units again, thankful for the power of the little forklift. He was panting when he came back to the door.

The revivalists had been calling to him. Some of the things they said were very irate in tone. He had never been able to elicit such deep reaction from the *Condor* crew in class. As he came close to the wall he caught Edward Pierce in mid-sentence. ". . . like sperm cells, or even brand-new embryos, Red. Very few of them are destined to live. Most fade off before the mother is even aware and no one wastes a tear on them. What's going to happen is that eventually we will cut our way in and then we'll have to space you, and all for a pile of boxes of unknown viability."

Hearing his death described as inevitable moved Wanbli not a whit. Everyone's death was inevitable. Edward thought he could be the servant of that fact, but others had thought that too. Heydoc, for instance.

Wanbli cleared his throat. "The viability part is pretty good, considering how old the *Commitment* is, Eddie. It's about four out of five. Of course, you flyers might be able to save more; I'm just doing it by rote."

"I already waked them up, you see."

There was a wail and lament on the other side of the door as though he had announced catastrophic death instead of life. He heard the thin woman, Kalliope: "Oh my God, my God, that's seventy people!"

"About," answered Wanbli bravely, although he had just a few more than half that number dozing in his nursery. "And they're alive, alive-o, even by your standards. What do your funny laws let you do with all of them?" He wished he had better Old Ang; it was impossible for him to be eloquent or even persuasive in his words of a few syllables.

"I don't know what to do with them," shouted Khafiya. "But I know what we'll do to you."

Wanbli didn't respond. He was tending his machines.

Once they tried to burn through the wall to one side of the hatch, but Wanbli pressed his fingernail between the two bones of Guillermo's elbow and the resultant shrieks were enough to stop the attempt. Evidently the revivalists were tender of their own. Or else they had another plan in mind.

* * *

There were sixty-eight various-colored sleepers on the floor and a sad row of bodies resealed in their glass coffins.

"Red?" Edward again. Wanbli turned from the contemplation of his work and walked wearily to the sphincter.

"Red, we're going home. Fastest. We've got a direct string out to the *Big Ball.*"

"That's nice," said Wanbli's voice, in the service of that small part of him that knew what he was doing.

"We're going to leave you all in there until we land." There was a pause. "And then there won't be much you can do to keep us out."

"And then what? Sixty-eight people without friends, relatives or government just disappear again: invisible as they were these three hundred years?"

He could hear the thump of Edward's shoulder or back against the vanes of the doorway. "No. They're alive now—God help us. And they're innocent of this. Just one person without friends is gonna disappear."

It was not the threat that made Wanbli grimace. Not the threat exactly.

"Damnit, Red, I vouched for you. I went on the line."

And Edward had been the one to push against them all for a small gain of mercy. Eight instead of seven. A manageable gain.

"You never told me you were ghouls, Eddie," Wanbli called through the door. His voice cracked once.

"Ghouls?" There was more emotion in the single shout than Wanbli had heard out of the revivalists in his entire sojourn. "Without us there would be no sleeper alive. Who else bothers to find us—them—let alone wake them up? And who has the better right to make the decisions?" Now Edward Pierce was screaming. "Damn you, damn you, you ignorant muscle-headed barbarian. You kill your own kin! What revivalist has ever done that?

"Didn't you ever hear about Accibos settlement, where the supposedly lost sleeper ship came down, right on target, in the most logical place to build a city? Where, in fact, they had built a city? Annihilation! Since Accibos *no one* has stood in our way. The entire populated galaxy needs us!"

"The entire populated galaxy doesn't like you, though,' answered Wanbli, as mildly as he could get, shouting through the vanes of the door. More quietly he added, "And I really can't blame them."

"I don't know whether you're protecting us or you kidnapped us."

Wanbli spun around, for the words came from behind him. There was the man of the large features: first on the dais and second into the revival unit. He was blinking with effort but standing on his own. Behind him the splendid young woman was sitting curled, knees to chest.

Wanbli opened his mouth to explain, but could not find a beginning. "Are you okay? Not going to fall over or anything?"

The man's legs were straight and braced, but he was hugging himself and trembling. "I'll make it. How long? How long have we been asleep."

It struck Wanbli as odd that this question should take precedence in the sleeper's mind over all others. "Something like three hundred years."

For a moment the brown face flushed bronze in triumph, but then it darkened. "Not long enough. We can't be there."

"Sit down," said Wanbli, but he was not surprised when the man did not. "You can't . . . you never *can* be there, flyer. Your equipment isn't right and then, things have changed."

On the floor behind, a young man was gagging dryly. The awakened sleeper turned and squinted at his naked company in a manner both helpless and proprietary.

The sick fellow hauled himself up onto his knees. His face was gray under its black pigment. "Oh dear Jesus," he whispered, and he folded his hands in front of him.

Wanbli pulled up a chair, and when the other wouldn't sit in it, he used it himself. "Listen to me and remember as much as you can, because I don't want to have to repeat this for each of you . . ."

Then Wanbli told him three hundred years of history, or at least as much of it as he thought he had to know.

Fiddlehead engines, which followed the minor strings

from system to system. The seven sentient races, among which hoomies lived longest, dayflowers the shortest and humans were by far the most expansionist. He did not mention the two interspecial military exchanges of the last century, because he did not even think of them, and it did not occur to him to tell the sleeper that men, nations and planets were constantly striving with one another in violent and unkind manner.

What he did tell them was that the great world grab of the last two hundred years was over, that string-served real estate was the most expensive commodity existing and that travel was the next. All this was in preface to Wanbli's explanation of why they were all where they were, scattered on the floor behind a broken door in the middle of a hostile ship, with no one in the universe on their side and nowhere to go.

When he was done the sleeper had sat down and was holding his chin in one hand. "No planet?" he asked. "No . . . money? Nothing?" Musing, he added, "We might as well be dead."

"Thanks! Thank you very much!" Wanbli stood up, sending the chair skidding. "That's exactly what I needed to hear!" Three angry steps took him across Medical to where the small package that was Guillermo lay, feet and hands touching behind his back.

The revivalist despaired as Wanbli loomed over him, bright and bitter, with a scalpel in his hand, but the stroke of the knife cut the cord that bound his arms to his legs. With a pull of the bandage tab Wanbli freed the man's mouth.

The medical attendant was weeping with the pain of returned circulation. "Sorry, ratchett. Forgot you were there," said Wanbli. Guillermo scuttled on knees and elbows to the jammed sphincter door and crouched there, glaring at Wanbli and all the lawless lives he had brought into being.

NINE

THERE WAS no food in Medical; this was the second day. It was not as hard a situation as it might have been, because the sleepers woke with empty stomachs and went from their hibernation to a fasting state without much perturbation to the system. Wanbli felt it more, but that particular hardship was among those he had been trained to handle. Guillermo, the medical attendant, was not fasting, strictly speaking. He was living on ethyl alcohol and anesthetics from the stores.

Two things were worth thankfulness: being naked did not seem to bother the sleepers as much as Wanbli had feared it might, and the revivalists had been kind enough to leave the water open.

They were heading at top speed toward the *Big Ball:* their home base. It would be only another two days. What would happen there no one in Medical knew, except that they had promised to kill Wanbli. For that reason, the awakened sleepers regarded him with almost superstitious awe. There

210

had been three cases of hysterics, as the sleepers understood they were not to have the lives they had chosen and risked for: that they were to be outcasts if anything. There were many more storms of weeping and lamentation for the friends, lovers and family who had not made it through, but these were responses in a different category.

Three hysterics out of sixty-eight seemed a magnificent record to Wanbli, considering these people were not Wacaan.

He himself did not regard his death as inevitable, though he was buried in the heart of his enemies' vessel and heading for their stronghold. It was not that he could not imagine himself dying; he had known and encompassed his own death at the age of seventeen, sitting cross-legged in underground darkness, fasting (as he was now) and his lungs filled with ceremonial smoke. It was more that he could not regard any particular death as unavoidable, save that self-willed, or from old age. There would be a confrontation of some sort, and he would live through it or he would not.

In the meantime he tutored the sleepers and wished he himself had a better grasp of human history. He could tell them that there was a planet called Nashua which called itself the Heart of Empire, but he could not tell them of what that empire was composed. Not armies, certainly (in answer to the question). Nashua was far away: at least twenty-five strings' connection. The whole idea of empire was no-never-mind to the people of Neunacht, his own people, and most particularly the Nashuite Empire did not deal with such things as lost or preempted sleeper ships. He had to repeat this to the sleepers many times. No. No army. No police. No help coming from outside.

Especially not from Wanbli's own people.

The sleepers waved hands or drummed fingers helplessly and met each other's eyes over Wanbli's head, feeling extremely guilty but also relieved that they were not individually under sentence of death. Happy that the unknown revivalists—kidnappers or rescuers—no longer thought them suitable for trade or fodder. So grateful were the sleepers that their hosts' peculiar ethics spared them, they were almost reluctant to judge them for condemning Wanbli.

He sat in his morning ritual, though his hands were empty. His mind was empty too. For the first time since the age of seven, when the obligation to help raise and lower the sun had been placed upon him by his elders, Wanbli could not call to mind any of the sacred words: not even his own heretical emendations. He was locked in ringing silence, while the sleepers of the *Commitment*—perfect name, that—talked and touched and moved with one another to make up for their lost pasts and unknowable futures. In the single examination room, and behind a rigged line of sheets, a few couples were using the time more intimately, but most were content to hold hands.

The browns stayed with the browns, the darker browns with the darker browns and the few pales were a group of their own. Guillermo, of course, was a group unto himself, and he glanced often from his desk with real fear in his eyes, as though the awakened sleepers might mob him.

Wanbli, always fascinated by people who looked different, wondered why people who had slept together for so long should be so divided. Were they worried they might conceive babies with health problems? No, they didn't seem worried about conception at all, and matching color to color didn't make it as scientific breeding. He found it curious, the way they clumped.

When Wanbli closed his eyes, as he did often under the strain of fasting and of worry, he saw a face: not that of a sleeper, nor yet one of the incomprehensible revivalists. It was a face of heavy hide, stone gray in color, with small blue eyes set so deep they appeared to be tunnels into sky. Wanbli wondered if Digger had felt like this just before the end: thrust flaming down a path of fate where effort could not slow him down and there were no turnoffs between now and the end. He had judged Digger for his suicide; for Wanbli, there had always been alternatives. That was Third

Eagle belief—that there were always undiscovered alternatives.

The announcement system came on with a pop. Everyone in Medical looked up, even Guillermo.

"Red." It was Edward again. Wanbli dispersed the ghosts in his mind and answered.

"There's a communication for someone: not one of us. Came through New Benares."

Wanbli thought of Audry and threw the thought aside. He thought of Reynaldo. He just waited.

"Anyone ever call you Wobbly?"

First disappointment faded. "Yes, I have to admit it. It's for me, all right. You mean you'd read it to me?"

Guillermo interrupted, crying loudly over Wanbli's words that he had to be let out. That it was unbearable. That sooner or later they were going to kill him. Wanbli bellowed him down.

"I'm not going to kill him, Eddie. He's drunk. What's the Elmira have to say?"

"I haven't opened it, of course." Edward was scandalized.

Wanbli settled back against the wall behind him, chuckling. "You have no objections to dusting me, but you won't read my mail. That's very . . . uncompromising of you, Eddie. I'd be very pleased to have you read it to me, even though I'm not one of your favorite people anymore."

There was a moment's open silence. "I'll read it to you. If I thought there was anything you could do in exchange, I'd trade for it. But you don't have anything we want."

"Not Gilly? Tell you truly, Eddie, we could do without him easy."

"Sorry, Guillermo, but we've voted to keep the room sealed until docking."

Guillermo stood with the aid of his desk, clutching a clear pouch in his right hand. "Voted? But I didn't vote. It's not consensus if I didn't agree!"

"N minus one consensus. You know." The voice of Edward Pierce sounded slightly shamed. There was the hissing of a printdoc relaxing its seal. "Here comes, Red.

"Dear Wobbly,
*   What a surprise to hear from you, and traveling*
again. Wasn't being a face in the shimmers enough for
you? I REALLY miss you and your wonderful little butt
end."

At this point Edward rattled the film and cleared his throat. Wanbli put his head in his hands and thanked all Nine Protectors that the message was in Hindi, for all the awakened sleepers were listening intently.

*   "There isn't anyone on all of Duden that can keep the*
game going like you, lover.
*   "But as for your questions and your funny little plea*
to me for old times' sake, do keep in mind that I'm not
at that level of Elmira that makes the legal decisions
and companies restructure every day and you can't take
it personally.
*   "And you know, asking me for favors like that is not*
how a real friend would treat me. Friendship is sort of
sacred and so is business.
*   "Keep it clean, but keep it up.*
*   "Ducelet."*

After Wanbli had sat silent for perhaps ten seconds, Edward Pierce beeped an inquiry over the broadcast.

"I'm here," said Wanbli. "I suppose you know what that was about."

"Parts were obvious. The rest: not at all."

Wanbli switched back into Old Ang. "I told you about the station we paid toward for seventy years, that they're not going to deliver. Well, it's her company, but I didn't know that, back . . . uh, then."

Edward snorted: a sound which seemed to envelop the room. "You seem to sleep around in high society."

Dully Wanbli answered, "Money doesn't rub off between the sheets." It was an old Wacaan saying. "Eddie," he added. "Eddie, will you send a printdoc for me?"

Edward cursed into the broadcast. "Will I do what for

214

you? You have so much goddamn gall, Red. I won't do fuck-all else for you and you know it!"

Wanbli listened carefully to the tone of the man's anger and decided that he knew no such thing.

"This is just a little favor, Eddie, and it's not really for me at all but for a whole planetful of people."

"Don't call me Eddie. No one calls me Eddie!"

"I just need to tell my folks at home what I just heard. That we're out of luck. No station. No hope. No money, no better life. That was the message I was going home for, remember? If you're going to snip me into little pieces, then I can't deliver it, and it's real important. See?"

Edward Pierce did not submit gracefully, but he took the message.

Wanbli woke from a dream about his mother to racket and tussle. One of the pale sleepers had discovered Guillermo sucking a bag of dextrose in the Medical lavabo. As was made evident, he had been concealing a stock of mixed sugars and honey and had been tapping them constantly, as well as the alcohol. This explained why Guillermo had been living in alternating hysteria and depression, while the fasting sleepers were only a bit lethargic. It took a good deal of earnest persuasion by Wanbli to prevent the assemblage from denuding the shelves and having a high old time.

Later that same night, he was roused again to watch Garland Medicine-Bear punishing one of his group who had been found appropriating the alcohol bottle. Wanbli watched the fisticuffs, not with a critical eye (they didn't deserve it), but rather wondering why the man should be so upset by one of his company's being drunk. The hangover would be enough punishment, surely. But Medicine-Bear kept bellowing long after the miscreant had folded in front of him, to the effect that he would not have it, would not have it, would see them all in hell before he would have them degenerating into drunks before his eyes.

It was remarkable.

The dream chased at the edge of things all night. Damasc came calling upon him, looking as she had last time he had seen her. She did not try to hide the fact that she was dead;

that was understood. He tried very hard to explain to her why he had left home, and why things had turned out the way they had, but she was always busy with something: the jewels in her short hair, their dinner, her bone-handled blunderbuzz. And there was a schedule on the table to which she kept referring—bus routes perhaps. Wanbli then remembered that it was his schedule, not hers. He glanced at it to see how far he was going, and one more time was awakened by Guillermo's pounding on the wall.

Garland formally introduced some of his people: Frederic Standing-Elk, Victoria Whistocken—she was the splendid young woman—Mary Standing-Shoes and William Ollokot. They were not of the same nationality and had not the same language but they were all still of the same large group, he explained very carefully, around Wanbli's lack of English.

Most of the colonists were of this large group, but there were also eight Baptists and four political dissidents. The Baptists were darker and the dissidents were for the most part much paler, leaving the large group, which was popularly called Indians, in the middle.

Indians they called themselves, yet not one of them could speak 'Indi. Wanbli laughingly averred that he himself had the better right to be called Indian, but none of them found that funny. They tended to stare at him.

The last day before landing, the fast began to tell on everyone. Guillermo slept all day. Wanbli would have been happy to sit in the corner under the bulk of the revival units and meditate on things, but he dared not let his body grow stiff and cold: not while things might happen. He forced himself to sociability. He pursued the acquaintance of Victoria Whistocken. He ran through his forms for her, though only at quarter speed. She was very appreciative.

Victoria had been the daughter of a ranch owner. (A ranch was an estate, like Tawlin, he guessed.) She had lost one cousin aboard the *Commitment* so far, but though she grieved for Lennie, he was no more or less dead than everyone she had left at home. She wondered whether a person could live through that: losing everyone she had ever known.

Wanbli said she could, and she nodded, distantly, with the dignity of indifference. But a moment later she was asking him about himself.

He explained Neunacht, and how the T'chishetti and his own clan were locked together, needing and not liking each other, and about the poverty of the place and the station which was not coming, though it had been promised and they had paid for so many years.

She was a marvelous young woman; she seemed to understand everything and she nodded and nodded. A real listener. Wanbli had met very few real listeners since leaving home. By the end of her first day of waking, she had begun to lose that distant look.

"And before Neunacht, Red? What part of Earth did you emigrate from? Surely you are one of the red peoples—I mean, the Amer-Mongolian race."

Wanbli smiled. He was hearing many new words from the sleepers, though he hadn't the energy to ask what they meant.

"We didn't come from Earth, Vikki. We came from Novare Colony, which didn't work out. The first elders got together there, and managed to buy the right to Southbay on Neunacht. It's not far away from here along the strings. If you had the money you could be there in a few ten'ys And we weren't then what we've since . . ."

"What about genetic surgery?" she pressed him. "Do you use it?" He pressed her back, physically. "Your eyes and hair, and the—exceptional color of your skin. Did your ancestors have their babies changed?"

Wanbli shrugged. "Didn't everybody's, some time or another? I hear there used to be a lot more of"—and he flicked his eyes across the room to where one of the dissidents squatted beside Guillermo's curled form, seeming to lecture—"them. People like Eddie—though you haven't met Eddie yet—with no color to speak of. Gamma rays played hell with them and they couldn't take suns. So they changed."

She looked warily at his face and hands. "So you might have been white?"

It seemed such a strange thing to say. "So you might have been white." Meaningless. "I might have been a hoomie, or a dog, but what I actually am is Wanbli Elf Darter. Of the Wacaan."

Victoria Whistocken's splendid face went blank and her mouth opened. She touched his arm with significance of manner and rose to her feet, calling, "Garland, Garland. Garland!"

"Lakota!"

Garland Medicine-Bear's excitement was suppressed into dignity. He sat on a chair in front of Wanbli (for his knees were bad and made squatting painful) and announced in the ceremonial language of the Wacaan, "So it is. You are Sioux."

Wanbli didn't mind the attention. He never minded attention, and he was amused by the seriousness with which the group took this identity of language: of names. "I'm sorry, but that can't be. I am Wacaan. We are ourselves."

Unmoved, Garland answered. "There are many branches of the Sioux, and all are sacred. That is what the word means: sacred."

The other sleepers of his group gathered around. Those who called themselves Sioux tended to look complacent. Others tried to appear not to care much. A few of the Baptists glanced over the shoulders of the assemblage, since there was nothing much else to do in the sealed medical pod, but they turned away again. They really *didn't* care much.

"Sacred? That's interesting." Wanbli resting his fist on his knee and his chin on his fist. "Really presumptuous too, isn't it?" He glanced at the faces around him, which were smug, portentous or tickled, according to nature. For a moment he wondered if he could work this discovery into an approach to Victoria, who interested him enough to outweigh the effects of a three-day fast and impending doom. But no, Victoria Whistocken had retreated behind the first

anks; she herself was not Sioux. Besides, everything was so
public here.

". . . and your name—Wanbli—means eagle."

"Oh, I know that. Named after the clan tattoos."

Garland growled a laugh. "Named after the great hunt-
ing bird, largest predator in the air."

This was interesting. "Larger than a swan?" He remembered the swan in the travel holo. Of course, such things
might be faked . . .

The Sioux laughed again. "Not like the swan at all."

Wanbli continued using Old Ang. He really had never
been comfortable in Wacaan Ceremonial. "But I wouldn't
put too much . . . belief in the fact of the language. People
can learn any language. Any human language, that is. If
they have to, or even just because they like it. And as far as
the color of the skin goes—well, I know a man who is as
black as the inside of a closed closet and he claims to be of
pure Anglo-Something-or-Other blood, which I guess is
white with pink eyes."

There was a laugh from one of the Baptists.

Garland looked almost ready to be offended. "So you
don't believe we are your brothers—ancestors?" The Sioux
glanced at their leader and sat up a little straighter.

Wanbli put out his hand. "Everyone of Old Earth was my
ancestor, I think. Go back far enough. And every human is
related to me now, even the T'chishetti."

Wanbli fell silent with his jaw open, realizing what he had
just said. He had resisted Tawlin's claim upon him so vio-
lently he had dropped his life in its tracks to avoid it, and
here he was, admitting something like it in order to resist
someone else's claim.

Here. He had hold of the tail of something. What was it?

He put the thoughts aside and said, "I don't say these
things because of not wanting to be one of you, but because
you will be making a mistake if you think there is a likeness
which is not there."

"You are a warrior." It was not Garland, but Victoria
who spoke. (Wanbli had, of course, been spinning yarns to
the woman.)

"I'm . . . I was . . . a bodyguard. Then an actor Then . . ." He didn't want to go on.

Garland Medicine-Bear grinned. "And you don't cal yourself a warrior? The life you learn and live; isn't that a warrior's life?"

"Oh, the Wacaan call themselves great warriors!" Wanbli dropped his hands in his lap and laughed. "That was what they are all about. That's what makes them such push-overs."

Garland cleared his throat. "So now you are disassociating yourself from your own people. You seem to have that habit. But yet I would call you a warrior. The care you take with things. You are alert. You are in control of yourself. You are alone though you are among us. That is perhaps the biggest part of it. You will do for a Sioux."

"Not Dakota: he's too skinny," came the call from Fred Standing-Elk, directed to the room at large. There were giggles and everyone speaking together, very warm and welcoming. Wanbli found it hard to resist.

He stood up. "The revivalists thought I might make a pretty good crew member too. Now they think I have betrayed them. And there were people on New Benares who thought I would make an actor, and on Poos . . .

"Well, before that there was a whole clan on Neunacht who had my life planned out for me. And they had most claim . . ."

He slapped limp arms at his sides. "So. Don't expect great things out of me. It doesn't work." He walked over to where a sleeper of the group called Pan-ethnic Socialists was pinching the skin of the comatose Guillermo with his thumbnail and fingernails and demanding to know the locations of the rest of the edible stores. The tormentor rose when Wanbli came near and went off without a word. Wanbli looked down at the small, sad, drunken crew member and wondered if he might lift him off the cot and use it himself; Guillermo wasn't feeling anything anyway. And if Edward was to be trusted, they still had most of a day before docking at the Big Ball. Surely someone would wake him up if the revivalists attempted entry. And he was so lethargic.

In the end, he lay down under the cot, without disturbing Guillermo. The floor, at least, wasn't cold.

Fatigued and light-headed, Wanbli tried to sleep. His brain was moving very fast, he thought, but like a simple engine with the clutch not engaged. If he could harness the various thoughts that spun about him, he would learn something worth knowing.

His betrayals: he had spoken them right out, so that the sleepers would know. So that he would not do the same to them. But at the same time, the secret was kept close inside him, in some airless, lightless place, that he had betrayed no one.

His betrayal of the revivalists was only keeping faith with the humanity of the faces in ranked coffins: with Garland Medicine-Bear and lovely Victoria and even the large, stern-faced Socialist who pinched Guillermo's fingers. And his break with the . . . the artists on Poos (Wanbli was finding it harder and harder to use the word "whore," even to himself) was the result of their misdirection and betrayal of him. And for the sake of the humanity of a young boy. Hopeless.

But it wasn't fair to claim that the Patish had lied to him. It probably had never occurred to it that Wanbli would object to the drugs. After all, wasn't he supposed to be a killer? And what do people (of all species) think of killers?

Killer. Warrior. What enormous, meaningless difference between the words.

The revivalists had never actually lied to him, either. They had just underestimated his ignorance. No one had come up to him, looked him in the eye and said, "You know we really kill most of the sleepers we catch, don't you?" That was not the sort of thing anyone *would* say.

And the Wacaan had never come out and said he was not permitted to leave the planet and the clan. He had only been careful not to ask.

What about the betrayals of which Wanbli was the recipient? He stared up at the underside of Guillermo's web cot and considered. It was both a less and a more painful undertaking.

Digger. He had thought the Dayflower's death a betrayal: a negation of their friendship. Without asking, Digger had rejected the thought that Wanbli, the great manipulator, had any power to help him.

Maybe he didn't. The list of people Wanbli had not been able to manipulate or even help was growing steadily. Wanbli was willing to admit that if life without Wanbli was unbearable for Digger, life with him in it might also be unbearable.

But then there was Audry. Sad to say, that was a definite betrayal. Wanbli could forgive her, especially with her so far away, but still . . .

Still. She had decided to conceal the truth and force a man with a bad job in a place he didn't like to leave job and place. If she had told the truth, she might have lost her own job, which she didn't like either, but which allowed her to take care of her mother and little sister, and would possibly have made her leave the place of her birth.

So Audry hadn't acted heroically, but then she did not live with a heroic ideal. Watching the shimmers produced a lot of heroic ideals in a person, but working the shimmers took a lot out of them. No betrayal, really, except to the stored passion Wanbli had dedicated to her. Of which she may have been completely ignorant.

He was able to wonder, halfway objectively, whether part of her duties had been to bed-partner her boss.

Even the old toad of a Technical Authority probably believed by now that he had not asked Wanbli to hit him.

No betrayal. No betrayal anywhere. People trying their best. Soon they would break in and try their best to kill him. Or maybe they'd flood Medical with an anesthetic and dust him neatly in the middle of the sleepers. Sleepers asleep again.

It wouldn't be that easy, thought Wanbli. He would not let it be easy, but whatever, it would be no betrayal.

It came to him with great force that there was no such thing as betrayal. It was all misunderstanding. And there was no such thing as . . . Something else. Much more important. Something to do with all he'd been saying to Eddie, or to Garland.

I only need one more piece, he said to himself, and then I'll know something worth knowing.

They came to him while he was talking to Victoria; one was black, one was ivory and one was Garland: of the color the sleepers called "red." "You have met the Reverend Godslove Thompson and Henry Larssen," said Garland in Lakota. Or Wacaan. "Each of us represents one group of the *Commitment* colonists. We have discussed the matter thoroughly and we have no intention of letting them kill you." The other two nodded.

Wanbli tried to keep the proper straight face. "I also have no intention of letting them kill me," he said. "Tell me, though, what is it you plan to do about it? We'll be caught in the middle of the *Big Ball,* which is as close as these flyers come to having a home. By the way—are you aware that they are certainly monitoring our conversations from Central?"

"We are aware of that," answered the Reverend Thompson, in bad Ceremonial Wacaan. Wanbli did not laugh now, at the sounds coming out of the young man's throat. Garland said self-consciously, "We of the Native American community voted on a language for our new settlement, and since the Sioux are great in number, it was decided that it be Lakota. Later, when we decided to take people of other origin with us . . ."

"It was scarcely charity." Larssen's Wacaan was also faulty, but his expression made him eloquent. "You charged us four times what . . ."

"I did not mean to imply it was charity. I am only explaining why we can all discuss our future without courting interference from our captors. It is a very good thing"—and Garland fixed a stony gaze on the dissident—"that we did insist on a second shared language."

"No argument."

The Reverend Godslove Thompson sighed.

"And as for being in their mother ship, I can only say that people have escaped from equally impossible places. Hostages give one great power."

"I am very grateful, certainly," said Wanbli, leaning companionably against Victoria Whistocken. She was very warm. "But they will probably shoot the air with some sort of sleep drug and haul me off while everyone is sleeping. What then? What can you do about that?"

Wanbli himself wondered what he was going to do about that, but it felt better to offer it as a challenge to someone else.

"We also suspected that," answered Garland, and Henry Larssen cleared his throat. "Mr. Larssen was the first to suggest that as a possibility. Therefore we are having the air system put on emergency: removed from the rest of the ship's circulation."

"Who among you knows how to do that? Is your ship so similar to the *Condor*?"

"Not at all. It is the medical attendant who knows, of course. He will tell us."

"Gilly? He'll tell you? I hadn't thought it of him. These revivalists stick together."

Garland smiled. Henry Larssen grinned. The Reverend Thompson did not. "Guillermo went back behind a sheet with Mary Standing-Shoes. This is what the visual monitor saw. He now wears a piece of tape across his mouth and he is communicating by means of paper and pencil. He knows that he must disconnect us, tell us how to disconnect, or die."

"I promised Eddie Pierce I wouldn't hurt old Gilly," said Wanbli thoughtfully. He put his arm over Victoria's shoulder in absentminded fashion.

"And so I hope that *you* do not," answered Garland. "It is a terrible thing to break one's word."

"We wouldn't really kill him," added Thompson. "I don't even like this business of threats, but it is an extreme emergency." He was a very young clergyman, with a heavy manner and a stiff, shy smile.

"We, however, never promised zip-squat to the buggers." It was Larssen speaking, and although Wanbli was not familiar with the words "zip-squat" and "buggers" and doubted they were even Wacaan, he understood Larssen perfectly.

224

"Can we do this without alerting Central?" asked Wanbli. He was beginning to enjoy the conversation.

"That's more difficult." Garland made a face.

"Pray God they don't notice," said Thompson under his breath. He didn't seem to mean it as advice.

"Why don't we put that responsibility on Guillermo?" asked Victoria. The three sleeper men glanced at her in faint surprise.

"I mean, think what a great position it will leave us in if they dance in here and think we're all unconscious! We just tell the little drunken rat that if there's any sign that the crew knows we're going off-line, we cut out his bowels and show them to him."

"That's horrid," said Thompson.

"I like it," said Larssen.

Wanbli liked it too. He felt very comfortable around Victoria. She was not exotic, like Audry, but she had sound ideas.

"Good so far, Vikki, but then what? You've got a dozen or two of revivalists with weapons in here. Surprise or no, what do you do?" Something occurred to him that made him giggle. "Hey! You know, I've been training these flyers in self-defense!"

Victoria's dark eyes widened. Garland gave a grunt. "And are they any good?"

"Wretched. Absolutely wretched."

"Then don't worry. I have been training my people for over a year—I mean a year three hundred years ago, but yesterday to us. They are not wretched."

"Ah." Now Wanbli understood Medicine-Bear's emphasis on warriors. "You have your own fighting arts, then?"

"I teach Hapkido."

"In my home, we have a large spiny animal called the stunk, which preys on ratchetts, which are no bigger than the hollow of your hand. The stunk is faster and much stronger, but nine out of ten times, when it chases a ratchett it loses, gets tired and gives up. This is because the stunk has many opportunities for supper and the ratchett only this one for life. In fact, sometimes the ratchett turns and tears the stunk's feelers off, which is an act of great madness and bravery. I myself would not try to tear off the feelers of a living stunk.

"When a weaker group takes on a stronger group," said Wanbli to the assembled sleepers, "it must be like the ratchett, or"—and he dragged the word out for suspense—"it must be able to convince the stunk that it is.

"They must think we are fearsome. They must be convinced we are mad: that life and death mean nothing to us. That we are complete savages."

The roar of laughter that greeted Wanbli's last statement was a complete surprise to him. He looked inquiringly at Victoria, who was as convulsed as the rest.

"No problem in that, brother," she called over twenty heads.

Wanbli didn't want Victoria to think of him as a brother. It made him feel inhibited.

"Don't you mean we really have to be those things?" a man sitting on one of the empty coffins shouted over the noise. "Fearsome, mad, savage?"

Wanbli considered, shifting from foot to foot. "If you cannot act them well enough, then perhaps you must. I myself would rather keep my madness as a bluff. Intimidation."

The questioner—he was one of the horse-symbol people, as was Victoria—made an uncertain sound. "But your own people, Wanbli. Aren't they taught to be ruthless and fearsome? To kill on command?"

For a moment Wanbli felt insulted. "We are taught to fight on command, Lucian. It's a matter of poverty."

Now Lucian stood up. "But you have a lot of land. You said so."

The discussion seemed to be going far afield, and any minute now the revivalists would move against them. "A small continent, yes, but . . ."

"And aren't there animals on this continent? Isn't there soil? I don't think you people are so poor. Not poor at all, in fact."

One last time Wanbli tried to explain. "It isn't so simple. Few of the animals of Neunacht are much good to human stomachs. The deserts of Southbay need a lot of watering before they produce crops. And then they salt up. We used to subsist, in the old days, but a few changes in weather patterns nearly wiped out the settlements. And when we were self-sufficient, it was a poor and strengthless life compared to our neighbor countries. Who themselves are fairly bad off.

"We have no metals. Poverty isn't so simple, Luce. In fact . . ."

"Poverty is having no land," shouted Lucian.

"Poverty is having no string station," replied Wanbli, slightly heated, and then he stood still, one hand raised in a frozen gesture.

The irritation smoothed out his face. All expression went. Sixty-eight people sat, slouched or leaned against equipment and watched Wanbli respectfully, for no man wears such a look of blank thoughtlessness unless he is thinking very hard.

"I have it. I have the other thing." He whispered these words but then he took one step closer to his audience. "I know the way out of our problems," he announced, and then he sat down on the lid of a coffin, staring at his own hands and grinning.

There was rustle and restlessness as the sleepers stared at Wanbli. Garland Medicine Bear stood up. "As I see it, we have two choices."

Wanbli's head jerked up. "No! Never say that, flyer! That's half the trouble in life: people believing that there are only a few possibilities. Possibilities are infinite." Now Wanbli hopped over to the shorter, broader man and spoke to him, not to the audience.

"Most Wacaan are so willing to believe that: that paths only fork into two. They think there ought to be a right way and a wrong way to go, and when both ways look punishing, they feel cheated, but they choose one of the two.

"The training of the Third Eagle is to look for forks three, four and five off the path. Or blaze a new path." He gave Garland a rough little shake.

"Flyer, I can give you what you want," he said. He glanced at the puzzled audience: at Lucian. "I can give you

227

what you want. I can give you all what you want, because *there is no poverty. No shortage. No poverty at all.*"

"Hallelujah!" shouted Godslove Thompson and all the sleepers echoed. "Hallelujah!" Wanbli did not know the word. He doubted it was Wacaan.

TEN

EDWARD PIERCE was always glad to be back on the *Ball;* he could usually convince himself that the docking was equivalent to planetfall, at least for the first few days. He was glad to be back this time too, because now it was less likely that the red man was going to do the one more stupid thing—who knew what—that might blow them all up. Edward had been worried about that.

He was not in the good graces of Captain Brezhner. He had not had a good time in the string-com meeting that had decided what the revivalists' responses would be to the catastrophe introduced by his barbaric protégé. But Edward's anxiety was not for his own sake as he paced the length of his own "home" quarters in the *Ball.* Edward was not an egoist.

He was worried about the fate of the sixty-eight unplanned-for, unfeedable people a mile away, locked in one pod of the *Condor.* He had poked at the computers until his eyes swam in the last three days and now here in the greater facilities of the *Ball,* to see whether a system of one hundred and eighty people might stretch to care for two hundred and forty-eight. It could not: not for more than three Earth months. And even if it could, most of his own people wouldn't agree to it. They lived with belts tight enough.

They would have to be dropped on a planet somewhere. Illegally. Oh shit, illegally. They had all worked so hard to avoid breaking other people's laws. Unpopular enough already.

It would have to be some backward or isolationist world with no enforcement treaties, especially with Nashua. And what made it even worse was that you couldn't expect awakened sleepers to conceal where they had come from and who had dumped them there. They were undoubtedly unhappy with the *Condor* crew and all the revivalists in general. Awakened sleepers needed to be reeducated. Edward himself had needed it more than most.

Perhaps they would starve where they were put. Perhaps they would be murdered. About the sleepers, Edward worried.

But it was for Red that he sweated. Red: boisterous, jolly, elegant in movement, good company and utterly (after all) untamable.

Red was Edward's campaign and his great folly. He reminded Edward of a story he had read as a child, about a boy who tried to tame a deer. At first it had seemed to work . . .

Edward had volunteered to be the one to kill him. Of course. He had been voted down on that. Everyone knew that Edward, of all the revivalists, had the hardest time when it came to jettisoning a "spoiled" crew. Someone from the *Big Ball* would do it. Someone who had never taken one of Red's classes.

"Delia," he whispered, not knowing that he had spoken at all.

Soon now. Within the hour. Edward sat down in one of the wall chairs and stared at his hands in his lap. There was something unusual about what he saw and his blinking blue eyes narrowed. It was his belly. It was not hanging over his waistband, as it tended to do. He had lost weight. No—he had gained, according to the last weigh-in. It was muscle tone. He flexed his arms and felt muscle tighten beneath his shirtsleeves. For a moment he felt vaguely complacent, and then he remembered how he had gotten that flat belly, those (slightly) swelling shoulders.

At least his distress—distress of mind, stomach, bowel and even bladder, real distress—proved one thing. There was an immense difference between a living man and a sleeper.

One only knew for sure once one had killed both.

Edward checked the time and rose from the chair, which retreated back into the wall. He would have to be there.

Twenty revivalists with breathers entered the medical pod the instant the jammed door was forced open. One, a doctor from the *Ball* itself, had the job of disposing of Wanbli, while the rest were to begin hauling the unconscious crew of the *Commitment* out to a more practical place of detention. Edward Pierce followed in the rear, wishing he could summon a trace of the anger that had supported him for three days.

The door closed again behind them all, cleanly this time, and was sealed from the outside. It would be reopened for them only when they could announce that Red was dead. He was too tricky for them to take more chances.

The limp forms, naked except for the improvised modesty wraps torn from lab smocks and hammock sheets, lay in a disarray that seemed in itself angry. He had watched over the monitor from Central as the occupiers had become aware of the anesthetic being leaked into the air. A few faces had reflected the shock and dismay natural at such a surprise attack, but most of them had erupted into blind fury, throwing bottles at the camera strip which ran along the top of the area wall, shaking fists, making really horrid faces at the monitor, which had begun to fail from this treatment. No one had even thought to try stuffing blankets into the air ducts. It wouldn't have worked, but that would have been the sensible move.

Perhaps there really was something to the idea that Indians were primitive.

Among the various colors of body he could not find the distinctive shade of skin that belonged to Red. It would be easier if they hadn't fallen in heaps as they had. Dr. Kassik was depending upon Edward to identify him. He had a hypopunch and it would be over very quickly.

He would look like a sleeper. That was a mercy.

There were perhaps twenty bodies scattered in the front reception area, including all the Baptists, who had fallen together, praying (probably) in a circle. Edward noticed that these wore more than their share of the scavenged clothing. One young woman wore both a skirt and bra affair made of the heavy puckered paper used to surround glassware in storage. What could be seen of her was very pretty.

No Red. No Guillermo, either. Edward would have liked to remind the rest to keep an eye out for a small, medium tan man in skivvies, but they were supposed to keep the breather tubes in their mouths. He wasn't sure just how potent this gas was, and he didn't want to be carried out himself.

There were three bays in the facility, each open in front to the reception area. On the left was the examination area, to the right was stores and in the middle were the heavy viral filters and the row upon row of revival units. Edward followed Dr. Kassel toward the neatly ranked coffins.

It was terrible and daunting to see the coffins yawning open and the bodies that had been in them draped or curled, abandoned at all angles beside them. It was like the remains of a great vampire feast. Edward's skin tightened and crawled over his shoulders.

Right at his feet, her head thrown back theatrically over the open mouth of a coffin, was one of the women he had expected to be chosen for awakening. This one had felt no need to cover her breasts, or couldn't find the material. One of her eyes was imperfectly closed, as will sometimes happen under anesthetic, and the strip of white and brown glittered up at him. He wanted to push it closed for her, but as his hand moved he remembered her as one of those throwing bottles at the camera, and the impulse died in him.

They had reached the end of the bay and not found Red among the sprawled bodies. Either he was in one of the side bays or he was hiding somewhere. Vain effort: there was nowhere to hide in a place like this. He could be in one of the coffins, or in a revival unit, and if the latter, then possibly he was not asleep with the rest of them. But the revivers had glass doors, and each of the twenty intruders had come equipped with a pocket pulse pistol, so that was really no problem. And if he was not in one of the revivers or in a coffin, then he would have to be . . .

The lights went out.

No space traveler could be prey to claustrophobia or fear of simple darkness, but Edward Pierce leaped six inches into the air and tried to draw his pistol. Another hand met his on its way and hurt it, badly. He spun around in time to receive a punch that snapped his teeth shut and lifted him once more. In the faint green glow that was emitted by the backup power for the revival units, he saw the fist and the face of the naked woman whose eye he had wanted to close, and who had thrown the bottles. Now her eyes were wide open, but still glittering: green in the faint green light.

He came down and saw nothing more for a while.

Wanbli hopped up from where he had been covered by the bulk of both Garland Medicine-Bear and Henry Larssen. Garland was already in the newborn riot, while Henry held a length of plastic tubing in his hands, garrote style, and was snapping it thoughtfully as he stepped over the empty coffins. Wanbli clapped him on the shoulder.

"Don't kill anybody, Hank," he said into the man's ear. "It isn't necessary." Wanbli himself stepped up onto one neat row of boxes and ran along the top of the walls, like a boy on a board fence, using his stick as a balancing pole. He ignored the fighting around him; there were two or three enthusiastic scrappers from the *Commitment* to each invader. Help from him would make the odds still more unfair, and would ruin his protectors' fun too.

He heard a cry and a snap coming from the front right. The cry sounded familiar and he sprang down at Victoria's feet in time to witness Edward's lurch and collapse.

"Hey, hey!" He yanked on her long hair. His teeth

gleamed green. "Take care of my pal Eddie, okay? Tie him real comfortable."

"Tie him with what?" Victoria was breathing heavily and rubbing her knuckles with her other hand.

Wanbli considered. "With your . . . whatever you call that." He pointed to the strip of cloth wrapped G-string fashion around her nether parts.

Victoria glared and snorted, and Wanbli hit her lightly on the upper arm. "Hey, I like you a lot, Vikki. You're one real flyer!" He walked on.

There was the snap of a pulse pistol and shadows leaped and fell again. Wanbli heard an angry curse from one of the other bays. He invoked the First and Third Protectors and went on.

Here, where the bay opened out, he found the man whom he guessed had been assigned to kill him. He had pressed himself against the wall and was holding off three of Garland's students with a simple hypopunch. A hypodermic punch was a useful tool for murder but a poor weapon; it had to touch skin and could only be fired once without reload, but such was the respect it engendered that none of the three dared risk approach.

Wanbli came quietly behind them. "He's mine," he said in Wacaan. The three looked, recognized and stepped back, enclosing him within their circle.

The doctor pointed his hypo and Wanbli raised his stick. "This doesn't have to touch," he said in Old Ang. Kassel stared down at the stun stick and Wanbli knew the man thought he was about to be killed. This seemed a proper sort of irony to Wanbli. He pressed the handle.

At that moment the doctor was moving, throwing the hypo at Wanbli's chest. The man fell but the poisonous hypopunch came on. Scarcely knowing what he did, Wanbli blocked it with the stick.

There was a smack and a howl as it hit one of the three fighters behind him: a tall, thin man with a large nose and chin. Lucian. He sank to his knees, staring with glistening face at the deadly thing which had hit him. Wanbli squatted down in front of him. His two companions stared.

"I . . . I'm okay," said the man shakily. "Embarrassed, is all. I think it hit me backwards." He grinned.

Wanbli retrieved the hypopunch, which had somehow discharged, and stood again in time to hear the thud as Lucian fell stone dead on the floor.

Edward felt himself being passed, pushed, booted along. As the woman had tied his eyes as well as his hands, he did not know where they were herding him, until his legs were lifted and he felt the sides of the coffin around him. Then he started screaming.

In the green glow of the emergencies, the young woman's blood looked much blacker than her skin, even where it soaked through the absorbent paper of her skirt. She had been perforated by the repeated pulse-fire. Almost cut in two.

Wanbli looked from her body to that of the revivalist equally dead beside her and up. "Why did you go for him if you're not allowed to fight?" he asked, keeping his voice level with effort.

One of the surrounding faces was that of Godslove Thompson. The green glimmer behind gave his round face the look of a moon's eclipse. "We surrounded him peacefully. I thought if there were enough of us . . ."

"It doesn't work that way." This time Wanbli had less success in controlling himself. "How'd you dust him, then? Break his neck?"

The Baptists glanced widely at one another. None of them remembered.

It was inevitable, he told himself. Unrealistic to expect that these—or any group—could take on twenty armed invaders without losing some. Without killing some. But it was still new to Wanbli, this business of having friends taken out under his nose. Because of him.

Now it was over in Medical, and in truth, it had not taken more than two minutes. Twenty revivalists were stored, still breathing, neatly in coffins. The two dead *Commitment* crew members were laid, not in the coffins, but on a table, and covered with paper sheets. One of these sheets slowly wicked up blood. The dead revivalist had been dragged out of the way. The body had been abused somewhat.

Garland was in front of Wanbli. In the dim light Wanbli could not see the man's expression. He was glad of it.

"Next—the door?"

Wanbli grunted. "Get Gilly again."

The attendant looked lost between the two men who hauled him to the door. He smelled of vomit and he had been crying, but now he was very calm. "I can't," he said. "If the door has been sealed from outside, it will have to be opened from outside."

"So tell them to open it. There's still a local com-box on the panel. Speak."

Guillermo cleared his throat as Wanbli slapped the speaker on. He called for the door to be opened. He called louder.

"They don't believe me," he told Wanbli, once they had given up on that method. "They must have a code, or someone else has to give the signal." His head sagged sideways against the shoulder at his right hand. "Let me go back to sleep."

Guillermo's words brought back to Wanbli the fact that he too had not eaten in three days. A quick glance around showed him that his crew of warriors was folding like so many alios. There was Victoria, slumped against the fat-ratio scale, yawning and yawning. It was too damned contagious.

His shout brought them all upright again. "Hey! Red calling the *Commitment*. Alert, *Commitment*. Anyone drifting off now is going to be under a paper sheet himself pretty soon. We've still got over a hundred fifty opponents out there, and they're not about to be happy with any of us. Got it?"

The yawning spread and there was a sound of faces being slapped. The Reverend Thompson invoked his savior and Henry Larssen uttered the same words with different emphasis.

"Okay, Gilly. Now you ask them who it is they want their command from. I don't want them thinking we've slaughtered their entire squad here."

Obediently, flatly, Gilly spoke his words, to no more success. Nor could threats move him to override the seal on the door; emergency unsealing had not been part of his training. They let him go back to sleep.

Wanbli tried a pulse pistol against the gasket rim of the door, but such weapons are useful on board ship particularly because they cannot cut through construction materials, and all that he gained was a sizable burn on his wrist. Mary Standing-Shoes, however, came forward with a small bone saw that worked perfectly and with very little disturbance. They left the door in place, hanging by slivers.

Each of the front row of the assault was to hold a captive as a shield. Wanbli hoped the revivalists would not be so panicked or so ruthless that they would slice up their own people. He himself chose Edward. He took him from Victoria.

"Up again, Eddie," he called, flipping the clear lid up.

Edward Pierce's blue-gray eyes were wide and glassy, unblinking. Wanbli believed him to be dead, but then his mouth worked and he swallowed.

"Up, Eddie. No one's hurt you. Much."

His flesh was like a soft plastic, and his skin as cold as wet plastic. There was no way Edward Pierce was going to stand alone. Wanbli slipped his forearm between the man's back and elbows and hefted him. He could scarcely feel a pulse, even along the man's neck.

"These fellows are not in good shape," called Garland.

Wanbli used his other hand to slap Edward over the ear. The blow did no good. "What's wrong with you, Eddie?"

"Dead," said Edward Pierce.

Wanbli glanced back at the empty coffin. This one bore the imprint of the spotted horse. "Huh! I imagine you flyers *do* feel a little funny being put back in one of those, don't you? I might say it was a perfect revenge—I mean, if I were the sort of flyer who did say things like that."

The taunt roused Edward no better than the slap had

done. ". . . won't wake me up," he said very clearly, and then he closed his eyes.

"Hup! Let's go," shouted Wanbli. "While they're still with us."

They got to the door, dragging prisoners in all degrees of shock. Garland Medicine-Bear dropped his weeping captive in disgust, and the man lay where he fell.

Garland took three running steps, leaped, kicked out the door vanes and landed rolling on the other side. "Howl," he shouted, and the crew of the *Commitment* surged through behind him, howling.

There was no resistance, no battle. First the hall seemed to be empty, but there were at least as many revivalists in it as had entered Medical. They were merely slumped over the floor.

"Retreat!" shouted Wanbli, and they all piled awkwardly over the broken door again, dragging the feet of the captives.

"If it were still active, we'd all be knocked out at this moment," said Victoria. "The air is circulating between the two rooms now." She was not a front-liner, because Wanbli had taken her human shield. She was inclined to be resentful about it.

"They wouldn't try the same trick on us we tried on them," added the crew member who had pinched Guillermo.

Wanbli tossed Edward at Victoria and leaped over the shards of the door again. He reached the nearest body, picked it up, let it drop with a nasty thud and finally put one hand over the woman's throat. "It's real," he said. "Pulse about forty.

"Let's go."

Medical Facilities on the *Condor* had no direct connection with the ship's skin because it shared the pod with Kitchen Facilities. Wanbli found the door at the end of the long hall unsecured. He and Garland Medicine-Bear ran into the kitchen a hundred feet ahead of the hostage-bearing crew. Wanbli had his stick at the ready.

The smell of the place, as always, was something like broccoli, but reminiscent of yeast. It was very clean and empty and filled with scales, and the sign on the wall said "More for one is less for another."

"Wrong!" Wanbli plucked a paring knife from its magnetic grip and threw it at the sign. It stuck.

He heard the door behind him suck shut and at the same moment the stuttering spit of a pulse pistol. His stick flew out of his hand. While Wanbli's arm, already burned, was beginning a message of pain, and while his brain was registering that he had been attacked, he had already dropped to the floor of the large aisle and was crawling toward the source of the attack. Behind him, he heard Garland go into another dive and roll, taking him further along the aisle.

There was another burst of fire and Wanbli, certain now of the angle of attack, hid behind the wall of a storage table, thankful now that the pulse pistol could not penetrate ferrous polymers. The thin metal buzzed and grew hot under the onslaught.

"Thanks. Now I know where you are," shouted Wanbli.

"That's all right, Red. I know where you are."

The voice was that of Captain Brezhner. A pistol spattered once during the words, and Wanbli guessed it had not been the Captain who fired. An empty bottle, thrown by Garland, skittered down the long aisle and shots pursued it.

Would the *Condor*'s captain choose to hold a position with only one other to cover his back? Wanbli had his doubts.

Out of the corner of his eye he could see Garland, wedged between the plastic side of a simple reconstitution vat and a huge sack of dried prunes. Evidently he suspected enemies on both sides of the aisle. Wanbli did not. He didn't think that the revivalists' innate conservatism would allow them to shoot in the direction of other squad members.

Besides, had there been gunmen posted on the left, amid the knives, boards and induction cookers, Wanbli would have been dead already.

"You have fucked up our whole settlement, asshole," shouted Brezhner. "You're as good as dead!"

Wanbli had picked up the Old Ang idiomatic for sexual intercourse, but this usage made no sense. "Asshole," however, was a common insult in every language he had studied, so he got the gist of the statement. As long as Brezhner seemed to know where he was, he saw no reason not to answer.

"Truth is, you don't *have* any settlement, Captain. But I —we—can do something about that."

The reply was a burst that rang the storage table like a gong. It did not seem to be coming from the same angle. Either the Captain was moving—more quietly than Wanbli thought the big man was capable of moving—or there were more than two of the *Condor* crew in the kitchen. Wanbli thought perhaps it was time to find another spot. He flung himself in a long, low frog leap, away from Garland, back in the direction from which they had come, and a shot burned hair on the top of his head.

The man was hiding behind a tread-wheel plate caddy. He fired once more, wildly, as Wanbli came on, and then two hundred white dinner plates smashed out of their stacks and onto his head. Wanbli grabbed the gun in one hand and smacked the fellow unconscious with a back-knuckle from the other. He heard a shot, not directed at him, followed by a horrifying whoop, a scrabble and a thud.

Garland, he thought with some satisfaction. Probably got the flyer alive too.

Wanbli took cover again before calling, "Captain. We don't want to hurt you. We actually have a proposition for you—for us all."

"Bullshit!" Evidently the Captain had moved further back. Did he have more guns at his command? Wanbli fingered the squeeze of his captured pistol gingerly. It wasn't his sort of weapon, especially held in the left hand. And he didn't want Brezhner dead.

"Indian!" Wanbli leaned forward, then realized that Brezhner was addressing the man who spoke no 'Indi. "Indian. What did this guy tell you? We didn't mean your people any harm. It was only him we were after."

Garland answered from far back in the kitchen, almost behind Brezhner. "No harm at all. You just meant to murder us."

"Not true. That's a lie!" The Captain spoke with spontaneous anger.

"They don't call it murder when it's sleepers," called Wanbli. He felt and heard a buzzing back at the entry door, and quietly he began to creep toward Captain Brezhner.

Garland laughed. (He had such a great sense of humor, thought Wanbli. They all did. And they laughed at the strangest things.) "They didn't used to call it murder when it was Indians, either. But I know who to believe, Captain, and I'll put my money on the Eagle."

Wanbli was only ten feet away from the Captain, who was crouched behind the inadequate protection of an aluminum barbecue. He raised the pulse pistol and aimed it at Brezhner's wavering gun hand. The Captain was still trying to locate Garland. He spoke again. "That way you'll wind up spaced along with him, fellow. Look. We were all sleepers here. It takes understanding . . ."

Wanbli raised the pistol, which felt odd and unpracticed in his hand. He decided against it. He tossed the pistol away as he leaped for the Captain bare-handed.

The rest of the *Commitment*'s crew had the door sawn open before Garland could open it for them.

"I want to speak to everyone aboard the *Ball*," said Wanbli into the ship communicator. There was no response, so Wanbli blew into the ear of the thing and tried again, louder.

The speaker popped on. "Everyone in the *Ball* does not want to hear from you, Red." It might have been Khafiya talking.

"I know that. You should know that we have taken your little 'boarding party' hostage. We've got Captain Brezhner. We've got Eddie."

Again there was silence. Wanbli, out of the corner of his eye, could see Garland begin to slump against the wall. The burst of activity, following three days of fasting, was telling on him. Wanbli put his damaged hand over the primitive little pickup and told him to go eat some bread, like the rest of the *Condor*'s crew. They were making a great deal of racket at it.

The man did not move. "I want to see how things go," he said. "Besides. I've got to keep an eye on your captain here."

Brezhner's hands were tied with kitchen twine in front of him. He looked ready to make trouble.

"You can look with one eye while . . ."

The speaker sounded again. "I don't believe you," it said. "Pierce, yes, but not the captain. He wasn't involved."

"He is now," Wanbli said, and pushed the man forward. "Talk," he whispered into Brezhner's ear, but the Captain was as silent as if he had been gagged. Wanbli pinched his ear, but the strangled grunt that issued from Brezhner's throat was not identifiable.

Wanbli laughed. "He won't talk. That alone ought to be enough to identify him, Khafiya. But if you won't believe me about the Captain, you can't deny twenty assorted revivalists, all tied up neat and under the care of some very impetuous flyers."

"How did you sweet-talk them into helping you do this, Red? They themselves were in no danger from us."

At this Garland Medicine-Bear heaved himself off the wall, his face blotched with anger. "No danger? No, you were just going to murder us in our sleep!"

There was a moment's silence. "You can't be expected to understand, but we simply haven't the resources to take care of every sleeper. There are tens of thousands of you. Of us."

"There are tens of thousands of habitable planets, you smug bodysnatcher!"

This time Khafiya had an immediate answer. "Not in this quadrant. And not on the strings, there aren't. And the price for transport is something you don't understand."

Garland smashed his fist into the wall beside the speaker, deforming it. "I don't understand! I don't? Well, let me tell you, lady, I organized a colony ship! Do you think I don't know about finance? Do you think I don't know about compromise? I weighed and saved and scrimped and compromised till my jaws hurt!"

"Your ship shows it," answered Khafiya with a touch of rancor.

"You're not sounding much like a savage," interjected Wanbli in Wacaan.

Garland thumped the wall again and turned away. There was Frederic Standing-Elk standing before him, holding a breadstick under Garland's nose like a club. Garland took it.

Khafiya was oblivious to the assault upon the metal wall, and to the rejection. She continued: "Our society is tiny, and cannot absorb over fifty new people without breaking down. Nor can we drop you somewhere without losing the tolerance of the planet governments—tolerance we depend on. And without us, there will be no more reclaiming of sleeper ships, because no one else in the whole galaxy cares. That's thousands of lives, thousands of dead hopes—because as long as one member from a crew is saved, the journey was not entirely in vain."

"Not so," answered Wanbli, though she had not been talking to him. "You may pump up a few warm bodies, but the hopes—no. You never wanted to be ship people. Your own hopes are dead."

"We did finc until you came along."

Wanbli smiled and scratched his Third Eagle. "Not true. You're so down about things you don't even dare have children; that's not doing fine in any world I know. And you got no sun. No light. No warmth, not even in your spirits. But you might do fine now that I have dropped in. I know the answer to everything." He paused, knowing how obnoxious that sounded.

"Call a meeting. Let me talk."

Wanbli entered the *Big Ball* for the first time chewing on something stringy and gray; he was not sure it had been cooked. But for his small involvement with this culinary question, the march to the Greater Assembly Room might have been more dramatic. There were guns pointed at him.

Captain Brezhner behaved himself befittingly as hostage

in chief; he stood very tall and looked to neither side. Garland Medicine-Bear, with his stolen pistol in the Captain's back, also kept an appropriately solemn demeanor. It was Edward Pierce who ruined the effect, for he would neither open his eyes nor stand up straight, and he kept muttering to himself. He was neither seeing nor hearing what was around him.

Wanbli was not oblivious to the guns, but he had seen so much of guns lately, and the food he had grabbed in the kitchen, whether uncooked or merely unappetizing, had stuck in shreds between his teeth. He danced from foot to foot to keep awake, and he noticed certain things as he went by.

—The *Ball* was much more comfortably built than the *Condor*. The halls were wide and they did not echo.

—Men and women were blinking roundly at him from doorways, like so many toads in their holes. They were frightened, not furious.

—Khafiya. Coordinator Khafiya looked just as she had the night she had slept in the crook of Wanbli's arm, and he was certain that she was ready to kill him. That was curious. That was remarkable. In an odd way, it was Wacaan.

—It was a long way to the Greater Assembly Room.

There were almost two dozen people from the *Commitment* in the march, each with a prisoner. All but two were Garland's people. The rest of the sleepers had been left in possession of the *Condor*.

Entering the assembly room, they made a semicircle at one carpeted end: an area which was big enough to dwarf the company. Forty others followed in wary procession. An equal number of revivalists were waiting, standing against the walls.

There was a chandelier, with crystal. Wanbli found that too quite remarkable. Good hall for a dance.

Khafiya preceded them to the proscenium end of the hall.

"Don't touch that switch," called Wanbli in sudden suspicion.

She glared her irritation, but her hand stopped in the air. "It brings the seats up," she said.

"I'll bet it does. Half of us are standing where the seats will come up, aren't we?"

The Coordinator didn't reply. Wanbli hopped up onto the dais beside her, his own gun at the ready. "Yes, we are, my sweetie. Did you think you could pull that without a number of hostages getting burnt?

"Or maybe you don't care. You flyers are so damn worried about the number of mouths you have to feed that maybe you'd welcome a big accident that left half of you dead. In fact, if you were all dead, you'd have no problems at all, would you?"

"Asshole." She spoke with feeling.

"Get away from the switch," answered Wanbli levelly.

They said he was being projected all through the *Ball.* Wanbli had no way of judging whether they had lied to him or not. He looked at the wall-built cameras and down again to the unfriendly faces ringed around him. He decided that it only made sense to talk directly to the people he could see.

He stepped backward, trying to meet as many eyes as possible. "Listen!" he began. "You think we're here to bargain, don't you?"

"You don't have to shout." It was Khafiya. "The acoustics are fine."

Wanbli ignored her. "You think we're here to bargain our lives for those of our prisoners, don't you?"

None of the dozens of revivalists answered this. They would not even give him that much, thought Wanbli, and he felt sweat prickle. He started again.

"And twenty-three prisoners, including a ship captain, do make a strong bargaining position, don't they?"

This was greeted by a rumble, neither assent nor dissent, but more like the growling of dogs. With a great sigh, Edward Pierce settled down onto the floor, legs spread out, and he covered his face with his arms.

"Delia," he said once more, with no particular emotion.

Wanbli stepped over to him. He ruffled the smooth blond hair.

"Well, that's not what we're doing here. We're not bargaining for our lives. We're offering you your own lives."

The rumble grew.

"As you meant them to be. What you lost when you woke up and found you'd been on your way to nowhere."

Now the rumble was unmistakably angry.

"Your Eddie is really sick," whispered Victoria in Wacaan.

"I know," Wanbli murmured back.

"Who is Delia?"

Wanbli shook his head and shrugged. "We shouldn't have put them in the sleeper crates. Coffins. With them especially," he said.

Wanbli wiped a hand over his mouth and cleared his mind of the problems of Edward Pierce.

Again he shouted. "I know there isn't a one of you who would choose this life. Who did choose this life, in fact. Every single sleeper wanted to wake up on a world with air. And soil. With a sun."

"That was then. This is now." The words were hurled from the audience. They had the ring of a proverb, though it wasn't one Wanbli had heard before. They sounded tired.

Wanbli shifted from foot to foot. He wished he could make eye contact with whoever it was who had spoken. "And now you could join the truckers, if you really have given up. The Guild can use any intelligent person who doesn't lose his runners when too long off-planet. One who doesn't need a home. Hey, the Guild is rich. Nobody weighs out the food they eat. If you flyers were really content with string-ways life, you'd have all gone for Guild members."

"Some do." It was Khafiya again. "But the rest of us have a purpose here. We're revivalists. We don't do it for profit."

Victoria Whistocken left Edward collapsed on the floor. Coordinator Khafiya backed two steps from the red woman's outrage. "I don't think much of your purpose: killing ten people and allowing one to live and patting yourselves on the back. The purpose of the fox in the henhouse, that's what it is."

Wanbli reached out his hand and touched Victoria on the shoulder very lightly. He stepped in between the woman he had made love to and the woman he wanted to make love to.

"If you had a planet, Coordinator, wouldn't you rather live on it?"

Khafiya kept her eyes on Victoria as she replied. "Yes, I'd rather live on a planet. An Earth-type planet. But not at the expense of forgetting the sleeper ships. That's a duty."

Garland spoke for the first time. "Killing people is a duty?"

Captain Brezhner took that moment to aim a two-handed punch—more of a slap, really—at the Sioux's face. Garland Medicine-Bear swept the Captain's feet out from under him and put him down on his stomach. Coordinator Khafiya moved forward, but a warning glance from Wanbli sent her back. "Sleepers—oh hell, you don't understand. You can't understand."

"I understand. We're dead. We're all dead!"

Edward was standing. When he fell again Wanbli caught him, knowing how helpless he was with the crazy man in his arms. He locked eyes with Khafiya.

"We didn't do this to Eddie on purpose. I want you to know that. We just stuffed them all into the coffins to get them out of the way. For just a few minutes."

For the first time the Coordinator's expression thawed a little. "Edward has always . . . had trouble adjusting."

"Yeah. Well, I think I understand them. I was at your meeting, remember? I like Eddie."

Khafiya went cold again. "Then it is surprising how much damage you have done to his life these last few days, Red. You are very hard on people who try to be your friends."

Once, thought Wanbli, that remark would have stung. Only a few days before . . .

"And you, whatever your name is. We don't kill anyone. We only decline to revive more than we can support. Is that our fault? No one else tries at all."

Garland was sitting on Captain Brezhner's back, holding the man in a hammerlock. The strong planes of his face hid anger well. "Why don't you just leave us alone, then? To land where we had planned to land, or to fail. That's better than being hauled in and used for . . . fertilizer or spare parts!"

Khafiya shot a glance or recrimination at Wanbli, for betraying the subject of the *Condor*'s private meeting. "To come crashing down on someone's city? That has happened before now. And besides—your revival systems were inoperative. You were only going nowhere, dead in a state of perfect preservation."

Garland cleared his throat loudly, as though he were about to spit. "I'll tell you this, lady. I've been in sleep for three hundred years and more, and in all that time I was not dead. I am alive now, and if I lie down in one of those coffins again and let my core temperature down to nothing at all, I still won't be dead. Not half as dead as this poor sucker you've worked so hard to convince that life is death that five minutes in a harmless box blew his mind out."

"I don't agree," Khafiya began, but Wanbli put up his hands.

"Please, Khafee. Garland. It doesn't matter now. What matters is that I can take us all home."

This statement was greeted by silence, and then everyone in the room breathed together.

"Home!" The air filled with Edward Pierce's hopeless, animal wail. Then he said, very calmly and distinctly, "We have no home."

"What do you mean, home?"

"A planet, of course." Wanbli took a long breath. He hadn't been sure he would be allowed to get this far. "A habitable planet with one sun, two moons and more stars at night than you would want to count. It's not empty—not the blank page you originally hoped for when you left Earth —but we all found that the blank page gets written on very fast.

"It has room for another two hundred people, or two thousand or twenty thousand."

"Your own home planet, Red?" Khafiya lounged against the wall, distrust in her every angle.

Wanbli nodded. Khafiya's expression went more and more sour. "You damned con man. Neunacht is one of the most closed of closed worlds. Don't you think we know about things like that? You've got no immigration and the strictest birth control of any planet on the books."

Wanbli did not know what the Old Ang expression "con man" meant, but he kept nodding. "All true. We've been closed for years. Because we're a very poor planet. Low in minerals. Slow trade. But Neunacht would welcome you flyers. Hey, we'd throw a dance to welcome you, because you've got exactly what we need. And what we're not going to have without you."

"And what's that?"

Wanbli stamped his bare foot. "This. The *Ball*. A string station."

The silence was immense, and to Wanbli, heartening.

When the man opened his mouth, Wanbli recognized the voice as that of DeLorca, the captain of the *White Cockade*. He was dark, and of a slighter build than Wanbli would have guessed. He walked composedly over to Coordinator Khafiya and sat down on the carpet.

This man had confidence, Wanbli decided. He had swagger.

"Release your prisoners and we'll talk about it."

Garland Medicine-Bear growled. Crouched by the prone form of the *Condor* captain, he showed self-assurance of a different kind. Wanbli had only seen pictures of bears, but he could well imagine one in Garland. "Release them with what guarantees?"

Brezhner exploded from the ground. "Guarantees! You had guarantees! We guaranteed the lives of you and your sleepers back there, and you chose to attack instead. How many of my men did you kill, you bastard?"

Garland sat still. "One. That's half the number of my people your guns took out. We had no guns, remember?"

DeLorca spoke. "You have them now, sir."

Now Garland rose. "My name is Medicine-Bear. Garland Medicine-Bear. Of the Black Hills of South Dakota."

DeLorca rubbed his hand over a heavy growth of beard stubble. "Impressive. I am Augustin Patros DeLorca. Once of the broad pampas, but now of the narrower string-ways. I am, like Captain Brezhner, captain of a ship.

"We were talking about release of prisoners."

"Don't give them anything!" Brezhner stood again with his bound hands extended in front of him. The heat of his rage had driven the twine deep into the skin.

"We'll release every prisoner in exchange for a promise of safe release of everyone from the *Commitment.* And of course, of the Eagle too."

"The Eagle?" Khafiya glanced from Garland to Wanbli distrustfully.

"His name is Eagle Elf Darter of the Sacred People," said Garland to Khafiya. With a sly shift of his eyes he added, "Though I admit I don't know what an Elf Darter is, the rest fits him very well."

"You will embarrass me terribly," said Wanbli to the man in Wacaan.

"Another tall tale, Red?"

With a touch of his old smirk, Wanbli said, "You can't have thought my own people called me Red, did you? I mean, we are all very much the same shade."

"I don't know or care what they called you."

DeLorca cut her off with a look. "You're asking a lot from us, Medicine-Bear of the Black Hills. This man has done more to damage our society than any in our history."

"He has exposed your hypocrisy, you mean. Usually there is no one to stand up for your victims."

"Except poor Eddie maybe." Edward Pierce looked up at the sound of Wanbli's voice. "Eddie does his little bit, don't you?" Wanbli gave him a neighborly thump with his foot: one that rocked the pale man back and forth.

"Hey, Eddie. Who's Delia?"

Edward Pierce looked only at the bare feet. "Delia . . . was my wife."

"And they didn't wake her up?"

He didn't answer. Wanbli glanced at Khafiya, who did not look at Edward or at Wanbli. "Nobody knew. Usually married couples will have some sort of sign of it on the box."

Wanbli thought about this. "And do you usually wake both of them. Or neither?"

"Neither." Khafiya looked past him.

Wambli sighed, and again he raised his voice. "I don't want any guarantees for myself. Guarantees are nothing. What I want is a lot more out of you. I want you all with me. For Neunacht. For the Wacaan."

"Not terribly likely," said DeLorca.

"You're a great one to be talking for your people, aren't you?" said Khafiya. "You ran out on them."

Wanbli nodded. "Yeah. I know. But I'm what they got. Now. I'm the one who happens to be in the place and time with the idea. It works that way sometimes.

"Release the prisoners."

Garland stood up. "Now? They're going to have to give in sooner or later . . ."

"Untie them." Wanbli looked into the Sioux's face and realized that he could not make it an order. "Please. Your people are safe, and I . . . I need more than bargaining can give. I want more. I want everything in sight."

Wordlessly, the Indians backed away from their prisoners. Henry Larssen also dropped his captive—rather roughly, because he was never happy to be ordered about by Garland Medicine-Bear. It was Greta, whom Wanbli still thought of as one of his old drinking buddies, who came forward with a small knife to cut the cords.

"So you think you can turn an antique and obsolete colony ship into a commercial string station that would serve the needs of an entire planet?" DeLorca seemed to find the idea humorous, but Wanbli decided he was the sort who would pretend to, till the last. "If that was commercially feasible, bidding on our salvages would be a lot more sprightly."

"It's feasible if a place is desperate enough. Neunacht can't start all over again playing on a turnkey, ready-built station. We already blew our wad. And the *Ball* would handle our immediate need without much alteration. It's a thousand percent better than what we've got, which is nothing. You can berth four ships now. More docks and seals can be added. Once we have the big frame itself . . ."

"And then what about the sleeper ships?" It was Khafiya, of course. Wanbli turned to her with a hint of a smile.

"You really do care about those ships, in your own way, don't you? Well, I think once we have trade, my home will be able to absorb a lot more people. Glad to, in fact. Southbay itself has less than one human occupant per five square kilometers. We can't pay for them, but maybe you won't need the money so bad in the future.

"You could bring all the sleepers home. All of them."

He had their attention now. Even the crew of the *Commitment* stood frozen, attentive. Wanbli called the Protectors to his aid. He summoned the green twilights of home to be his shield. He surrounded his mind with the many-colored, weightless wings of the Elf Darter.

"Still, you can't make promises for your own nation, let alone the planet," DeLorca reminded him.

Wanbli laughed. "You still haven't understood how much I'm asking of you. I'm not trying to sell you the idea of joining your way of life to ours. I'm telling you that together *we* have to sell *them:* the Council, the T'chishetti, the entire world.

"With the Wacaan you will have no problems, because we're by nature gullible. Besides, we'll be real owners of the station."

DeLorca's quick bark of laughter gave way to a very straight face. "Oh. So now we're giving away everything."

"No. I said 'we.' All of you and me. You will be Wacaan too."

Garland Medicine-Bear made a choking noise.

"Just like that?" asked DeLorca. "I thought you were all red warriors."

Wanbli shrugged. "All red, anyway. Until now." He laughed again. "That was then. This is now."

Edward Pierce was standing. His normal fairness was blotchy, almost blue, but he seemed to be paying attention. "You said, all the sleepers?"

"That's exactly it, Eddie."

Khafiya left DeLorca and touched Pierce's hand. It was an awkward gesture. "Sleepers," she said to Wanbli, "do not adjust easily into different society. It could be . . ."

"Out of the way!"

Ten meters off stood Captain Brezhner, and he had a gun,

which he was trying to aim at Wanbli. Khafiya was off to one side of him, and she shook her head in shocked denial of his intention.

Three, then ten pistols were trained on the Captain, but the Indians were reluctant to begin the firing which would doubtless end in bloodbath.

Garland, standing off to one side, measured the distance for a leap.

Wanbli thought he could jump fast enough. Perhaps. But here was Victoria Whistocken sliding in front, daring the man to shoot her down, and if Wanbli moved now he surely would shoot . .

Less than half a second, and then Edward Pierce flung himself forward off the dais, shouting, "No! No more killing!"

The Captain stepped back, stumbled and shot him.

Neither sleeper nor revivalist moved, numb with horror and surprise. Brezhner stood staring dumbly down at his own crewman. Only Wanbli had the power to go to Edward where he lay on his back, with a neat russet spot spreading over his khakis.

"Eddie?"

Pierce met his eyes.

"Eddie, don't die. Hey?"

"It's all right." Edward was very composed. "I was a fool to be so afraid of it. Of the dark. Of a simple box. Every time . . ." He took a breath and winced. "Every time I close my eyes it's darker than that."

Wanbli pushed the limp hair out of the man's face. "Yeah. You don't have to be afraid of dying, but you don't have to die, either. It's only the stomach, Eddie. You can survive a shot in the stomach if you really want to. And you have to want to—all kinds of things are going to happen. Look, here's the medics coming now: they were ready for you." He let himself be shouldered aside by the technicians.

"Eddie. We can still have good times together. Even after all this. Don't die, Eddie. You don't have to."

Edward's eyes in the light of the assembly hall were gray-green, like the beautiful sky over Tawlin. They promised nothing, but as Edward was wheeled away, they were still alive and looking at Wanbli.

Victoria was at his shoulder. The crew of the *Commitment* stood where the last burst of action had left them. Some of them sat down. Everyone else was leaving. Wanbli stood there for a long time.

"What . . . what's going on now? I lost track."

"The big vote," she told him, and he remembered.

"Oh yeah. That."

The Sky of Home

To: Wanbli E. Wacaan
c/o Ship Big Ball
660 Pulsar North 137-11
East 489. Sub FTL Progress

From: Tawlın Akelind
Hovart, T'chishett
Neunacht, BR. 2-98

Dear 'Bli,

Sweet girl's gonads, fellow, I only asked you to find out about the station! No complaints, tho. Except you're a fool to put those rock-headed kinsmen of yours in charge of the most lucrative disturbance our little economy has ever suffered. How will you keep them from getting all fleeced from under them? You won't, you

*know. Winners keep winning. Losers keep losing. To-
gether, we could have made it a paying operation.*

*You say it's going to need alteration. Let me procure
for you what you'll need. If it's on the NINETY-EIGHT
I can get it. You owe me that much.*

*Two years, hey? That hard to keep the old boat cen-
tered on a string? Still, it's nine years before we expected
the Cynthia model. (We're trying to sue. With a refund
we'd really be in the pink.) Can't you give your old
father figure the exact numbers? I won't tell anyone.
You bet I won't. Split the profit down the middle.*

*Oh. Forget that father-figure bit. How in sizzling was
I to know I'd upset you with a little joke? I mean, you're
the original stone-face and all that. And anyway, you're
bright enough to be my son. Must be nurture, not nature, after all.*

In answer to your questions:
*Your damn clan council gave in about your revivalists—
out of ignorance, I think. (Nobody who knows anything
likes revivalists. Didn't you know that?) But it is still
debating whether a naturalized Wacaan will be eligible
for sire- or dam-promotion. Old farts, this council of
yours. They want me to be content with one paint. Ta-
pering down, they say. So what if I get squeezed in the
taper?*

*Regarding what's-her-name—your honey—they might
make an exception. If national gov't leans real hard. Or
you could both be T'chishetti. Wouldn't you like that?
We all love you here. Even Rall, sadistic bitch that she
is. You could have your valves permanently opened. Be
like me.*
This doc is going to break me. End.
Tawlin

Wanbli was still thinking about that letter when the sun-
lamps shut down. Victoria was watching him idly. "Your
people don't have permanent—uh—connections?"

He stared. His body radiated heat. "Connections? You mean the valves?"

"No. I mean husbands and wives."

"Oh." He was very aware of Victoria's nervousness. "Paints don't, as a rule. Not all Wacaans are Paints, by any means. But it's Clan Council that decides who has babies by whom."

"That's tyranny," she stated.

Wanbli flopped his shoulders against the padding in a reclining shrug, leaving Victoria no one to argue with. He considered a few more minutes under the tanner. She stopped his hand as it approached the controls.

"The pills are more effective if you want to keep your color up," she said.

"This is closer to sunlight, though. I like to imagine I'm home." He sat up and scratched through his black-red hair. "I'm never warm enough."

"Pretty hot in Southbay?" She tried to be casual, but Wanbli glanced up sharply.

"Nicely hot. And hotter still up by Tawlin. How about the place you come from?"

"Came from." She had a small habit of correcting his Old Ang grammar, not knowing the mistakes were on purpose. "Wyoming is not really a tropical climate." He was still staring. "But that doesn't mean I wouldn't . . . get used to the heat, Wanbli. Don't worry."

"Oh, I'm long past worrying," he replied sincerely and took her hand in his.

Wanbli Elf Darter SON OF DAMASC Branch-of-Flame
c/o Ship Big Ball
660 Pulsar North Merid. 99-02
East 406

Hovart Clan Council
Hovart, T'chishett
Neunacht, BR. 2-98

Wanbli
We have received your poetry and have recited it aloud

in Council and now must consider it. It is not objection-
able but you must not think of it as alternative morning
salute. You may make us station-keepers. You may
make us wealthy. You may free us of our servitude to
the goldmen. But you cannot make us change what is
basic to our people.

After long debate, we have decided to award you sire-
promotion. This is not to be interpreted as an endorse-
ment of all your actions of the past year. If this
Whistocken woman is found unobjectionable, there will
be no problem with acceptance.

Mychael Irradiate
Chief of Council

Wanbli rattled and rippled the uncreasable gram-foil.
Sire-promotion. Though he'd expected it (demanded it,
truth be told) it felt good. He only wondered how he would
explain to the medics the valves that were already wide
open. He'd think of something.

His smile began softly, reminiscently, but after a few moments it blossomed into a smirk.

Out of the black and shining vault,
The black void, the shining night,
To the golden mother, painted with light,
We were born out of the belly of our father
To the grace of two mothers,
Bright beads on the Strings.
We are like all others who live.
We are Wacaan.
We are the big ones. We are the small.
We live ten thousand years. We live a day.
Our lives are a single learning.
We are those who remain people.
We are Wacaan.
We are outlaws and we are presidents,
Teachers, saints and whores to worlds,
Defenders and betrayers at one stroke,
We are Wacaan.
I invoke the six directions upon this morning.
I invoke all life-giving suns.
I invoke the moons and their little sister, our guardian,
Who is my own little sister.
We are of the people of the sky. We are Wacaan.

ABOUT THE AUTHOR

R. A. MacAvoy is a winner of the John W. Campbell Award for Best New Writer. Among her novels are *Tea with the Black Dragon, The Grey Horse,* and three novels—*Damiano, Damiano's Lute,* and *Raphael*—that are published under the title *A Trio for Lute.* She lives in northern California, where she is at work on her next novel, *The Lens of the World.*

Editors Gregory Benford and Martin H. Greenberg
ask the provocative question

WHAT MIGHT HAVE BEEN?
Volume One: Alternate Empires

• if the Egyptian dynasties—and their Hebrew slaves—
had survived until modern times?

• if Joseph McCarthy had risen to the Presidency?

.e Hellenic states had not survived long enough to
pass
along the concept of democracy?

In the first volume of this star-studded anthology of
original short stories, authors include Robert Silverberg,
Frederik Pohl, Larry Niven, Gregory Benford, James
P. Hogan, Poul Anderson and George Alec Effinger
examine the different worlds in which we might have
lived. Here are stories that will engage the mind and
challenge the imagination!

Buy What Might Have Been? available wherever Bantam Spectra Books are sold.